FIRST CLASS RAVES FOR
JANICE MITCHELL AND HER BOOK

JADE

"NO MATTER WHAT ADVERSITIES HAPPEN IN YOUR
LIFE, THEY CAN BECOME MOTIVATING FACTORS, INSTEAD
OF OBSTACLES. A lot of people will find themselves in this book."
__Charles W. Porter, Publisher - The National Inner City

JADE

BY

J TYSON MITCHELL

SHE OPENED
UP HER BROKEN HEART
TO THE WORLD

authorHOUSE®

AuthorHouse™
1663 Liberty Drive
Bloomington, IN 47403
www.authorhouse.com
Phone: 1 (800) 839-8640

Published by AuthorHouse   03/18/2015

ISBN: 978-1-5049-0060-7 (sc)
ISBN: 978-1-5049-0063-8 (e)

Print information available on the last page.

In Loving Memory of

My Mother

Dorothy Grey
Who gave me a big heart! I'll always love you!
You will always be my hero!

My Great Grandmother

Mariah Wylton - "Big Mama"
Who nurtured my mind and body! I love you!

and

My Grandfather

George Knight, who saw the good in everybody!
I love you Daddy George!

Acknowledgments

Thanks to my best friend and life mate, who knocked twice, to indicate dinner was at the door - as the story unfolded. Knocked once, and left fresh juice which gave me the fuel to keep going. Thank you for your love and devotion. We are blessed as one. I love you.

My appreciation and love to my daughters Virhanda and Kytanja for making me feel like the greatest Mom, ever. I love you with all my heart.

To my Grandchildren, Kalen, Sidney Terrell, Sidney Donte, and Sidney Ar'Darrel...who loves me unconditionally and makes me feel like I felt about my "Big Mama."

Katrina, you kept me grounded; thanks for the ears when I needed you the most. Little Sidney - Thanks for always caring, sharing, and your love. Mario - I'm proud of your calling. Kiki – you are my inspiration. Kristi – keep persevering. Charles - thanks for listening and God bless.

To my best friend Brenda Waters, who was always there to lend an ear! Thanks for the diversions to the theater and the limo ride as we pretended to be celebs.

Hildridge Bluitt - Friends don't come like you every day. You read it and digested it. Thanks for your brutal honesty, which gave me the courage to go that extra mile.

To my friend Connie Bax - who motivates and encourages nothing less than excellence. Thanks for adding to my brainchild after reading it. Your interpretation was heartfelt.

Marlena Wells - I'm so grateful for your friendship. Thank you for staying up past midnight as I read excerpts from the manuscript during its fruition. I love you.

To my friend Edna Leggett, who planted the suggestion, persuaded the creation, and compassionately encouraged me to go full speed ahead. Thank you for strongly believing in me.

To Jeri Williams - Your friendship is unmeasured. Thanks for helping me to grow. I look forward to every New Year's Eve.

To my teacher, mentor, and editor - Mr. Charles W. Porter, who has always believed in me and continuously encouraged me to be all that I can be. I am eternally grateful to you. I love you soooo much!

To my sisters and brothers: Deborah - your comedy belongs on stage. The laughter you give brings inner peace. You make us all happy. You are the glue that bonded us all for life. Thanks for the input and your love. Vanessa's got the baton and really twirling it.

Dorothy - it's no secret - we're twins. I'm spell bound by your loyalty and love! You make me want to be a better person. I love you too, Prentiss. Kurt, Diedrick, Marquita, and Kevin - thank you so much for your love.

Cynthia - My darling, you are so hard to catch up with, but when we do connect, the love is unmatched. You and James are a good team. Tookie - you are amazing.

ShaValarie - When you read excerpts- my level of confidence was raised as you urged on to acknowledge that God has blessed us all with a special talent. I'm proud of your calling.

Angelo – You are our big brother now and a role you've made us proud of. When you flew down to take Val & I to dinner, I knew we had arrived. Thanks for the love. It's apparent to all, Anita & Kirsten, mirror our Mother. Brandon, Travis, and Demarcus - Your foundation has been laid - Keep it going.

Randy - Who would've thought you'd have all females out of the entire bunch! They are modern day reincarnations of your sisters. Treese did great! Thanks for the love and all your support.

Butchie, Darryl, Nina, JoJo, and Cliff - Thanks for the love.

Bessie - When I look at you, I see our Dad. Thank you for being there. Hi Tracy.

To my nephew, Damion Williams - You've been such a positive force in my life. Thanks for your use of the word beautiful. You've inspired me tremendously.

James and Henry Ransefore - You're the best cousins in the world. Thanks for the love.

My Dear cousin Henry...May you rest in peace!

To the rest of my family and friends - I love you all.

To Terence Jackson - I will always think of you as my son. Thanks for trusting and believing in me. I love you.

To my dear friend, Marjorie Jones - Even though you're in another country, you made a believer out of me - always forcing me to spell the word procrastination, and learning its meaning. Thanks for your sincerity and inspiration to put pen to paper. Therman, Marcus and Damon, you're blessed as a family!

To my friends - Ron Longmire and Bohdan Welch. Thanks for lending an ear and all the encouraging words.

To Lynn Arendell - Thanks for your encouragement when I...1st arrived from sunny California. Your words, *"you got potential - kid"* - were an inspiration, coming from a true poet.

To Larry Buffer - Thanks for the technical support. You gave true meaning to "cut and paste."

To Zelma Rosada and Sophronia Lytes - Wish I knew where you were.

To Douglas Motley - Thank you for unlocking the memory of how you led me by the hand to our 2nd grade teacher, Ms. Lewis, asking who was the smartest, of the two? Thank you for making me strive harder when we were rivals in those Oratorical Contests!

Special thanks to all of the MCTS Alumni - Class of '68

Gratitude to the following Post Offices:
Citronelle, Alabama - Roseville, California - Sugarland, Texas -
Missouri City, Texas - Orchard, Texas - Plantersville, Texas -
Anderson, Texas - and - Prairie View, Texas

I was inspired on a daily by the students and faculty of the incredible historically Black University - (PVAMU) Prairie View A & M University - and the fascinating campus radio station - KPVU - 91.3 FM

Prologue

This story is about a little girl who sets out spiritedly and diligently to make a liar out of a Grandmother who had decided her destiny, erroneously. Through fearless courage and perseverance, little Jade is determined to prove her self worth, no matter what the cost.

This story is very important to me and I'm telling it because I want it to be some sort of record of my struggles, my siblings and my Mother's suffering and the undeserved humiliation endured during her short life.

There are millions of little Jade's around the world. No one can decide who you can become and high you can climb in the world - *except you!*

JADE

It was 1950, and the moon was full that night as Aunt Lauren knitted the last bootee, begging little Jon Jon not to crush the crickets jumping everywhere. My Dad couldn't stop pacing the floor. "Did anybody buy the cigars?" "It's gonna be a boy," Uncle Delson said, "With a lotta hair like old ugly Griffin." My Mom screamed, "Help me please! Give me something! Somebody help!" She was beyond exhaustion as they wiped the sweat from her forehead.

The mid-wife yelled, "Try it again, Ms. Zoe. I believe this is it this time! Lord have mercy, child! Push! Oh God - it's coming!" Then, a real miracle happened. At 11:13 p.m., on April Fool's Day, I forcibly pushed my way into this world. My first screams scared Mama Terre, the mid-wife.

She laughed as she revealed to my Mother, "This here's gonna be a talker. She's got a set of lungs on her - my goodness gracious!"

My Father yelled, "A she! You need to look again Mama Terre! I know we got us a boy, and he's gonna be just like his old man." When Dad realized what he'd said, he covered his eyes and hung his head, appalled at his temerity.

"Nah! This here's a beautiful little girl who will always be your third child. You and Ms. Zoe really hit the jackpot. I'm gonna clean her up; Be right back."

Mom and Dad already had my oldest sister, Bria, and my oldest brother, Griffin the 3rd, whom we later called Junior. Little Griffin was restless as he pulled the multicolored quilt from my Mother's bed.

My Father yelled, "Boy! Get away from there and leave your mama be." My Mom, as drained as she was, gently kissed Little Griffin on the cheek so that he wouldn't feel left out and asked him to go see what the nurse was doing with the baby. The mid-wife brought me back and told Mom she noticed a green spot on my chest that wouldn't come off.

"I believe that green spot is a birthmark, Ms. Zoe."

My Mom asked, "Jade is green, right Griffin? Let's call her, Jade."

Mama Terre said, "I like that. I'll put it on the certificate and you both can sign it in the morning. Now, Get some sleep - and congratulations again. It's been a rough night. Thank God we made it through! You did good Ms. Zoe! Good night, now."

A week passed and my Father was glued to that darn radio again. He couldn't wait to tell us how the world was changing rapidly with the newcomer politician on board named John Kennedy. He was so impressed with Mr. Kennedy. He said, "Remember that name y'all cause that boy's gonna do great things!" He told us how they used to refer to Kennedy as "the poor little rich kid." He went on to inform us that Kennedy was incredible with his fight for slum clearance and really impressed the people with low-cost public housing. He told my Grandmother he was sure this man would be President of the United States one day.

It's 1955, and had not snowed this much in fifteen years. Dad chopped some wood for the furnace and Uncle Neal, Grandma, and Aunt Fran were all telling my Great Grandma about this Negro man that was all over the radio news. They told her about Martin Luther King, Jr., and how he was awarded a Ph.D. at Boston University.

My Great Grandma asked, "You mean he's a colored man? So what is a Ph.D.?"

Aunt Fran explained that this Negro man was now a doctor and was sure to be somebody great. As usual, my Dad interrupted to let everyone know his views. He said, "That's all well and good about that Mr. King, but you mark my words, I already told y'all - you need to keep an eye on my boy Kennedy." My Dad said, "Kennedy's been sick with back problems but he's gonna bounce back and do something great for this here country - "You watch and see."

My Father was a pretty smart guy. He was born in Pittsburgh, Pennsylvania, to Vera Rykiel. His Father was a painter from Pittsburgh named Griffin Lang, the First. Things didn't work out for Grandma and Grandpa, so she gathered up my Dad and her belongings and caught the first train smoking to Alabama where she met and married my Granddaddy, Alex Persaud.

It all started with *Big Mama*. She was my *Father's Grandmother*. Big Mama's name was Mariah Rykiel from Horoak County, Alabama. That's where my name originated. I used to think Mariah was the ugliest name in the world until recently, when Mariah Carey was introduced to the world as one of the greatest songbirds, ever. So now when asked, my chest sticks way out.

I never loved anybody like I loved my *Great Grandma*. She was my ace in the hole. Whenever I was in trouble with my Father, I'd run to my Big Mama. She lived in the house with us in the room across the hall. I remember countless nights when I would sneak into her room and climb into bed with her. When my Big Mama was awake, my Dad didn't seem so hard-nosed. He seemed to acquire a bit of gentleness that only she could bring about. Big Mama would save her food for me. I'd help her into her rocking chair and climb into her lap where she'd tell me stories about her two daughters. One of them was my Father's Mother whom we called "Mom-me." We'd laugh until she'd catch a cramp in her toes.

She'd always say, "Baby, pull Big Mama's toes. Pull hard!" I'd rub her huge, bow legs then look up at her to find out why she had a big dent in the right one. She said, "It's just made that way baby." Then she'd play in my head like nobody else could. She took my skeletal face in her hands and looked into my eyes and said, "Child, your hair sho is thick! Come on here and let Big Mama plat this stuff up." The way she twisted my hair, I was awestruck, but couldn't escape the fact that my head was in excruciating pain. Big Mama called it tender-headed. I wanted to know how she did it so easily. I looked up and asked with a big smile if I could practice on her pretty, white hair, and she gave me the comb. She said that because of the texture of colored people's hair, there was a special way you had to separate the hair with a wide-tooth comb to avoid tearing it from the scalp. She said, "The best way to teach a five year old would be to part the hair down the middle first, then part half again. You listening Jade? Now act like you're twining a pole, honey. That's it. Go over and under, over and under. That's right, my baby. Look like you gone be a hairdresser some day." Before long, I was actually platting hair. Wow!

Every evening, I sneaked into her room for my lesson. Pretty soon, I was really good at it. Little Zoe caught on, somehow. She saw me going into Big Mama's room and wanted to come, too. Big Mama yelled for her to take her thumb out of her mouth. I laughed at Little Zoe. She was so funny. We called her Little Zoe cause she was named after our Mother. Then, we heard this awful noise coming from somewhere. Big Mama asked, "Who's making that ugly sound? Is that you Zoe?" Sure enough, she was popping her navel and sucking her thumb at the same time. I remember Big Mama telling her it was bad for her to suck her thumb because it made your lips swell. The next day, right on target, her bottom lip was swollen. I'd never seen anybody cry so hard. I wanted to make her better so I'd kiss her, but the swelling didn't go away. That night in our twin beds, there was plenty of laughter. We rubbed and poked fun at her till she fell asleep. I managed to play with her swollen bottom lip but wasn't much fun cause she was out, like a light.

My Father came to the door and screamed -"Cut out all that noise!" I put the covers over Bria's head as he cut the lights out. Bria was the oldest of the girls. She was also the prettiest, the sweetest, and quite sickly. My heart sank every time my Mother had to lay her down to rest trying to avoid her becoming ill. We didn't know what kind of sickness, just that my shy little Bria was so frail. I wanted to stay with her forever.

There was lots of commotion in the other room. We didn't know what was going on. The door swung open, and in walked Grandmother. My Father's Queen Mother. I nearly wet the bed! I believe Little Zoe did, but I wasn't gonna tell on her. There she stood – my Grandma - hateful as ever, and just a plain-old, fractious, hell raiser!

My Mother was pregnant at the time and needed to take it easy. She called my Mom in and questioned her in front of us as if she was a little child, wanting to know if she had given us a bath. She replied, "No" and held her head down as if she thought she'd get a thrashing any minute from Grandmother. I yelled, "Good night Mother, I love you," and the old witch turned to me and asked if I had on clean underwear. I scratched my leg until it bled and she spanked me hard as she could on my backside. That was a diversion to get her off my Mom. I pulled the cover off Bria and kissed her forehead only to aggravate my Grandmother even more. She yelled! "Leave that girl alone and take your ass to sleep!" I had made up in my mind at the age of five, I'd never be like that mean old goat and that one day, I would do whatever it took to get us all away from her.

The next day, everybody came over, even "Tee", our Grandmother's, sister. She was the good sister. My Grandmother nicknamed her "Peanut". I knew in my heart, something must be wrong because everybody was acting kindda strange. Dad was hugging Grandma, telling her everything was gonna be okay. Tee couldn't stop shaking her head and chanting - "Mama, please be all right." I was right. It was Big Mama! "What's the matter with Big Mama?" Nobody would tell us anything. "We were too small to understand," they said.

There was a knock at the door. It was Dr. Franklin, our family doctor. Back then, doctors really did make house calls. So this must've been pretty serious for Dr. Franklin to come all the way to the house.

I ran to my Granddaddy Alex, the old Bat's husband. Now, that was a match not made in heaven! He was the sweetest person on earth next to Big Mama, and a real man of God. He was always happy - even when my Grandmother (he called Nanny) was treating him as if he repulsed her. I honestly believe my Grandfather invented the suspenders he wore everyday to hold up his britches – giving him that superb, Mafia, look. Of course, he was also known for his hats that covered his shiny, bald, head. His skin tone was real red, like Choctaw, Indians. That was, by far, the best- dressed man I had ever seen. He had the charm, and looks, to match. Now, how Granny reeled him in, till this day, we still don't understand what he saw in her. I guess we had to conclude: love truly is blind!

I heard Dr. Franklin say that Big Mama needed complete silence and plenty of rest and that he would be back next week. Dr. Franklin didn't return, because the unthinkable happened. My Big Mama was gone! I mean, she was really gone. I just stood there with my eyes bucked really wide. I felt like somebody had just run over both my feet with a car and stayed there. It hurt so badly! "What was I going to do? Who was going to protect me from mean old Grandma and my Father?" Big Mama won't be here to see another spring turn to summer, I thought. "How was I going to get extra food when I was still hungry?"

I looked out the window and noticed all the leaves had turned brown. The wind started blowing hard and I could hear the shingles on the roof making that awful noise. I wanted somebody to hug me. I wanted my Big Mama. Nobody even knew I was in the room. Somehow, with my head down and mucous dripping all over my clothing, the flooded tears I shed blurred my view and caused me to bump into the lamp as it broke. I thought it was lights out for me, but nobody said anything, thank God!

That was the first funeral we had ever attended. We all wore black. I tried to be a big girl by not crying in public, but I could see my Grandfather make that awful squeal, then covered his face with his handkerchief, so I couldn't hold back the water from my own eyes. I used the bottom part of my dress to wipe my face. I remember lots of people coming over and bringing food. I never saw so many cakes in my entire little life! My Aunt "Tee" was still crying so Trevor, Jr., and Bumper, her two sons, and our cousins, took her back home. Trevor and Bumper were such hunks. They had girls falling at their feet, but they still treated them with civility. Aunt "Tee" taught them well.

She used to have us come over to help dust her big house and I admired her good taste in decorating. If you opened the back door to our house, you could see my Aunt "Tee's" house and my Grandmother's house next door to hers. There was a field of sugar cane, approximately an acre, which separated our house from theirs. I looked around at all our kin people and thought why hadn't we seen these people before? Granddaddy Alex walked over to us and stooped down to my level and stared into my eyes and said, "You know dear, Big Mama is still gonna be with us. She's in a better place where she can keep an eye out for us all. You can still talk to her. Just mention her always when you say your prayers at night. She loved y'all children a lot, and so do I. Now, give Granddaddy a big hug." I was able to release most of the tears I'd suppressed earlier because I knew he really did love us so I felt a rush of calmness that would help me get the sleep I desperately needed.

A year had passed and I was six years old. I thought I was really grown. This was my special year in the first grade and I was indeed a trip. Our first week in class, our teacher read us a fascinating story with pictures about how the Post Office got started and about the Pony Express. She said that the mail service remain one of the most popular, inexpensive, and simplest means for people everywhere to stay in touch with one another and to transact business. I raised my hand. "Ms. Badelt, will I be able to get a letter to my *Big Mama* up in heaven?" She said, "You can write as many letters as you'd like. I'm sure God will get the message to her, for you." I decided, right then and there, I was not going to be an Animal Doctor; I was going to be in charge of getting letters to people. My teacher called that person a Postmaster General. I remember as tiny as I was, her telling us how the Articles of Confederation, was adopted in 1777. She said it gave Congress the exclusive right and power to establish and regulate Post Offices. She went on to say that the President of the United States at that time was George Washington and he appointed Samuel Osgood as his first Postmaster General. I couldn't wait to get home to practice being in charge of my own mail house. I found three large boxes and cut them up to make a building and called it my Post Office. I made Little Zoe ask me for a stamp. Bria put her hands over her mouth to suppress the laughter because it was really funny to her. The boxes collapsed and my office was gone.

Suddenly, we heard a siren and ran to the door. There was lots of commotion going on and we wanted to know what the fuss was all about! Smoke was coming our way! The smell of something burnt was definitely in the air. Mercy, be! It was our Aunt 'Tee's" house. It was on fire! We had never seen a real fire truck, and policemen were everywhere. People were whispering that Aunt "Tee" must have accidentally set the house on fire with a cigarette. I remember thinking, "How could this be?" I found out that the awful rumors that were being spread were a major lie, and I made sure Milla McLaury and her friends and relatives understood as such. They put the fire out and "Tee" was okay but we stayed over to make sure she was gonna be all right.

I'm now in the 3rd grade and President of my class.

Miss Irwin called me to the front of the class.

"Jade - the Principal wants to see you in his office." Everybody was amazed and wondered, as I did, what was the problem?

"Run along now and hurry back when you're finished, said Ms. Irwin." She pushed her glasses on her nose and I could tell she wouldn't waste time looking for me if I didn't show up in the next ten minutes or so. She was what people referred to as a fluffy girl, and nobody messed with her cause she was a no non-sense kind of teacher.

Mr. Russell, our Principal, saw me standing in the door. "Come in little lady. We're having an assembly program day after tomorrow and I want you to read the program for me. You'll be my little Mistress of Ceremony."

"What do you mean by that Mr. Russell?"

"Go back to Ms. Irwin and have her help you. She'll explain."

"Yes sir."

"Hey Jade. Where you going?"

"I'm going to class, Trudie. You better get back to your room. Here come Mr. Russell. Run, Trudie!" My heart was beating really fast from the excitement, but I had to use the restroom.

I wanted to rush home and tell my Mother that Mr. Russell chose me to be on his program, but when I got home, my Mom wasn't there. She was down the street getting her beer on – on, what I remember as Crain Street.

I peeped out the door and there stood Ms. Lolita. "What's wrong Jade?"

"Nothing. Can Sean come out to play?"

"No. He's sleeping right now. Maybe tomorrow, okay?"

Ms. Lolita was our next door neighbor and her son, Sean was dying of cancer. Sean was so light, he looked white, but I knew he wasn't cause his Daddy was dark as me and Ms. Lolita was – what we called - high yellar. Her daughter's name was Mary Gale. Directly behind Ms. Lolita's house was Ms. Becca Gilchrist and her daughter Joyce. Down from her was Lonette Rose, and her sister, Delia. On the other side of our house were our neighbors Erica, Karyn, Ms. Daphne, Robbin, and her rotten sons. I can only remember Skipp's name. Ms. Daphne had a goat that constantly ate our clothes off the line.

To make matters worse, we still used an out'house, in which, on occasion, our neighbor, Skipp would open the door and peep in when it was in use. He tried to push me down into the bottom of the out'house.

"Help! Somebody help me!" He was such a sickie! He finally let go. I ran over to my Grandma's. This was the only time I ever wanted to be rescued and protected by the old, battle- ax. She went to see Ms. Daphne. All I could see was her finger pointing in Ms. Daphne's face with the other hand on her wide hips. Skipp never did it again.

When my Mother came home, my Father was waiting. I leaned up against the china cabinet with my hands over my ears. I knew my Dad was about to do something horrible to my Mom. Sure enough, as she walked into the door, he knocked her into the next room, screaming at her to never leave this house again. He accused of her having an affair and told her he'd kill her if he caught her cheating.

I flinched, scared out of my wits. I felt really sorry for her. I couldn't stop myself, as I yelled, "No!! Don't you hit her anymore, you hear me? Don't you hit my Mommie! I hate you! I hate you! Stop it!"

I thought to myself as I watched my Mother gasp for air and sob hysterically - "This woman, who bore nine children for him! This woman - who worshipped, and married him, at age thirteen! This woman, who he swore he had to have because she was so beautiful, was now being threatened to death."

I wanted to run to her and tell her that I'd be there for her to make sure that no harm came to her. I wanted her to come to school with me and stay all day so that I could protect her. Suddenly...telling her about the Principal of the school and what he wanted me to do on the school program - just, wasn't a good idea.

I backed myself into our bedroom and fell on the floor to pray. "No more God! Why won't you help my Mommie? Granddaddy said you were everything, God! All I'm supposed to do is ask and you're supposed to take care of it for me. That's what my Granddaddy told me. So why won't you help our Mother?"

Later that night, we could hear the record by the Flamingos called, "I Only Have Eyes For You." That song always made my Mom melt, and that other record called, "Lonely Teardrops," by Jackie Wilson. She always smiled really big when she heard them both. Give me a break! I knew my Dad was in there trying to run a game. I could hear the bed screeching, so we thought, maybe everything's okay.

That night I sobbed and hugged Little Zoe trying to figure out why the law let my Dad marry my Mom at age thirteen, when truly, everybody knew this was considered statutory rape.

All I could think of was that she never finished school. How she didn't have friends or never went to a prom or a football game or a movie. All I could think about was how, since 13, she had baby after baby after baby (nine in all). She didn't know how to do anything. She never learned how to drive a car, either. She had been trapped and alone for so very long.

Alcohol had consumed Fannie Rhea, her Mother, to the point of no return. So the only Mother figure my Mom had to emulate was the woman who hated her guts for marrying her only son.

She put my Mother down every chance she got - calling her a cheap floozy with no backbone. She said my Mom came from the wrong side of the tracks, and that's not what she wanted for her only child. My Mother was an exceptionally, smart, and beautiful woman. She may not have finished school, but she was by far much more intelligent than anyone we knew with the most beautiful handwriting in the world!

My Mom finally started feeling better about herself. She'd dress up really nice before my Father came home from work. He was a Chef at the Air Force Base in town.

Every evening, a motorcade of military jeeps, approximately 2 miles long, would parade along our street right in front of our house. The men were all dressed in camouflaged uniforms observing their many, many admirers.

After much persuasion from us, Mother got dressed and sat out on the porch. I was so excited! I knew that once the soldiers saw her, they wouldn't stop whistling. Sure enough, you would've thought Marilyn Monroe was on that porch. We jumped for joy and couldn't stop laughing. Bria, Zoe, and, I, all hugged with excitement. We could hear the song, "There Goes

My Baby - Moving on Down the Line," by the Drifters, and I delighted in turning the music loud enough for us to snap our fingers and dance for joy. No one cared that the rain was coming down fast and fierce against the screened porch. We grabbed Mother up and spun her around and felt joy to see her deep dimples come to surface.

For the first time, you could see Mom coming out of her shell. This was a real lady with a lot of style and grace. She was truly not from this planet! From then on, sitting on the porch became the highlight of each day. I could tell Mother became engrossed with one of the soldiers and I became really worried. This was supposed to be just a fantasy. But the soldier wore his heart on his sleeve.

I couldn't concentrate on the assembly tomorrow. I was too afraid we had created a monster.

My Father arrived, angrily shouting, "Where's my food?" Well, Mother didn't cook because she was out on the front porch watching the soldiers in the motorcade, but we didn't tell him that. I ran to him before he made it to the porch.

"Mother's been sick all day – Daddy. We think she might be with child again."

"What you mean girl? Did she tell you that?"

"Naw sir. We just figured it out."

"Ah hell! I'm gone to Mama's."

My Dad went over to my Grandmother's to eat, so we had a chance to rush her in the room to change clothes before his return. You can only imagine the conversation he and she had against my Mother. He came back to inform us that we would have to go over to her house on a daily basis from now on, to help her around her house and learn how to cook.

Reluctantly, we went over to her house after school. She gave us a list of chores that had to be done on a daily basis. She taught us how to pump water. She wrung the chicken's neck, and showed us how to pluck and cut him up. I held back the puke.

Daddy Alex brought home fish he had spent hours catching and she showed us how to scale and gut the fish.

The next day, we were to learn how to cook corn bread. I wanted to be first. She said, "Break the egg open into the bowl, child." I did, but some of the shell fell off into the bowl. She became infuriated and pushed me out of the way and said I didn't have the knack for cooking and that I was stupid just like my Mother. My heart was broken that she would talk to me in that tone so I began crying.

She stopped what she was doing and ran in the back room and retrieved a very large switch she had been hiding for this very moment. A switch was a combination of branches from a tree tied together as a weapon to try and beat the living devil out of you. Next thing I knew, she was hitting me across my back, my head, and one of the branches cut my neck. She kept yelling to me that I was hateful and stubborn just like my Mama and she wasn't gonna have any back talk. I wish my Big Mama were still alive. She wouldn't let this happen to me. She would take those branches from her daughter, my Grandma, and make her think twice about hurting me again. I could see Bria and Little Zoe buck their eyes in disbelief. I started asking her why I was being beaten and she thought I was trying to sassy her back. She pushed me into the room and told me to go blow my nose and when I came out I had better not make a sound.

The next day she stood over me as if to intimidate me hoping for a repeat performance of striking me across my back and face like she was some kindda crazy person.

"You know you've got that crazy blood in your veins from your crazy Mama so you know what that means; It means you'll never be nothing! Huh?"

Right then and there, I wanted to drop her, but I kept saying, "And, this too shall pass!"

The next day she had something else in mind for us to do. The weather was scorching hot. I think the man said it hit 105 degrees. We had to go outside to learn how to hang up clothes. Of all days!

"Now, I mean all shirts need to be hung together; All pants – I want'em hung together; All dresses the same way. Ya'll listening? Don't have me come back out here and, it ain't done right. I'll make ya take'em all down and start over. You say something Jade? You always got something smart to say." I accidentally dropped a clothespin on the ground so she slapped me on the head. "Don't let it happen again, ol' big head girl."

Her telephone was ringing. I had given the phone number to my little girl friend from school since I knew we would be at her house. She went in to answer the phone then came out.

"Come to the top of the steps gul. I'm having a problem with you," she said. "You the only one out of all these children who acts like a fool all the time. Ya'll are not my children. I'm just helping out my son cause he asked me to. Now, why you gave out my phone number? - Don't you ever, ever, do that again, missy! You understand? Do...you...understand?"

"Yossum." I was scared to death!

The next day she showed us how to clean her venetian blinds. She warned that she would wear gloves during inspection and if a spot of dust were detected, she'd take action.

It was my sister Bria's turn to clean the blinds and when she wiped them down, they still had dust on them. Man! That lady saw smoke! Immediately, she assumed it was my doing. Bria tried to tell her that it was her turn, but she wasn't having it, so I went ahead and said I had done it so that my sister wouldn't get a whipping. That whipping she gave me wasn't so bad since I felt I was avenging what could have happened to Bria. She was too sickly and vulnerable. I was being like Granddaddy Alex told me to be. He said, "Be a little dauntless sometimes daughter."

That evening, she had cooked a possum with sweet potatoes.

"I'm sorry," I told her. "I don't want that stuff."

She said, "Ain't no such thing as not wanting any, heifer! Food is not to be wasted and there are folk starving all over the world; So, you'd better eat what I put in front of you."

The only thing that saved me from this situation was my brother, Griffin, Jr. He was a permanent fixture at my Grandmother's house. She had raised him since he was an infant, and he acted as if his elevator didn't quite go to the top floor. He would, on occasion, stand in front of me and buck his head into mine as hard as he could and fall out laughing whenever he saw my tears. He would then poke fun that I looked like an ugly little boy and that there was never any hope for me to have a boyfriend in this lifetime.

My Grandmother always knew I had no problem letting her know how I felt about her, so she asked me to wash the dishes knowing it wasn't my week. I became angry, so crazy me decided to speak my mind.

"It's not my turn!"

"What you say? Is your mouth stuck out, Jade?" Without waiting for an answer, she pushed me into the back room. I stumbled over the red chair as she reached behind the trunk and grabbed a switch and threw it on the bed until she finished tying me to the chair. I pretended like I didn't have a care in the world. At the age of nine, I felt like I could handle anything after witnessing my Father brutalize my Mother. She stood in front of me and I looked away.

"Look at me, gul! When I tell you to do something, I mean for you to do it. You hear what I'm saying?" Before I could answer, I remember trying to hold my breath, but it didn't work. When I looked up and saw her raise all those switches that resembled a tree, the last thing I remember, was those branches, cutting between my eyebrows and neck. This wasn't discipline; it was hate. I closed my eyes tightly and held my head back and prayed one of the prayers I had heard my Granddaddy Alex pray. He used to say, "God specializes, baby doll, and keep this in your heart now, cause - he will do, what no other power - I mean - no other power - can do!" Suddenly, the pain seemed to go away, but the tears kept coming. I knew there was no such thing as calling somebody, anybody, talking about child abuse. I kept holding my breath with my eyes closed tightly, thinking this is temporary. "God, please make her stop!" I thought to myself, "Soon we won't have to put up with this abuse. Pretty soon she'll slip up, and they'll throw her behind in jail where she belongs."

When we got home I told Dad how cruel she'd been towards me and he said she was doing the best she could and that she was an old lady and set in her ways and we should show some respect cause she was all we've got.

"I'm not going back."

"Now see here Jade, you either shape up little girl, or you could very well, ship out. Now get on outta here!"

I walked outside when he wasn't looking and started picking honey suckles off the tree. The bees started buzzing around me in a circle, so I backed off and started doing cartwheels.

My Mother called me into the room to confide in me. She said, "You're a strong little girl, Jade. I want you to understand I'm going through something really awful right now and I need your help." She wanted me to go down on Crain Street to the house that sold beer and get her two bottles. I didn't want to go by myself, so I took Little Zoe with me. I was glad to get out of the house cause it made me feel important to help my Mother. The dogs were equally glad to see us. We had to hurry before Daddy returned. We were coming out of Mr. King's gate, when this big German Shepherd decided we looked like two sirloins. He ran us all the way home. We looked at each other thinking a close call was an understatement. I knew right then and there, as a little girl, I'd never make it as a mail lady. Dogs hated me for some reason.

When I opened the screen door, Daddy was home and he could see the brown bag I had under my arm. "Lord, Jesus! I knew it was over for me."

"Where y'all been?"

"Down the street," I said.

"And who told you to leave this house?"

Before I could answer, impetuously, he turned around and slapped my Mom, then told me to get undressed. I started pleading with him. My Mother tried to talk to him. He snatched the bag, which contained the beers, then drank them.

He then took off his belt and started wailing on me hard as he could. He said, with the worst frown on his face - "You are not to run to whore-houses, or cat-houses and get alcohol for this woman, you understand?" At that moment, I hated his ass, and resented his Mother, (my Grandmother), even more. When he finished with me, he grabbed my Mom by the hair and dragged her into the room. I could hear her scream. I covered my ears wondering why were we born? Why should anybody have to go through this? Why was this happening to our family?

I knew in my heart, as a little girl, something was very, very wrong with us. I knew that I missed Big Mama. She wouldn't have tolerated my Father's insanity. I knew I wanted to run away, but where? If we thought we were living a stern life, the next four days were even more hell.

My Grandmother wanted us to wash four loads of clothes by hand on something they called a rub board. We had never washed clothes before. She had us to get three big #2 tubs and fill them with water. One of them to wash clothes in, and the other two to rinse them in. The third tub, we had to put bluing in the water and called it the final rinse. She handed me some octagon soap that smelled kindda funny and showed us once how to smear the soap onto the clothes and rub them on the board until they became clean. Then you were on your own.

She came out periodically, and threw clothes back that we had already washed because she said they weren't clean. My knuckles were swollen and blistered. Our hands, raw from being in the water too long; calluses from ringing out so many clothes. We were such tiny little girls. It was murder on our hands!

To reward us for our extreme hard labor, she'd gather us all up and take us down the street to Ms. Mitt's. I could still hear the laughter about big head Aunt Mary as she churned buttermilk and opened the sacks of peanuts she'd roasted the night before so that we could slap one another on the hand and try to guess which hand the peanut was in. How exciting!

The next week, we had to climb trees and pick figs and pears. They had to be peeled very thinly so that your Highness could cook them and make preserves. I was tired and wanted to crawl into bed, but she wanted us to go down the street and pick blackberries. That was it! I had - had enough! I ran home.

There had been talk about a Panther being loose in the city. My Mother said not to worry.

My Mother asked, "Where are the others, Jade?" "They're picking blackberries," I replied. "I came home to be with you. You want me to throw the dish water out?" "That's all right, baby. I'll finish it," Mom said.

Bria told me what I had missed. She said they had seen a snake and it was multicolored. I watched and listened to her closely. I couldn't remember hearing her talk so much and being so excited. Bria was clairvoyant. So, I felt like she really knew what she was talking about. Out of the blue, she said she had a feeling something bad was about to take place in our family. I responded by asking, "How could it be any worse than it already has been?"

Later that night I could see my Mother, worrying. Dad wasn't home yet. It was a Saturday night. Obviously, he'd gone out on the town. My Mother stayed up. Finally, about one o'clock that morning, my Father came home and tried to open the door. My Mom went over and opened the door as he muttered, - "Help! Please get me something!" By this time, it was too late. He had thrown up all over the kitchen floor. My Father had let whiskey and God knows what else, assault his brain.

This went on for the next three nights. Our Mother had gotten to the point where she knew full hand to have the bucket ready for him to just let loose. It was a pitiful sight!

But tonight is an unusual night. It's a Monday night, and he's drunk again. After he threw up this time, she put a cold towel over his head. Dad jerks the towel off of his forehead and punches my Mom in her stomach as hard as he could for no apparent reason. The sound that came from the bottom of her gut - hurt me! She screamed, "Oh please God, help me!" Right then and there, I decided I'm just gonna kill my Father. That was the only way to have some kind of peace or calm in our household. My Mom was still curled up in a fetal position so I ran and got her some water. My Dad had fallen out. He was totally inebriated. I told Mother I would make it up to her. She kissed my hand and whispered for me to go to bed and that she'd be all right.

I was in the fourth grade now and we were sitting in Ms. Cranpo's class and one of my classmates, Evie - yelled out that my cousin, Sonia, and her family were all alcoholics. She said very proudly that she was told by her Mother, that the whole family, were a bunch of lushes. My cousin held her head down, but, I told Evie to take it back and if she didn't, she would have to see me after class. I tried to refute the argument but her virulent behavior gave me no choice but to vindicate her accusations. She wanted to know why I was taking up for Sonia, and had no idea we were related. The entire class was in a state of shock because I was such a quiet little person, no bigger than a quarter, was considered a book- worm, and furious with Evie.

My cousin, Sonia said, "No! –You'll be in trouble with your Grandma." She said, "Don't worry, I'll go get Diedra!" Diedra was our other cousin. I remember a while back when Diedra and Sonia sneaked over to our house when my Father left for work and wrote down curse words on 3 ½ x 5 cards so that we could learn how to "cuss the paint off the walls." After living like we were in a convent, I thought it was fantastic! I'll never forget when Grandma found the cards under my mattress...It changed my life!

Evie turned around again, and said, "Yeah! Yo Momma is an alcoholic, too!" I heard somebody say, "Whoah!" There was complete silence. She was talking about my Mother, now. Little did she know I was about to kick her natural ass!

The only thing I felt, was retribution. Indeed, those were fighting words and they knew I was fuming.

The bell rang. Everybody was chanting, "Fight! Fight! Fight!" They were all guarding me until we approached the cafeteria, then I threw my books down and I heard a scream from the crowd. It was really happening. At that moment, I knew I was in a quandary. Evie caught me off guard and slapped my face. I then pushed her against the cafeteria wall and started choking her while hearing all the noise from the crowd. Suddenly, something snapped in my head. She was trying to really hurt me so I went berserk and went for her throat. Regretfully, I ended up putting three long, deep - deep - scratches onto both sides of her face. Blood was everywhere! The meat from her face was under all my fingernails. By this time, three teachers came running and broke up the fight. I heard someone say, "Oh my God! That child is bleeding to death!" Her face was all messed up.

They yelled to call an ambulance. Mrs. Ferrel said, "Who is that other little girl? She doesn't have a single mark on her!" Mrs. Harris pushed through the crowd and told them to clear out. I could hear her mumbling to other teachers that I was an excellent student and that clearly, she was sure I didn't start the fight.

They made me come to the office to try to contact my Father. He couldn't be reached, so they called my Grandmother as next of kin and told her they had to hold me over for an hour because of what I'd done. I was yelling in the background that it wasn't my fault. Ms. Harris told me to be quiet. I could hear the Assistant Principal, trying to explain to Granny her version of what she thought had happened.

When I got home, Grandma surprised me with laughter. I thought she was gonna kick my fanny, but she kept saying, "That's right. Don't you let nobody, I mean nobody put they hands on you, child. You betta hadda taken up for yourself or else I wouldda kicked your ass for losing. I didn't raise y'all to be scary, ya know?" I thought about all the violence in our household and wondered myself if maybe their behavior had something to do with mine. All I could do was stand there and stare at her uproarious behavior. I had never seen her behave so inane.

She called my Father to rush home. He had to go to the school the next day and was interrogated over and over again. The Principal wanted to know if there were any family problems at home. My Father let them know that I came from a well-rounded, Christian family.

My new nickname from the school was - "Tiger." In the cafeteria, the guys brought my food to me. My teachers came over one by one, expressing shock and disbelief considering I was such a reserved little girl with a lot of potential and practically unscathed by the incident.

Pretty soon, they had stopped talking about the fight and I was over it, already. Thank God!

The girl was not healing properly and we were told the scars were permanent and there was some talk that she might go to another school. I felt bad, but was sending a message – "You can't deliberately go around hurting people for no reason. So you gotta be careful what you say and how you say it."

Everything was really quiet around our house. My Mom was making a banana pudding, which she did quite well. She was the originator, banana-pudding- maker. The smell from the oven was invigorating.

We were dancing to the tune, "What I Say", by Ray Charles, and it was a happy time, I thought.

Out of nowhere, Daddy jumps up and goes into the kitchen and we could hear the loud cursing over the music, then we heard the most awful gut scream from my Mother and ran to her rescue. Unfortunately, there was nothing we could do as we stood in absolute shock as he stood over my Mom, blood running hurriedly from her nose. He had broken it with the iron skillet.

I put my hand over Little Zoe's face – shielding her from all of the commotion - hugging her tightly - feeling every beat of her heart. My sister Bria began to cry hysterically! My Dad jumped to his feet and yelled for us to go back to our bedroom. The only thing I could think of at that time was again, plotting to kill him. He brought her from the hospital all bandaged pretending to care for her every need. They found out she was pregnant again.

Little Zoe was 9 years old and very impressionable. I wanted to protect her from any harm. Even though there was a year's difference between the two of us, I felt we had more in common than any of my other siblings and I made a point of trying to protect her. She was malleable at this age, but quite charming.

At age 10, I figured I could rescue my Mother from my Father's possessive, neurotic, abusive and insanely jealous behavior. The only sanity in my dysfunctional family was my Granddaddy Alex – my Dad's Step-Father, and the only person I knew who was a true, born-again- Christian. He had "joie de vivre", which means, "Joy of Life."

We sat on the front porch of our home and patiently waited for Granddaddy Alex to walk home from work. He had the most beautiful smile I had ever seen. We made a tune up by singing, "Here comes Daddy Alex." He'd then reach in his pocket and give us all a nickel and a big hug.

Grandma found out about the nickels we had been receiving and told us in no uncertain terms we were not to take any money from him, because, as she so sickly put it, "He's a man and men always wanted something in return." At that moment, I knew I really did loathe her. She placed my Granddaddy Alex in an ugly category with other men who could never measure up to him.

My Grandfather was born in Newsvale County, Alabama. He was a Master Mason of Lodge #938 F & A.M. Old as he was (71), he was a very, active and energetic person, kicking his legs in the air, jumping down - doing the split, and playing baseball, as if he was twenty-years old. He could also raise the roof with a sermon that only God presented him with. Everybody loved him. The man was magnanimous! On the other hand, Grandma, whom we called "Mom-me," was just the opposite. She was a combination of the characters played by Betty Davis and Joan Crawford (both well-known actresses), rolled into one. Evil - and more evil, or should I say, iniquitous - was her middle name. She was an infamous ogre who was disliked throughout the community. Most of the time she was our guardian, because Daddy was always working, or gone.

At long last, we found out our Mother had filed for a divorce and it was granted. The courts awarded my two sisters, Little Zoe, Bria, and I, to my Father. Junior, the oldest of nine children, was already living with Grandma and Granddaddy Alex. The other five children were to live with my Mom. We wondered where in God's name were they going to live?

I was devastated! Mother gathered the portmanteau, and suitcases then headed out the door. My tears came uncontrollably. I yelled her name and she responded, "Don't ever cry after me, you understand?" All I wanted her to do was take me with her, but she couldn't. All I could think of was that my life was over. I knew the way Mom-me, our Grandmother, would treat us. She felt like my Mother was trash and we were no better. When Dad went to work, we were in her care.

As she approached the house, we would look out the window and run to stand in place for inspection. I had - had enough of her crap! When we talked at night while in bed, I'd often confess my plot to escape this hellhole and never come back.

Bria would try to make everybody happy by making us turn to the wall while we were in bed, then ball up her fist and make signs of cartoon characters. The shadows of the fist really did look like some people we knew. She made me laugh, but I hated that room. The brown walls were closing in and they were quite dreary looking.

A month had passed and seemed like an eternity. We had found out that the judge had granted us visitation rights to see our Mom and other siblings. I was aching to see her. We had heard she was staying up on the hill about a mile down the road with some distant relatives.

Another week passed. We walked to school everyday. It was a Wednesday, and we were almost close to our cousin, Allison's house when we heard a voice. It was our Mother hiding behind the tree. We ran to her sobbing like crazy. She hugged us all as we held back the many questions on our minds since we were running late for school. She kissed us all on the lips and asked me why I had all those welts on my legs. I told her, in my Grandmother's eyes, I was an atrocious little girl. I wanted to know why we couldn't come and live with her. She said to try and stick it out a little while longer and she would see what she could do.

I arrived at school very excited because we had just seen our Mother for the first time in three months. I forgot all about the welts on my legs until Diane pointed them out to me.

"I know that old lady tore into you, right Jade?" I didn't answer. I just wanted this day to be over so badly, I could taste it. All I wanted to do was concentrate on how our Mother looked and how I wanted to stay in her arms forever.

The next day, I stopped up to the catholic- church on the way to school, and took my hair down. My Grandmother had platted it, as usual, into six plats, predictably so, every day. I combed my hair over again into a ponytail, and made some bangs in the front. My head was already too large for my little frame and for them to plat my hair into so many plats exposing how horribly nappy the texture was, made me sick. I knew I was plenty ugly, but this was going too far. I was ten years old and still had my hair combed the same way I wore it when I was five years old.

The other little kids used to poke fun at us, especially at church. We always had to wear long, homely dresses and oxford shoes, almost as if we lived in a convent. We used to roll our skirts at the waistline so that it would appear shorter, and was caught red-handed.

In our Sunday- school class, the kids used to whisper how they were gonna steal our pears and figs, the first chance they got. I told Grandma, and she began sitting on the porch with her shotgun. It was always loaded with buck - shots. Man! She was serious about her figs and pears.

One evening while in bible-study, something we did on a daily basis, Granny asked me who was the oldest man in the Bible. I answered incorrectly, just so she could move on, when suddenly, the noise of the boys from down the street became obvious. They were stealing our pears! We arrived home hurriedly and Mom-Me headed for her favorite chair so that she could have a perfect aim. My Grandma reared back in her chair, removed her handkerchief from her apron to wipe her mouth, adjusted her tan stockings which had fallen way below her bow-legs, and fired two shots towards the trees. Boy! They ran like crazy getting out of the pear trees. It was cold out there, too.

She was the talk of town for a while, and I assure you, nobody tried to rob us of our pears and figs, ever again. That old bird was plenty tough, I tell ya. She had everybody scared to death.

It's Friday, and I went through the same rituals as usual, combing my hair over and rearranging my clothes to appear more modern. This time, I forgot to plat my hair over and came home to an outraged witch. She took one look at me, pushed me against the bed and told me to strip. I took all my clothes off and everything after that was a blur. My Grandmother whipped me so bad, my hands swelled, my knees were cut, my lip was bruised, and I couldn't move because my back was hurt, too. I knew in my heart this was child abuse, but who was I gonna tell. I stood in the window and stared at her rose bushes. They were so pretty. I went outside to smell them because they seemed to be a bit of healing medicine for me. I swore that I'd always surround myself with beautiful roses the rest of my life.

I had no idea how bad I must've looked. I scared the dog cause he ran away. Granny really put a beating on me that time!

Later, that evening we found out that our other sisters and brothers were coming by to visit us. My joy was heightened, and I decided to put what she had done to me on the back burner.

Coda was the eldest of the younger set of children who were awarded by the courts in my Mother's care. At an early age, she developed a keen since of money. She knew how to economize and save when necessary. She was quite frugal. Coda had the most beautiful, innocent eyes I had ever seen in my life. My Grandmother questioned her, and out of fear, her response was "Yah! Yah! Yah!" We laughed, really hard, cause Grandma was grilling her about everything, and poor baby was trying to do the best she could. Our Grandmother came right out and called her a hypothetical liar. How dare she! My little sister was frightened senseless.

Then, if that wasn't enough, she walked towards my baby sister and told her not to put her hands on any of her little raggedy whatnots. Mace ignored my Grandma, being the inquisitive toddler she was. When Grandmother tapped her legs, she started screaming. She was so helpless. Mace went into hysteria. Since Mom-me couldn't stop her from crying, she decided to give her a reason to scream even louder. She tore into my baby sister with a switch to her little legs. I yelled to Grandma, she's almost two, and just a baby. Mace started screaming for help and muttering everyone's name as she held her little hands out for help -"Bri - Jade - Jade - Zo – Zo - Ian - Ian - Coda -Coda - Bri - Bria - Dino - Dino!" Her screams were heartbreaking! The sounds made us cry, too. Yet, we couldn't run to her. We were in hell. It had to be hell!

My little brother, Dino looked up at us, as if to say, "One day - it's gonna be me and that Broad." People were already talking about my little brother, saying, how, as a little boy, he had pernicious mannerisms. They kept saying that he didn't act normal. We couldn't understand why our Mother constantly took up for his obnoxious behavior. It was rumored that our Dad was not his Father. We often pondered, considering at age five he threw a knife at one of us when he couldn't have his way. The little snot! I whipped his tiny behind, but good!

It's Saturday. My Father had found a new girlfriend. Her name was Nicole. We were prepped before her arrival and told not to misbehave. We wondered what she'd be like and began to hate her already. We heard the car. My Dad had gone to pick she and the kids up. Yes, she had kids. Five of them, to be exact! I figured this would be short–lived since he already had nine children, so a ready-made family seemed, not an option. Then, we found out, two of the children were our Father's. Imagine that! This was insurmountable! The cheap bastard! He not only treated our sweet Mom like she was an alley cat - he had been cheating on her big time! I was repulsed! There were not enough words to describe how much I disrespected this man! His witch of a Mother thought he could do no wrong. She knew about this mess all along. I felt it my duty to confront Grandmother. I'm sure she would be impervious to reason.

The car is pulling up! Bria, Zoe, and I ran to peep out the window. We hurriedly dashed back into the room as if we weren't excited about the first meeting. There she was. My first thought was to be a complete bitch. My allegiance to our beautiful Mother was unparalleled. God knew I would never betray my Mom; she was my heart. Now, here stood this absolutely, gorgeous – stunning woman named Nicole. Her kids were Neal, Angus, Darrius, Alem, and Hans.

It was obvious they were from the other side of the tracks. I mean, the good, the very good side of the tracks. What could she and my Mother possibly see in this man, our Father? He was short in statue, with average looks. My first incline, as an eleven year old was, he must really, be packing!

It was January and my Father was ecstatic. He had the radio and television blasting with the broadcasting of Kennedy winning the Presidential Election. Man, you would have thought Dad was his Campaign Manager, the way he carried on. He told everybody to be extra quiet because they were playing his speech again. President Kennedy said that he wanted the people "To bear the burden of a long twilight struggle, year in and year out against the common enemies of man: tyranny, poverty, disease, and war itself." He told Ms. Nicole to look at the President's wife. He said to her that Mrs. Kennedy was almost as pretty as she was. He was such a liar. He jumped up and down as he called his best friend, Mr. Hickembottom.

My Dad asked us to take Ms. Nicole's children and walk them down to the hot spot of our little town. It was called Craig's drive-in where the best ice cream in the world was sold. All the major hunks, and, anybody, that was anybody, hung out there.

As we approached the hang out, we could hear the juke box playing -"Kansas City, Kansas City, Here I Come", by Wilbert Harrison. We started singing along, skipping and holding the kid's hands. As soon as that song finished, Gladys Knight and the Pips were a smash as they sang, "Every Beat of My Heart." Then, came "Tutti-Frutti," by Little Richard. Everybody shouted the words - "A-wop-bop-a-loo-bop...." What a great song!

I was eleven now, and thinking, it sure would be nice to have my first kiss tonight. Once we were inside, you could see couples paired off, smooching all over the place. I couldn't wait to reach the ripe old age of twelve. It seemed like an eternity. I figured this would be the age to get some real action, since some of the older kids I knew from school were inside getting their freak on.

The jukebox played on with, "Stagger Lee," by Lloyd Price and I wondered, "Why would Stagger Lee shoot Billie? What was this song really about?" Everybody's dancing. Then it was time to return home. I'll admit, I had fun, but those darn mosquitoes were monstrous!

It was late at night, and we weren't afraid because the neighborhood was relatively small and everybody knew everybody. There was no mistaking our house because we lived up on a hill. My Father was always in the yard. He was responsible for the landscaping in front. I can remember when he designed the tall, cemented steps that led to the front of the house. He took different colored marbles and inserted them into the cement and came up with a pretty classy little finish. At first, I thought it was kindda country, but when he completed the landscaping - it was quite charming. It was a small little house that my Father painted every three years to try and keep up. I can't imagine this being the little house where the nine of us were born.

Some of the houses were considered shotgun homes. It was one way in and one way out. If you stood in the front door, you could look straight through to the back door. On the left, approximately three miles down the road was The Paper Company. It was the famous company that manufactured paper towels. A little ways back was International Paper Company where my Granddaddy Alex worked.

My little community was a small suburb, of Mobile. Mobile is the second largest city in Southwestern, Alabama and a thriving seaport on the Gulf of Mexico. It's approximately 160 miles Southwest of Montgomery, the capitol, and about 130 miles east of New Orleans, Louisiana. The city maintains a system of free museums portraying the history of Mobile. The Azalea Trail, which is about 37 miles of breathtaking flowers is what I remember seeing on Sunday afternoon after church, when Daddy had enough spare money to fill the tank of the pretty green Buick. He almost took the paint off his car trying to maintain a shine.

Bellingrath Gardens is a 1,000 acres of beautiful flowers and trees about 20 miles south of Mobile. The Battleship USS Alabama and the Submarine USS Drum are on display at the waterfront.

The Municipal Auditorium in Mobile was the home of the famous Junior Miss Pageant, and some very memorable concerts. My Father used to tell me that the manufacture of wood pulp and paper was the leading industry. Because he was a part of the Air Force Base there, called Brookley Field, he said that aircraft engines, aluminum, naval stores, shipbuilding and oil refineries was another way that Mobile survived.

Further back towards our home was our church - the First Intermediary Baptist Church, where Granddaddy used to jump from the pulpit as he became filled with the Holy Ghost. My God! That was a sight to see. It was surely one of the reasons why some folk came to church. Speaking of which, since Granddaddy Alex was one of the ministers of the church, we had to attend church every night. If it wasn't revival, choir rehearsal, bible study, it was "BTU".

It's summer, and we must attend Vacation Bible School. I kindda felt we were being groomed for the convent, no doubt.

Down the street was the Elks Lodge, where the older folk, got their groove on. Speaking of the Elks, the Masons would sometime congregate here for their meetings. My Father and Granddaddy Alex were both

Masons. They would wear those hats with the tassel hanging on the side. It looked as though all the men wearing them carried around some kind of secret amongst themselves making them more than, unified.

My Grandmother was an Eastern Star and held the office of President and, feared by all, I'm told.

It's Sunday again and Ms. Nicole is back. This time, she cooks dinner. I was sure not to like whatever she prepared. Boy! Was I wrong! She not only cooked a full course meal - she made a mean, lemon-meringue pie, too. I couldn't find anything I disliked about this woman. I just couldn't understand what she and my Mother saw in my Father. I do know he was a pretty smooth operator.

The moment came, when he announced we were going over to her house. The majority of her family was at her parent's home. They had a pool table and a very large, striking living room. We all sat outside at the picnic table which accommodated about thirty people. Somebody put on the oldie but goodie called, "Mother-in-law" by Ernie Doe, and Dad seemed paranoid. It was obvious these people had a little money. Impressive, to say the least. It was apparent to all, that Dad was pretty serious about Ms. Nicole.

Christmas came. I wasn't excited about this holiday because it only lasted for a day. Grandmother never bought any presents. She always made the same cotton slip and quilt as the year before. I was grateful, no doubt, and was advised by her that we should be on our knees thanking the Lord every minute for her being in our lives. Okay. That's all well and good; I just wanted a doll that I begged for every year. A doll! I swore that when I became an adult, I would always keep dolls in my presence at all times! Christmas was the only time that all of the family congregated together. I was energized because it was the only time I would see Grandma take a sip of something home-brewed then watch her become a much nicer human being.

You couldn't move my Granddaddy Alex from the television. He was so excited over the new boxer, Cassius Clay whose name was later changed to Muhammad Ali. Granddaddy would sit on the edge of his chair and box as if he was in the ring himself. "Look Nanny - listen to him talk. He's talking bout how pretty he is. He beat the stew outta everybody!" Granddaddy's on the floor now with excitement. He's holding both legs in the air as he yells, "Boy, that Clay makes me happy cause he can sho punch!" I wish I could've been around when Ali knocked out Sonny Liston, I thought. I'm sure Granddaddy must've jumped to the ceiling.

That following week, my cousins came running to us from down the street to let us know that it was told to them by Mary and Eileen that our Mother was very ill and not expected to live.

"What do you mean - not expected to live! What the hell are you talking about?"

"Jade, y'all better come quickly!"

"Tell me again. This time go slowly. Now, who said what? I'm, not believing this crap. Our Mom is too young to be talking bout dying, so what right do you have to come over here and upset us like that?" Unbelievable! The news was much too much to handle.

Our Father was getting ready for work so we told him what was told to us and asked to visit with our Mother three hours instead of the, one hour, suggested by the courts.

"It's all right by me, if, Mom-me agreed," he said.

"We shouldn't have to ask for Mom-me's approval since Mother's illness is life - threatening. My God Daddy!"

"Watch your mouth Jade." You still have to have her approval." Our Father was married to this woman and she bore nine children for him and he couldn't make a decision. I didn't get it.

After he left for work, we walked to my Grandmother's house to inform her of our Mother's condition, and to let her know that Daddy had given us permission to stay at our Mom's house for three hours. She then responded, "I can only let you all stay one hour since you'll have to finish dinner for your Father."

I was outraged! Who did she think she was? It was no secret to all that knew my family that Mom-me hated my Mother. I stared at her, then yelled as loud as I could, not giving a damn about the consequences, - "Daddy said we could stay three hours, old lady." She then slapped me hard as she could, like I was another woman she wanted to fight, and not, a little child. She pointed her finger and swore - "You bitch! You ain't gone never amount to nothing, you hear me? I'm cursing you in the name of the Father! Now go do like I told you before I beat your ass!"

Killing her at that moment would have been too easy. In a matter of seconds, I had flashbacks of her trying to slaughter me with her homemade switch she declared as discipline. That wasn't discipline. I ain't crazy. She was acting out her loathing towards my Mother by half killing me. I thought if I retaliated, I would probably spend the rest of my life in prison and she wasn't worth it. I mean, really!

She then told the others to go home and finish cleaning the fish. She said, "Put some lima beans on, then, prepare to stay at your Mother's for an hour and come on back here." I tried to hold back the tears, but couldn't. My heart was broken because I knew that if our Mother was critically ill, there was no one available to take care of the smaller children at her house. Granny looked at me in disgust as I turned to leave and said with her finger pointed in my face once again, "Nothing good's gonna come of you – I promise you that!" Right then and there, I knew since she said it twice, she meant it and I had to do everything in my power to prove her wrong. I mean everything!

We ran back across the sugar field to get to our house. I knew when we left to visit our Mom - I sure as hell wasn't coming back.

I began putting can goods into as many pillowcases as I could find. I took most of my Dad's towels and linen, and put them into other pillowcases to take with us to my Mother's house. Bria and Little Zoe were scared.

"Mom-me is gonna kill you Jade and she's gonna be furious. I don't want you to get into any trouble, so why don't you put that stuff back," asked Bria?

Little Zoe said, "Yeah Jade - put it back!"

"No! It doesn't matter, I'm never coming back."

We walked up the street on the way to my Mother's little house on the hill. Kenny and Rodney were passing and wanted to know what we were carrying. I looked to the right and saw Ms. Ginger Mae, our insurance lady, on her way to my Grandma's house. Man! Was it hot! When we arrived at my Mom's house, I knew in my heart I was never going back.

The small children were crying from hunger. The house was filthy! Coda was nine years old at that time and was trying to cook. She was the oldest in the household when Mom wasn't there. The flies had taken over the place and not a clean dish in the house. My Mother had been rushed to the hospital in an ambulance. She was hemorrhaging. What a nightmare! I can't even be with her, and on top of that, the baby needed changing; No clean diapers were in the house, so we cut up a sheet till we could wash some clean.

I looked at the clock. It was time for us to go back to our Grandma's house and my sisters were very afraid.

Again, I shouted, "I am never going back to that place!"

Little Zoe said –"I'm with you Jade". My oldest sister finally agreed, reluctantly. Three, long hours had passed. My Dad drove up on two wheels and sent my brother...Junior, to the house to tell us to come on out. Junior looked at Bria and appealed to her good senses and told her Dad needed her to come to the car. I told him we weren't coming.

He went back to the car and we watched in horror as my Father yelled, "I'll be back goddammed!" He bucked his eyes like he does when he wants to kill somebody, then started blowing real hard like he was a mad man. We thought he was gonna turn his car over as he tried to make the curve.

Minutes later as he returned to his Mother's house, Dad called to tell us how much trouble we were in and to tell us that Mom-me would forgive us if we would just come on home. I wasn't hearing it!

The rest of the family found out and began to go crazy. My sisters quit worrying so much, and that made me a lot calmer.

The next day we went to the hospital to see our Mom and was made aware by the doctors that she was gonna be okay. Ah man! I was half free from anxiety and looked towards the sky to give praise to the Lord for saving our Mother.

The day after that, was the hardest. Bria was weakening. God, bless her soul. She was so sweet and wanted desperately not to disobey Mom-me, our Grandmother. We knew how wicked that woman was, and, if we were to return to her house, we knew she'd plot something evil and nobody would be there to rescue us.

The next day was Sunday. I called up our Uncle Phillip on my Mom's side of the family and asked if he could come over and take us over to our Dad's home so that we could get our clothes. He looked stunned. He didn't have a clue as to what was going on. He just knew that we'd always stayed with our Father and my Dad and his relatives never associated with he and the rest of my Mother's family. Aunt Penelope told him to be careful. When we arrived at Dad's house, we didn't want Uncle Phil to know that our Father and Grandparents were at church.

There was no way to get into the house, so I cut the screen, broke the window, and climbed in to open the door. We were hastening, knocking over things, but managing to gather most of what we needed. We then packed everything my Father had in his pantry to eat. I, then, went in to get as many clothes and linen as possible. Three trips in my uncle's car sufficed.

Two hours later, church was over. I was expecting the inevitable. Just like clockwork, Dad showed up with a Police Officer, a Truant Officer, along with Grandfather, ready to throw me into the Reformatory School.

Mom had made it home that day and was lying on the couch looking as if she was just visiting because she knew there was nowhere else to sleep.

Our Daddy yelled -"Come on out here! I know y'all are in there! You don't have anywhere to hide. It's that Jade! That heifer broke my window and tore up my screen and I want her put away!" My Granddaddy and Mom begged our Father not to let the Truant Officer take me away. He didn't want anyone else to go away – just me! He said, "Nobody else was capable of such hell in them, except Jade."

He looked at Bria and said, "I know you didn't have any part in this, baby. You either, Zoe. You are much too young to conjure up such treachery and I don't hold you responsible."

Granddaddy stood up and said, "Come on son. Leave the girls be. Leave Jade alone. Let'em alone, I said!"

The Truant Officer, Police, and my Father stood up to leave – and after much persuasion, Daddy gave us the okay to stay a few days. A few days! Little did he know we had no intentions of ever returning!

The next week, we convinced our Mother to try for housing assistance. She took our advice and was awarded a five - bedroom apartment in the Projects. This hellhole was called, "Cheerful Cliff," but we soon found out there was nothing cheerful about it.

I had my own room. All I could think about was getting a turntable inside my room so that I could practice dancing since we weren't allowed to do so at Mom-me's house.

There was much talk about a new, sexy artist with a deep voice and a new 45 single out called, "He Will Break Your Heart." That man was Jerry Butler. I think I played the record fifteen times before they all became agitated. So I shocked them with the song - "Party Lights" - by Claudine Clark. I could really sing that song. "I see the lights, I see the lights. I see the party lights, they're red and blue - and green".... I'm talking some serious dancing. What I really wanted to hear was some Jackie Wilson. My Mom seemed happy when she heard him say -"Work Baby, Work Out." Then, she'd scream over Brook Benton, as he sang "Any Day Now," - now - that was the song!

It was time to get serious. Right away the first thing on the agenda was helping to get our Mother a job. She had never worked, so she had no work experience. Luckily, on her first interview, she got a job at the Factory down the street. Duh! I wasn't gonna be bragging anytime soon about this occupation. But, to look at my Mom, you'd thought she'd won the lottery. She had to wear plastic over her shoes, hair, clothes, and no makeup. The factory wasn't too far away, so she walked everyday.

It was Friday and she got her very first paycheck. Everybody at her new job went to celebrate - making it through the week. Surprising to us, when she returned – Mother was plastered. Boy! Was I furious! But, we let it slide since this was a celebration of her first actual payday.

Three days later, she was plastered, again. Then, the next day, and the following day, too. We discussed it among ourselves and decided, Mom needed this off- the-wall behavior because she never had a life after giving birth to so many children and was constantly trying to please Dad, and, after being so sheltered, this was like a future shock.

The following week, a beer became an everyday thing. Right behind the Projects was a house of ill repute. They did everything in that house. It was widely known as a Cat-house. We were all very concerned! Things never eased up. They got worse.

I spoke to my Mother about the situation thinking she wouldn't mind a concerned ear, instead - she picked up a chair and hit me across the back with it and screamed –"I hate you – you ugly - ugly, Muthaf..ka. You look just like your damn Daddy!" I begged her to stop. I'm dumbfounded at this point and shocked beyond belief that our Mom would have such a temper. Where did this come from? This sweet, demure person, enunciating, so perfectly, the worst language imaginable! Little Zoe tried to come to my rescue, but got some too.

School was out at 3:00 and when we came home, my Mom was already there - she wasn't alone. The door was shut to her room so we opened that door – Lord, have mercy! A bald headed maggot. We beat and kicked him out. We called the police but knew they'd never come to our rescue living in this hellhole. Mother was under the influence again.

I began to cry but pulled it together as I thought of my Grandmother and her threats to me that I'd never amount to anything. I cried a lot; not because I was weak, but because I was a little kid - we all were little kids trying to make adult decisions and trying to hold it together so that we could all stay together under one roof. We wanted to make sure that no authority would come in and separate us no matter how difficult the situation was.

Mom had to throw up so I helped her to the bathroom and rubbed her head with a cold towel. We had a long, long, talk with her. We thought she was listening about how she was supposed to be a role model and how our Pops and his Mother were hoping the worst for all of us and how she needed to pull it together if we were gonna show them all.

I stressed to her that the terrible things they were saying about her were not true and that she needed to stay sober so that we could make sure we proved them wrong, but she became angry and asked me to get out.

The next day I noticed she was still home, so I asked why she was just sitting there. She was reticent about her reasons for being there, then, finally confessed.

"I was fired!" My mouth flew open wide!

Did I hear you correctly? "You what?" It was over! She no longer had a job. She couldn't find another so she drank her problems away. When she was inebriated, she came after me in a fit of rage because I resembled our Dad and the man she was married to for so many years.

On this day, September the 6th, I will never forget it as she started choking me and I couldn't breathe. This was it! I knew it was the end for me. My Mother, my sweet Mother was actually trying to kill me! She really wasn't responsible for her behavior. She was out of her mind. I was tired of all the abuse. I was tired from watching my Father abuse her. I was tired from her turning on me. I was plain ol' tired, so I decided after this episode, I couldn't take it anymore.

I ran to the bathroom and got as many bottles of prescription medication, as possible. I opened and took all the pills I could find because I wanted to die!

All I ever wanted was my Mother's approval and her love. It seemed no matter how much I tried, she resented my presence. I couldn't help it that I reminded her of the only man she'd ever loved since she was thirteen years old. It wasn't my fault that I was an ugly kid and mirrored his image. As it turned out, all the pills I took were prenatal vitamins. I was kind of relieved that I got another chance to live. I was so little. I weighed in at 85 pounds.

As a form of celebration, I went through the neighborhood and told all the kids we were having a party, and they were all invited. Sabrina was the ring -leader for the females in the Projects. She had the largest rear end I had ever seen. She informed everybody she knew about the party. I told Dexter, who was the ring- leader of the male gang in our Projects.

Jesus! I was terrified of these people, but thought if they were invited, we wouldn't have any problems.

The night of the party, I remember the song – "Money - That's What I Want," by Barrett Strong, blasting throughout the neighborhood. They were jammed in the little apartment like sardines. Some of the hooligans were on the porch because it was too crowded on the inside.

Then, I heard somebody say, "Y'all got that song by the Contours, called - "Do You Love Me?" I thought they were losing their minds when we played it. Half way through the song, when the man said – "Now That I can Dance, Shake it Now, Do you love Me" - my Mother burst through the door, drunk as usual, screaming, "What's going on up in here? Y'all - - - jooking in the dark. Git the hell out!" I was so embarrassed! Everybody scattered. Where did they all go so quickly? Little Zoe and I ran out the door holding hands. Bria stayed and tried to soothe Mom. We finally found humor in all that happened and we never heard a word about the incident ever again.

The next week Little Zoe and I had found out about a big hay- ride going across the Bay to the beach, on Friday. We stayed out till past one o'clock. How were we gonna get back into the house. We approached the house with a plan in mind.

I whispered to Zoe to stand up in my hands and climb up to the window and open it and get into the house and run and open the door for me. She whispered, "Okay." Little did I know that when she got through the window, she ran and got in the bed with all her clothes on, pretending to be asleep. I didn't know what was going on so I jumped up to the window softly yelling, "Zoe! Zo!" Before I could finish her name, my Mother came to the window in a frantic. You could tell she was mad as hell! I looked up into her bucked eyes as she asked, "What the Sam hell are you doing out there?" She grabbed me and pulled me up through the window, with one hand and demanded a response. I told her that Zoe and I had gone on this hay- ride and she slapped me and told me in no uncertain terms, "Stop lying on your little sister. She's in the bed sleep, where you should've been." I ran to try and show her that Zoe was still wearing her clothes, but she pushed me away from her and told me to get in the room and prepare for a beating. I looked back, only to see Little Zoe smile, then pulled the covers over her head. I was so mad I vowed never to have anything ever to do with my little sister again!

After Mom couldn't find work locally, she finally concluded, she had to go out of state in order to find work. She ended up getting a job in New York working for a rich, White family.

I was still 12 years old, my oldest sister Bria was 13 years old and Little Zoe was 11 years old. The rest of the children were a year apart and there were nine of us. My oldest brother was 14 at the time and living with Grandma.

Since my Mother was taking up residence twenty-five hundred miles away from us, it was a scary, scary thought living in the house without any adult supervision. We were not to tell anyone about this arrangement so we called a meeting with all the siblings and explained that this was our special secret and that no one, but no one, must ever know. Our Mom was to send a little money home whenever she could. I tried to be brave and pretend that I wasn't afraid, but my heart was leaping from my chest. I finally contained my emotions and decided we were definitely gonna make this thing work.

During this time, we, sometimes, subsisted on just bread and water until we could hear from her. I remember once sneaking next door when they all were on the porch, stealing our neighbor's loaf of bread so that we could make mayonnaise sandwiches. Sometimes we just sucked on sugarcane.

I would walk through the Projects, knocking on doors to see who needed their hair pressed and curled in order to make money. I was paid $3.00 from each customer to style their hair and the money went towards food and throw rugs for the waxed floor.

While in New York, our Mother's drinking became more profound. Her appetite for alcohol became insatiable. She hung out at the Seamen's Club where she met a man by the name of Humi Lyle.... Little did she know that this person was in deep involvement with someone who practiced witchcraft!

Her first night with him, she swears he cut some of her hair, then, went to someone that practiced voodoo with it.

She began to speak in another language claiming that someone had put a spell on her and she had no control of her actions. She came home for a visit and God help us - it was a major mistake! She was acting very strange. I didn't know who she was. She looked like our Mother, but the sweet, decorous lady we knew and loved seemed to have disappeared. I was frightened. What was gonna happen next. Bria said, "Let's call Uncle

Delson, her brother." Then we all concluded it would be best to just call the doctor, instead.

No sooner than we could get our thoughts together, Mother sneaked outside in broad daylight, took off all her clothes, walked backwards down the street of our neighborhood passing by four houses with a crown on her head – screaming she was King Hussain's woman. Jesus! I wanted to die! What happened to my Mom? We called the ambulance. People were shocked beyond belief. Cars pulled over. The police showed up. Everybody was astonished. Mom was totally irrational and tried extremely hard to fight anyone that put their hands on her. Nobody could hold her down. She was finally contained and taken to the mental ward at the state hospital.

God! - Please, help me to stop crying. I was in so much pain for my Mother. She never had a good life. Never finished school; never went to a fancy restaurant; never went to a ball game; never went shopping with a friend; never accomplished any short or long term goals; never took time for herself; too busy having babies. I just wanted to go to that hospital and stay with her until she was released. I loved her so much. She was such a fragile, beautiful lady.

I remembered the times I would fit my fingers into her dimples when she smiled because they were so pretty. I wanted to lay her head on my shoulders and let her know it was gonna be all right. I wanted her to relax for once in her life and let somebody else take care of her instead of her always doing the nurturing.

Bria reminded us all that, at least, this way, she would get help and we could go and see her as often as they would let us. The next day was pretty gloomy. I was kindda depressed, but knew I had to concentrate on me, now.

I finally made it to the eighth grade. So much was happening. I was working two jobs. One of the jobs consisted of hot - shotting tires at the new car wash. Tips were kindda good. My other job required me to hitch hike thirty miles away from where we were living. Most of the time I was really scared. Nobody in their right mind would let a thirteen year old hitchhike alone at night with strangers to get to a job she was already too tired for and not old enough for either job.

Tonight as I wait for a ride, I could tell something was wrong. There was something strange in the air. Wow! The truck went up the street and came back around. I was scared to get in, but I knew I had to get to work across the Bay. When I got in he said, "How you doing little lady?" I told him about getting to work and he said, "You know, you don't look no older than them little girls got bombed today. They was Negro girls just like you, child." I tried to act like I knew what he was talking about. He kept talking and finally disclosed that four little girls had been bombed in a Negro church in Birmingham and he said, "They put that Martin Luther and some of his associates in jail." While in jail, we found out that Dr. Martin Luther King wrote his moral philosophy, which became known as, his "Letter from Birmingham Jail."

I was a year younger than the children that were killed in the church in Birmingham. They were just little kids like me. What a scary thought! At our age, kids usually looked to their parents for guidance. At age thirteen, most of the time there's a parent or guardians at home preparing meals and helping with homework or just somebody there to say, "I love you." I wanted to know that kind of love. I wanted to be cared for and hugged and talked to. I wanted to hear somebody say something nice to me for a change, something encouraging to motivate me to be all that I'm supposed to be. But, there wasn't anybody. I'm so lonely. I wanna let somebody know, but I can't.

After work, I had to hitchhike back home in time for school.

The money I made helped to buy fishnet stockings, clothes, plastic curtains, and two- for- a- dollar, throw rugs. The little ones wanted some popsicles and stage planks. I bought sardines, potted meat, cookies, hot dogs, Royal Crown Cola's, and Nehi drinks. Tired! I was truly, truly...tired!

All I could think about was that it was almost Thanksgiving, and I had to get across that Bay one more time so that I would be able to afford a turkey. I tried not to think about it in class today. A tear fell because I wanted to tell somebody our secret but I promised the rest of my sisters and brothers that I wouldn't, and you never break a promise. All of this was my fault anyway so I had to suffer the consequences. I was undernourished and lacked sleep. I needed a hug somebody. I needed somebody to take care of me.

"Ms. Jade have you been asleep in my class?"

"No sir. I'm not feeling well, sir." If he only knew I hadn't been to sleep all night. I had to work the 11 to 7, shift across the Bay, then hitchhike to class this morning. Nobody could tell. Nobody ever became suspicious. Imagine that!

Suddenly out of nowhere, all the bells started ringing. We heard a scream. People were breaking down crying. I wanted to know what could possibly be going on.

Finally, somebody came into our building and told our teacher to let us know President John F. Kennedy had been assassinated.

He turned on the radio and we sat in silence that afternoon as everyone sobbed uncontrollably. The news traveled across country, even in West Berlin when Mayor Willie Brandt said, "A flame went out for all those who had hoped for a just peace and a better life." I think I was torn into a thousand pieces and became frightened. I didn't have parents to run home to. There wouldn't be an adult at my house to finish discussing the particulars of this tragic incident. So, we tried to calm each other.

My Father was ordered by the courts to bring food over to our house as part of his child support. The five bags of groceries he brought over, always but always, included the same things every month. He would buy three loaves of bread for a $1.00, five cans of pork and beans for a $1.00, four packages of wieners for a $1.00, a pack of fish sticks, and whatever else he could get in large quantities for a small amount of money. He asked where our Mother was and we lied that she was still at work.

He and the rest of the family had no idea that we were in the house alone. No one knew about my Mother and we kept it that way. Usually, when I got home and there were a bunch of boys hanging around on the porch with my sisters, I would often run them away for fear somebody would get pregnant, then everything would go down the tubes. I didn't mind at all that they referred to me as a cock- blocker. I wanted us all to remain a family without interference.

My little sister, Zoe was so cute. I was worried about her because she had the body of an eighteen year old and she was only thirteen and I'm now fourteen. Little Zoe had great legs, very busty, a round butt, and a smile that oozed - s e x! Nobody could tell her anything. The girl was fine. She often came in my room and listened to some of my oldie- but- goodies. Music was very comforting for me. It took my mind off of our Mother.

Tonight, one of my favorite songs was playing - it was called - "Cry, Baby" by Garnet Mimms. I would often close my eyes and imagine what it would be like to dance slowly with someone of the opposite sex during a song like Cry, Baby. It was so beautiful. I stopped daydreaming long enough to catch the beginning of "Green Onions," by Booker T. and the

MG's. I found an oldie by Jackie Wilson called, "Lonely Teardrops" and, "It's Just a Matter of Time", by Brook Benton, and fell to the floor, in awe.

My imagination ran away with me as I pretended I was being held tightly on the dance floor as Brook Benton continued to say, «It's Just a Matter of Time." We remembered this was one of our Mom's favorite tunes. Enough of that! It was time to do the Cha- Cha.

Zoe wanted me to show her a new dance. For a minute there, I almost forgot Mother wasn't here with us since we were having so much fun swinging out and two stepping. As Zoe was leaving the room, "Mr. Postman," by the fabulous Marvalettes was blasting. She couldn't go then. We pretended to be the Marvalettes. We stumped and hollered --laughing as we sang - Please, Please - Mr. Postman, Look and See - is There a Letter - a Letter For Me. Our little brother, Dino, and, Ian came in to dance. It was too funny. I held Dino's hand as I spun him around, and Ian placed his hand over his mouth as he almost choked from laughter. Then, our favorite record, of all times, was blasting. It was "Duke of Earl," by the great, Gene Chandler. Ian held both of Mace's hands, as he swung out, danced, and chuckled. Little Kendrick, the baby, bopped his head from side to side, also. Coda came in and sat on the bed and joined in. We had great harmony.

Out of nowhere, Dino hit Ian in the head and we broke them up as we talked to them and explained to Dino that violence is unacceptable, and definitely not an option. As they left the room, Dino was still trying to latch out at Ian. Ian was so quiet and very much wanting to be like Dino. I knew from the start that Ian was something really special. We were all special, but there was something really mystical about Ian. He often sat in a corner and tried to read everything he put his hands on. When he wasn't paying attention, Dino would sneak and put on Ian's good pants, splitting the seams, because they were too small for him. We had a talk with Dino, even spanked him, but it didn't do any good. He was a little shit! We often tried to propitiate his anger. He'd pretend to whimper and we wondered if the terrible experience of our Mother had unhinged his mind.

Bria came upstairs and Dino seemed to calm down. She was like our Mother - kind and humbly, sweet. Baby Kendrick jumped into her lap and started kissing her and wouldn't stop. He kept trying to kiss and kiss her some more. I wondered where he learned that kind of behavior. It was hilarious, and became a daily thing with Kendrick. He was in awe of Bria because she was so pretty. We sometimes joked with her that Daddy wasn't her real Father, and that perhaps our Grandfather was really her Dad. We'd all laugh uncontrollably at the thought, as she'd let us know in no uncertain terms, we were nuts.

In school today, we found out that the same man, Dr. Martin Luther King, Jr., that my Aunt Fran and Uncle Neal were telling our Big Mama about, when I was just five years old, was recognized for his efforts to bring peaceful change to America. He received the Nobel Peace Prize. He was the youngest person ever to win such an honor. My Dad's prediction that he was going to be somebody great one day really came true!

Today, little Kendrick isn't laughing. He won't stop crying. We all got together and decided we should do what our Mother would do if she had been home. We tried to remember what Grandma and Dad did every time we weren't feeling a hundred percent. I went next door to Ms. Sarah's and asked if she had some black draft and cod liver oil. We gave some to Kendrick and watched him throw up.

Coda told us to tell the story to the little ones about the castor oil Daddy used to put in our grits, and how Grandma didn't disguise her tactics, either. She poured castor oil in a big spoon and made us chase it with a lemon. "Ooooh! Gross! Sometimes, they would even put it in our cream of wheat."

Since we were reminiscing, Bria and Zoe wanted me to tell them about the time I had sores in my head and Daddy shaved it and used some sort of home remedy to rub my scalp daily and my hair grew back really long, and too thick to comb.

Little Zoe said, "I betcha I can top that y'all. How bout the time when Daddy had to go to work and couldn't find his military shirts." She had everybody scared as she went on to tell how our Dad finally found his shirts bundled up and carefully hidden by me. She told how he made me strip butt naked in front of everybody, then took my head and placed it between his legs and wore me out. Bria said, "Yeah, Jade, that was the worst!"

Dino said, "How bout that time when somebody left the iron on and it burned the wooden floor and Daddy was so mad he couldn't get a confession, he beat everybody in the house." We screamed with laughter. How did this little boy remember such torture? He was much too young!

I fell across the bed as everyone left the room and had a moment of calm. This time I'm daydreaming about how someday I'll be a singer and no one would have to know from whence we came. Then I could rescue us all and it would make up for all the bad, bad memories. I thought about, maybe as a reward, God would give me a perfect world after all of this. I wanted perfect children, a perfect house, and a perfect man. I knew these things were non-existent, but it felt good to say them out loud.

I'm fifteen now. It's hard to concentrate on my math. Mr. Chedson is getting on my nerves at school. He had a talk with me after school. There he goes, staring at me with those big eyes, looking at me like I'd stolen something. He told me that I was hanging around people that was gonna cause me to fall behind in my studies. He knew I liked hanging around Dedra, and to me, she was more than good people. He also knew I liked Stacey. His justification was unfathomable. Where did he get his information? He said he knew I smoked cigarettes and desperately wanted me to stop. I was stunned. No one knew I smoked except my sisters. I started when I was thirteen. I thought it made me look mature since, I weighed in at only 85 pounds. During this time, my sister Zoe, my cousins, and I often drank Mad Dog (M-D 20-20), Boone's Farm, and plenty of screwdrivers. It made me crazy and enhanced my cravings for cigarettes.

The following week, Zoe came to talk to me in private. In all I stood for, my little sister Zoe admits she's pregnant. Everybody felt sorry for her because they said she didn't know any better. They were all convinced that since she tried to emulate my every action, and must have seen me do terrible things. Lord knows this was far from the truth! I was still a virgin and had no intentions otherwise. She tried to tell them I was not at fault, but no one would listen. They thought that because I was gone all the time, I must have been up to no good; instead, I was trying to make a living so that we could live.

I begged and begged for us all to keep a low profile so that others wouldn't know what was happening in our household. Everybody was interested because it was so many girls. Zoe was soon to deliver the baby so she and the Father of her baby got married against my will. Man – was he a jerk! He constantly made passes at all of us. My sister Zoe was much too good for this asshole.

Aunt Yelma and Uncle Delson, my Mother's brother and his wife, came over and said they wanted to help. They said they wanted to take Bria to live with them because she wanted to graduate from their district. They were considered the better side of my Mom's family. I prayed that Bria wouldn't get pregnant. She was away from me and I couldn't keep an eye on her. I still had a point to prove to that troll. My prayers were not answered. She got pregnant but it was much later during her last year of school.

I continued to work really hard, but my schoolwork had fallen way - behind.

Still, no one suspected we lived in our house alone without anyone to take care of us. I was doing the taking care of for everybody. At night I had two pillows. One, to lie on, and the other to cuddle with. I often pretended that my pillow was my Mom or just somebody holding me and helping me through the night. I was so scared. There were many nights when I wanted to call my Granddaddy to help, but knew since he was a man of the cloth he couldn't lie to his wicked wife, so I never called.

It wouldn't be long before somebody found out. What would happen? Out of the eight of us, not counting Griffin Junior, since he lived with Grandma, they would split us up and put us into different foster homes and possibly, we would never see one another again. I couldn't let that happen.

Gunshots were very loud tonight. I jumped to my feet with eyes bucked wide. Glass shattered in the bathroom. Someone was breaking in! It was more than one person. I recognized the voices. It was the worst gang in our neighborhood. They had stocking caps on their faces, kerosene cans in one hand, and knives in the other. My heart was pounding, and I knew it would explode. They were looking for the small check my Mother received every month, and the check she sent us from her job she landed in New York taking care of rich folk. The intruders looked at all of us, in each bed. "Please God! Don't let any of them rape or kill us," I said to myself! Remarkably, they never touched us! They just wanted the money.

Every month - the same thing would happen. They're breaking in again. Won't somebody help us? It was unheard of for the police to show up. To this day they never realized we knew who they were, but were too afraid to admit it. The gang leader's name was Dexter. He thought he was God's gift. And I'm sure he's responsible for the others not harming us, when they very well could've.

Today, as I fall on my knees, I'm taking all the blame for all the things we're going through. My Grandma threatening that nothing good would come of us. Lord, I'm so afraid and tired. Please help us!

I must tell my teacher what took place last night or - should I? Mr. Walsh was the only teacher on the face of this earth that I would entrust with any of my personal information. He truly believed in me as a person, always encouraging me to become a Journalist. He took interest in me during the beginning of the 7th grade. I would compete in Oratorical Contests for the school and almost always won first place. He often took me to perform at places like the United Way, where I had to represent my high school, then turn around in assembly at school, and repeat the same performance. He was so proud of me and made me feel like somebody. I confided in him a tiny bit of what was happening at home. He couldn't believe it.

Me holding down two jobs, helping out at home with no time for me personally, he wanted to know who was taking care of me! He said, "You're just a child, Jade!" I knew he felt sorry for me, but didn't let it show. He kept saying, "Someday young lady, you're gonna make everybody in this town proud." Wow! My confidence shot to a new level. I won another contest and convinced myself that I was going to be a Journalist just like Mr. Walsh wanted me to...so that I could get out of this place and take my family with me.

It's a Thursday, and I'm feeling really sick. My private parts were hurting something awful! All I could do was recall when I turned eleven years of age, a couple of months before we ran away.

My Grandmother was cooking her usual buttermilk cornbread to go with some butterbeans and hamhocks and I was suffocating from the wonderful aroma. I asked Grandma if Griffin, Jr., and I could go up to the Catholic Church and race our bikes. She surprised me with an okay response.

My brother came up with the idea for me to ride his bike and he, ride mine. His bike had a hump in the front made for boys. The race was on. I was winning the race with my Brother. I looked back to gloat, riding very fast with him trying to warn me, but I thought he was being bitter that I was winning, and I ran into a tree. The impact sent me flying way up, then back down on the front of the hump in the middle of the bike – splitting my vagina. Jesus! I bled like a hog. Oh yeah. I knew I was dying. My Brother ran home in a panic to let Grandmother know that I had been injured really, badly. She explained to him that it wasn't anything wrong with me and told him to calm down because it only meant that I had started menstruating and that it happens to all little girls.

She ordered him to hurriedly run to Ms. Russell's family store and bring back some sanitary napkins. I tried to tell her that I was in a lotta pain and that it was not my period – but she wasn't hearing it. I never went to the doctor, and was constantly hurting. I was forbidden to ever talk about it, so I learned to live with it.

As I looked back on those events and how much pain I was in, it would have been really nice if I had someone, preferably, a female to talk to – to help me. I felt so lonely! I needed someone to help me with - just - life itself. I need some help God! Just somebody to tell me about the facts of life and hug me in a way that would be sincere love and admiration. I didn't know what that was. I didn't know what it was like to look up to somebody - I mean, in a motherly fashion and want to emulate that person. I didn't know what it was like for somebody to lovingly say, "I'll always be here for you." I just wanted somebody to brush my hair for me. Someone to experiment with new styles, as I got older. I never knew what it was like for somebody to say, "Wow, you really did well in school today, sweetie!" When I was winning contests, and being on program, no one ever came to represent me. There was never a support team. My teacher, Mr. Walsh was my only support group. He was like the Father I'd always imagined having.

My teachers would often ask where my parents were, but because we were minors, living alone without supervision, I didn't dare tell the truth. I would hold my head down, and say, "They are working."

This particular night, I remember being hungry, but didn't want the fish sticks and pork 'n beans, anymore, so I fell asleep dreaming that I was eating hot biscuits and apple butter. I remembered waking up crying because I felt all of this was my fault and whatever happened to each and every one of us - I was the blame for it. That morning my eyes were swollen from crying all night. As I stared in the mirror, I decided I must continue to be strong so that Granny wouldn't say the infamous words, "I told you so!" I vowed to start thinking positive as often as I could. Besides, my breakfast and lunch for today...was a slow poke. It lasted a couple of hours. I kept sucking on that chocolate till it was gone. It killed my appetite. I was so little, I decided to buy some "Weight On." My neck, arms, face and butt blew up like somebody had been pumping air inside of me. God! What had I done? I looked like a football player without the shoulder pads. I needed to look older for my job, anyway.

That evening, I saw the guys putting tat-too's on their arms. Diego was the ringleader. He was a cutie with a very large head and pigeon toes. He kept coming over to our house because he had a thing for my older sister, Bria. She didn't seem to pay him any attention. His tat-too came out really pretty. One of the boys in my class from school was there also and I wanted to impress him. I'd do just about anything for his attention. He didn't notice me, so I begged Diego to put a tat-too on me to gain his interest. He said, "It's not for girls, now go away." I told him "I can do it, pain, or no pain." They all started laughing. I held my arm out as if I knew what to expect. "No ma'am! If only somebody had told me!" They took a needle, and ink and started sticking me with it. Diego asked what I wanted my tat-too to be? I said, "I want my initials on my arm." Then I became really bold, and told him to draw a fancy line underneath it. Big mistake! Not only, didn't the little boy from my class notice me, but, Ms. McCord from our school said that if I wanted to continue representing my school in Oratorical Contests, I had to have that contraption removed from my arm, immediately!

I found Diego and told him what she said, and his response was, "No problem. We'll take it off just like we put it on." Wrong! They got some goat milk, alcohol, a match stem, and rubbed my arm until it burned badly. My arm was swollen for two months with the aid of a sling.

I was walking down the street with my arm messed up, when Lyle, from my class approached me. He wanted to know what had happened. He started coming over every day to see how I was doing. He was kindda cute. I had no idea that Dakota was his cousin. Chelsea would often bring me messages from her Brother that he decided he was my boyfriend. He showed up at the door just before I went to work to give me a ring and I was already entertaining his cousin, Lyle. I felt really bad. I couldn't understand why anyone would be interested in me anyway. I was an ugly child, but determined and ambitious to the point of exhaustion.

My first period was math and my teacher was very vocal and enjoyed class participation. He called on me to participate in the class. Surprising to the entire class, I cracked a funny. One of the members of the football team commented, "She's not only a brain, she's a comedian, too." Oh my God! He was staring at me soooh much. Instead of me appreciating his advances, I became annoyed.

Everyday for about a month, he was cutting me off so that I couldn't get to my locker. The other jocks with him kept saying, "Man - ain't no way you gone get no play from her. Not this year! You might as well forget about it. She don't talk to nobody man." Jeff leaned over me with a sly smile and a long stare and asked, "Are they right?" I walked away without a word.

The next day, he came to me and asked, "Jade, would you wear my ring?" I wanted to know why, since it didn't belong to me. He laughed and wanted to know why I was always alone and never associated with anybody in the class. I didn't want him to know that I was hiding a major secret. I didn't want anyone to know that we lived in the most notorious Housing Project in the world and alone.

I always carried myself like everything was normal so that no one would become suspicious.

Today is the day for the election of the Thespian Society. I was voted as one of the officers – I nearly flipped. Jeff sat next to me every day and brought attention to all of our classmates. Soon, the whole team was asking me to come to house parties and calling me Jeff's girl. I tried to tell all of them that I wasn't interested, but it was like no one, was listening.

By this time, I heard rumors that some of the older females in higher grade levels, were having sex with some of the football players and I became furious. I was paranoid thinking – this must be the reason for the interest. Everyone was anxious to find out who was going to pop my cherry, first. I tried to stay busy and out of his way. He asked if he could call me since I wouldn't let him come over. I saw no harm in it. My heart was pounding so loud it embarrassed me because I thought he could hear it.

As I made conversation with myself, I convinced me that I was strong enough to be with the opposite sex and not engage in any sexual activities until marriage. I had something to prove.

My head was down with a big smile as I walked home from school. As I approached the apartment, this voice came out of nowhere.

She said, "Why the smile?"

I looked up at her and said – "Hi" –

"Don't you live in that first apartment?" she asked.

"What's your name?" She replied, "I'm Marcia and what's yours?"

"Jade."

We continued to talk and she asked what school I attended and she told me her school was about 10 miles away and that they were having a big dance Friday night and asked if I would go with her. I pretended that I had to ask permission and would get back with her. Man, I couldn't believe it. Everything was changing. I met this wonderful girl a couple of doors down from me and one of the football jocks was trying to get me to wear his ring. The sun was shining and it was a beautiful day.

I immediately quit my job where I had to hitch hike 30 miles away. I had more time on my hand and more time to think.

My little Sister Mace met me at the door to ask if I would take her to the park so that she could swing. Her hair hadn't been combed and she had been crying. It brought back memories of when we first moved to the Housing Project and she was so hungry and trying to cook bacon at three years of age. The hot grease fell over and burned her with third degree burns on her leg. The ambulance was not gonna come over to this particular Projects – it was too horrible! The police even took a very long time to answer a call. So I had to think, hurriedly. I immediately grabbed Mace as she screamed to the top of her little voice. My heart went out to her. I started to cry, too. I was so scared. I didn't want my little sister to die. So I picked her up on my side and ran outside and kept running – she was too heavy for me to keep running. I finally made it to the doctors. He couldn't believe I had traveled that far by foot carrying her alone, and afraid. She was still yelling. "I want my Mommie!" I told her it was going to be okay and I would buy her a pickle if she'd stop crying.

He repaired her burned leg and I felt some relief. From then on, my little Sister was very attached to me. If I approached leaving the apartment, she would scream for me to take her with me. I would always make her stay and try to convince her that I would be back soon and that I would take care of her. But, she would fall to the floor and have major fits. Just watching her react so uncontrollably would break my heart.

It's now Friday, and I let Marcia know that I would go to the party with her. Boy! Was I nervous! She wanted me to stick close to her because her friends were a wild group. She was well known at her high school, and every where we went, people wanted to know who I was. Guys? There were about five hundred. All I wanted to do was sit back and admire others and, hope they wouldn't notice, but the guys kept on coming. They all wanted to dance. I kept saying no, but they weren't having it. This was quite different from my school. They appeared, more mature. Marcia is really laughing now because they are all asking who I am and wanting to get a date.

Jim knocked over my punch and commented to Marcia that he was surprised some of the main team members weren't there. In walks one of the captains of the football team and everybody's cheering and he's having a field's day from all the attention. So I asked Marcia, "Who's that guy?" She smiled really big and said, "That's Dylan."

Chris came over again and wanted to dance. This time I agreed. They were playing my song – "Dancing in the Street," by the fabulous

Martha and the Vandellas. I was a good dancer and decided to dance very innocently, but the others didn't seem to think so. "Yes ma'am, I was showing out!" They wanted to mimic my steps, then before long, everybody was doing my dance. I was having a blast!

As Chris walked me back to my seat, Dylan grabbed my arm. I was amazed as Chris announced to him, "Un ass my woman, man!" I turned to him and said, "I'm nobody's woman." Dylan followed and asked Marcia to put in a few good words for him. He said he wasn't leaving until I agreed to give him a phone number. He leaned over me and said he had never seen anyone move like that before and wanted to know where I got my moves, from? He also wanted to know how much I weighed. He claimed, I was very petite like he liked them – whatever that meant. I was not impressed in the least, just ready to go.

Another female friend of Marcia's came over and we all laughed as she gave us the run down on all of the so-called wannabe Don Juan's. That was a welcome change, and, a lot of fun.

Just as we were about to go, the last song began to play - "I've been - Loving You - Too Long - To Stop Now," by Otis Redding. Dylan grabbed me and held me really close. I could feel his heart beating. Come to think of it, he kindda looked like Otis. That was unfortunate. Nevertheless, I had big fun.

My Sister Zoe finally got rid of her dead weight of a husband. She finally met the man of her dreams. His name was Tinsel. When he came over to the house, we were all there to welcome him. Tall, and exceptionally, good-looking, was the perfect description for him. He was about to go to Vietnam, and we were hoping and praying that he would come back in one piece. So many people were dying. We had heard that Calderon had gotten killed. He was a really good friend and a great guy! He will be greatly missed.

A year passed, and by the grace of God, Tinsel returned. He lost an arm. He and Zoe got married. My brother-in-law, Tinsel, was awarded some years later, the Coast Guard Silver Life-Saving Medal for his heroic actions in rescuing a couple whose vehicle was forced off the Dauphin Island Bridge, with one arm. They had their second little boy. A real cutie, he was! This same little boy later became a Chaplain (Officer) in the Marine Corp. During the fruition of this book, Zoe and Tinsel have been married over 46 years.

Marcia came over every day and repeatedly talked about the party, and how many people were interested in me. She came over to bring me a note from Dylan. He wanted a date.

On the news that night, 8:00 curfews were in effect. What a drag! The phone rang. It was Dylan. He wanted to come over tomorrow. He was so persistent. Dylan crawled, ducked and dodged until he made it to my house. He didn't want to leave and now it was past 8 o'clock and if caught, he could go to jail.

Now, he's gotta do the same thing to get back to his house approximately seven miles away from me.

Three days later, I had just celebrated my birthday. We turned on the television, and I couldn't believe my eyes. They were saying that Martin Luther King Jr. had just been killed after talking with his staff on the balcony of the Lorraine Motel, in Memphis, Tennessee. Say its not so! Tears flooded my eyes, as did the rest of my siblings as we watched in horror. Dylan called, but I couldn't talk. The news was too devastating. I need a hug really badly!

Two months passed. Dylan insisted it was really time for sex since he felt like he was in love with me. I still wasn't ready. I was much too afraid to get pregnant. I didn't know how to do it anyway. What was all the commotion about? It didn't look like much fun. I remember when we first moved with our Mom, and our cousin would bring over one of his girl friends, and we would hide in the closet and peep through the crack. We'd watch, as our cousin would lie there waxing his carrot. "What's he doing," asked Zoe? "Shhh. I don't know. Be quiet before he hears us." We wanted to know a few minutes later why the lady was always screaming - "You're hurting me! It hurts! Please stop!" Well, it looked like he was fighting her instead of loving her, and to me, that sex thing everybody was talking about seemed overrated. Why would anybody wanna participate in anything that involved pain anyway? Go figure!

Marcia informed me of another party and Dylan called to tell me he wanted us to attend. The same crew, were there again. Some of the guys were happy to see me and wanted a hug. Dylan saw me hug one of his rivals and went ballistic. He walked over to me without warning and slapped me as hard as he could. I kicked him in the groin. It didn't seem to hurt him in the least because he turned around and hit Chris in the stomach really hard for jumping to my defense. By this time the biggest brawl had started! Everybody started screaming and running and then there were gunshots. I was frightened out of my mind. He then grabbed me and we started running and when we made it to his car, he started to cry. He continued to babble on, how sorry he was. He said it was love at first sight for him. I seriously did not want to talk to this person again. He freaked and I thought he was gonna kill himself. That should've been my cue that he was a crazy person. Don't ask me why, but I felt sorry for him.

Dylan wouldn't go away. That night, the sirens were in full force in our territory, in the Projects. Two people were brutally murdered right down the street, shooting a game of pool. Then, that morning, they shot Mr. Joe, the vegetable man that came around every day with his vegetable truck. He always gave me free grapes and tangerines. I couldn't believe Mr. Joe was dead. I don't know how much more of this nightmare I can take!

Dylan called and told me all the things I wanted to hear. He said that it was a crime for me to have to under go so much pain and indignity living in the place where we were. He admitted that he wanted to show me a better life and show me how wonderful life could be if he was looking after me. He appealed to my every need and I so desperately wanted to feel like I belonged and that I was loved. I wanted to be taken care of for once in my life. I was so tired from the two jobs and keeping house and watching over the little ones.

Another month passed. He came over and took me to a really nice restaurant. The waiter came over and gave me a rose. Attached to it was a ring. He then got down on his knees in front of everybody and asked me to marry him. I said, "Yes!"

My Sisters were thrilled. I asked him to accompany me to my Grandmother's so that he could ask for my hand, and, he did. She wanted to know what he would do about my schooling and he said that he would make sure that I still went to college since it was my dream to become a Journalist.

I was informed by the principal of my high school that I was to speak at graduation along with the Valedictorian, Salutatorian, and, President of the Student Council. I didn't want to do it, but Dylan insisted I continue to do what I had always done in the past.

I informed my teacher, Mr. Walsh that I was gonna get married two days after graduation and he begged me not to. He said that he had big things in store for me and that he wanted me to be that writer I had always wanted to be, and that my dream wouldn't be fulfilled if I had a break from my education. Wow! If only I had listened. But, I was too determined to take a rest.

There had been plenty of nasty rumors on campus at my high school, regarding Mr. Walsh and me, but none of them were true. Mr. Walsh was my only true friend. He tutored me for most of the major oratorical contests and made sure that I would win. He also tried for a scholarship in Journalism for me at one of the prominent Universities. He displayed all the editorials I had accomplished as co-editor of the newspaper for our school, and I can still here him telling me, "You've got talent Jade. Don't let it go to waste."

I was to be married two days after graduation and Dylan was to go straight to the Army. We were having a big Graduation Party after Class Night and as we were on our way Dylan turned up to announce that he had a 4-F classification from the Army meaning he was disqualified from entering the armed services. He wanted us to go home and celebrate the fact that he wasn't gonna have to go to the military, but, I wanted to be with my class to celebrate our graduation. What a bomber!

He pulled his act with the tears, and, I fell for it. We were all so elated over graduation. Everybody was hugging and crying. The majority of the football team apologized that the rumor that was started that I must be gay because I wouldn't have sex with anybody, was the highlight of my night. They told me that there was a bet on who would score first and as it turned out - no one won. They said that I just happened to be a very nice and determined young lady, and hoped that I wouldn't let anything stand in the way of my dreams. Dylan looked like he wanted to throw up. He said, "Let's go!"

The next day he asked his neighbor to sew my wedding dress and his Mother got everything else ready, on such a short notice.

The wedding was very nice. I finally thought my life had changed for the better. I thought I would finally live normally and be able to watch television and eat a normal meal with my husband and have my own apartment and then attend school so that I would get my degree.

Big mistake! Dylan decided he wanted us to live with his Sister. He wanted to finish technical school and get a job when he graduated. The moment of truth! I had to have sex with this man. Well, I was still a virgin and knew little or nothing about sex. I was truly afraid!

I went to the family doctor and asked if he would write a letter to my husband explaining my condition that I could not have sex right now. I didn't have a condition. I was just afraid and needed time to get used to the idea. No sex went on for about five months.

One evening after school, Dylan came home and found me dancing very provocatively to Tom Jones. Tom Jones was one of the most dynamic entertainers that had hit the stage during this era. I didn't realize he was standing in the door watching me perform. The next thing I knew, he was tearing my clothes off. Not pulling them off, he was literally tearing my clothes from my body. His strength - where did it come from? The brutal slap he gave me landed me against the wall and blew my mind. I didn't have time to think. God! What was happening to me? Who was this person? I thought he'd stop and show remorse, instead, Dylan punches me with hard force to the stomach. "Oh! My heavenly Father. Work one of your miracles and let this be a very bad dream!" The pain was excruciating, and I couldn't think straight. He plunges towards me and devours my virginity as if there was no tomorrow. It was the most God, awful experience of my entire existence!

My first child was conceived. I named her Paige - an African Princess, from the book I read, when hospitalized. I stared at my beautiful baby girl who amazingly came from my tiny body. What joy I felt! Somehow I knew I was going to give to her what was and had been nonexistent in my life - lots of love.

I forbade him to come near me again. My daughter was born during the week of the worst hurricane in history, called, "Hurricane Camille." My baby was very small, gorgeous, almost like a doll. I was terrified. I had no earthly knowledge of what I was gonna do with a little baby. I just knew I wanted a much better life for her, than what I had.

Three months later, he sexually assaults me again, and Toury, my little shining star would soon enter into this world. "Lord, what was I going to do?" I just wanted my life to be better. Now, I was bringing babies into the world and had no idea how I would take care of them. I was twenty years old, and, in a real bind. My husband had no job. I couldn't work because of the new babies being born and no one to care for them if I did work.

Everyday I looked at my babies very carefully, and even though they were conceived by force, they were magnificent and I loved them dearly. I wanted so much for them. I wanted to make sure they wouldn't have to suffer as I suffered. All my life as a kid, I always hungered for love. I got on my knees as I promised God I would always show them love. I wanted to be the parent that would nurture and love them the way a Mother is supposed to, letting them know that no matter what...I would be there for them. I wanted to teach them strength, character, compassion, sharing, love, trust, dignity and respect.

As I continued to daydream about my babies, the door opened. It was my husband. He sounded angry. The first thing he did was come in the room and started choking me in front of the girls. I couldn't breathe. As I struggled, he mumbled something about not being able to get a job and how he couldn't take it anymore. Toury started crying and I tried to reach her but he decided he would throw me across the bed. He didn't know his strength, because my head went through the wall. Blood flowed rapidly from my scalp as he suddenly came to his senses. When I regained consciousness, I could hear him scream -- "Jesus!" He was kneeling and swearing that this would never, ever happen again. Trembling, he repeated the words, "I'm sorry baby, I'm so sorry. Please forgive me." I'm thinking, at that moment, he really is a very sick person. I got involved with this man trying to escape the Projects. He was crying like a fool, and all I wanted to do was protect my kids. "Lord! What did I get myself into?" I had gone from bad to worse and shoddier! He grabbed me to try and wipe away the blood, but I wanted to be rid of him forever. I didn't have anybody to ever be there for me when I was growing up. Now, look what I've gotten myself into.

A week later, I called my Sister to see if we could come and live with them for a while. She wanted to know what was wrong. I didn't want to get into any details so I talked very slowly so that the tears falling from my eyes wouldn't give me away. I didn't want them to know that I had married a maniac. A truly deranged, thoughtless psychopath and I was so, ashamed. What was I going to do? My Sister reminded me of the amount of people already living in her one bedroom apartment. I had to tell her that it was okay, and that everything would be all right. Dylan came into the room, still sobbing and apologizing for his behavior the week before. He swore on his Mother that he would never do anything that bizarre again and volunteered to get professional help. Even though his actions were reprehensible, I fell for his lies.

Two months passed. I knew my husband had a natural talent for repairing cars and major appliances. The neighbors found out that he had these capabilities and began asking him to repair their automobiles. Tim wanted him to put a cam on his car so my husband did and charged him a beer for his time. When I found out I was furious.

The lady next door needed her air conditioner fixed. Dylan repaired it and told her to just give him two dollars to buy a six-pack. I freaked. This was his opportunity to bring some money home so that we could pay bills and prepare for a better home. Instead, he does these things for free! When I approached him with it, I wasn't prepared for what was about to come. He knocked me in my eye and mouth so hard I passed out. When I came to, he was on top of me ranting and raving about how I was never gonna leave him and how he would kill me if I did. This went on for hours. I no longer cared any more. To me, being dead would be an awful lot better than being with him.

The phone rang. It kept ringing. I managed to convince him that the persistence might be his family and might be an emergency. Sure enough, it was his Father calling to invite us to a barbecue. My lips had swollen so large I was unrecognizable. I could not see out of one of my eyes. My baby cried when I picked her up. She didn't know who I was.

He went to the barbecue and when the girls and I didn't come with him, my Father-in-law became suspicious because we didn't come along. He seemed to like me a lot. He said I was innocent and fragile. While everyone was enjoying the barbecue, my Father-in-law came to the house to bring us some food. I didn't want to answer the door, but had to. When I opened the door, he said "Nooooh! Lord - have mercy, Jesus! Did that boy do this to you?" I started crying and didn't say a word – he placed the food in the small kitchen and said, "Dear, he won't put his hands on you again, I betcha that." Then he left.

My Mother-in-law called and told me that his Father returned to the house and knocked Dylan almost through the living room wall and vowed to kill him if he put his hands on me ever again. She said, he told Dylan that I was the sweetest, brightest young girl he had ever encountered. My, my, my! What was going to happen? I had nowhere to run. Would he obey his Father or take it out on me again? When he returned, he said nothing. He grabbed a beer and went to sleep.

The letter finally arrived letting him know that he had been hired to build pre-fab houses. What a great day! He swore this would change everything and that now he would treat me like a queen because all our troubles would finally be over.

The job was an hour away from home. He decided for the first three weeks, he would take the children to his Mother's to give me a break, against my will. Then, he became paranoid. He said that he dreamt I was gonna leave him. Dylan decided he would tie me up every day and place water and crackers in front of me until he returned home. This was worst than slavery!

Every time I called the police to complain, the police turned out to be friends of his he graduated with. They would always take his side and say – "Man! You need to control your woman." I told them that he was physically abusing me and he would take them aside and give them some sob story, then, they'd leave. Finally, I found a way to leave him for good. I convinced him not to tie me up any longer. I promised that I would be good and that he had absolutely nothing to worry about.

When he left for work, I contacted the Air Force Recruiter that had come over to my school some years ago and wondered if my scores would still be good enough or, if I would have to retest to join the Air Force. The recruiter wasn't there, but the lady said he would return next week. I didn't give up.

The next week, I continued to try to be really good so that he wouldn't become suspicious about anything. I finally reached the recruiter. I gave him my name and the school I had attended and the year. He said – "Yes- here it is. You did extremely well, ma'am. But, you'll have to retest." I started to cry and he wanted to know what the problem was. I told him I was married and in a life or death situation with two small children. He asked if I could come to his office and I told him I had no way. He said, "I don't think it would be such a good idea to come to your home ma'am, considering your husband's history." He said, "If you could get a ride over to my office, I'd see to ya getting back."

Right then and there, my head started to pound. I almost chickened out until I looked in the mirror and saw the scars – I knew eventually, he would kill me if I didn't get away from him and start a new life away from this town. I knew I would have to reinvent myself and pretend that this part of my life never existed.

So much time had already gone by. My dream of finishing college and becoming a Journalist, was not a reality. Who had I become? My drive was almost gone. My ambition was at an all time low. Why on earth should I be subjected to such abuse? I hadn't done a thing to anyone; and had been through hell and back, already!

I mentioned my babies to the recruiter, but he said nothing about them. I wondered if this would be justification to disqualify me from entering into the Air Force? Who can I get to take me down there? My next door neighbor. I'll try her.

I ran next door and knocked. Nobody came. As I was leaving, the door opened and she said, "May I help you?"

I said, "I'm your neighbor, and wondered if I could get you to do me a favor." I promised to pay her the coming weekend, for gas. I explained that no one must know about my plan.

"Honey, I know all about your crazy husband."

She said, "Don't you have small children?"

"They're with my Mother-in-law."

"Um huh. Okay. Well, come on. You ready?"

I was so excited! She noticed the scars on my face and said —"Girl – you too young for this. I ain't letting no man disfigure me like that! Come on here fore he gets back."

I passed the test with a high score. The recruiter was very nice. His eyes were really sincere and he almost appeared angry when I told him my story. He made some phone calls and told me that there had been a waiting list, but he was going to try and waiver me on the list of 400 people and put me first since I feared for my life. I was to give him a call in three days and he would give me the final outcome.

It was Saturday. I wanted to get my children so that I could move with my Sister until the recruiter could get me out of town. I did make it to my Sister's. We all feared for our lives. Dylan was a crazy person. We all sat waiting for him to come from work knowing I had nowhere else to go but over here. He shows up. Everybody's running.

He knocks on the door and my Sister said, "I don't want any trouble so I'm going to ask you to leave, Dylan."

He said Coda – "Please tell her to come out and talk to me. I just wanna talk to her. Please! I promise you that I just wanna see my kids and talk to my wife and I'll leave. Please!"

Coda came and told me he seemed calm. She reassured me that she would call the law if he even looked like he was gonna act crazy. I held my head down and reluctantly walked to the door. I asked my younger Sister to watch the kids until I talked with Dylan.

"Would you come and sit in the car with me for a few minutes baby – please. I promise – I just wanna talk to you," he pleaded.

"Keep the door open and I want my feet on the ground," I said.

"Sure baby, whatever you want."

I got half way into the car, feet on the ground with the door opened.

"I really miss you, baby. Why you wanna embarrass me like this, huh? What's your problem?" By this time, before I could turn to look at him in disbelief, he took off in the car with my feet hanging out the car. He grabbed me with one hand and said, "Shut the door. I mean – shut the goddamn door!" I could hear a scream. I knew it was my Sister.

"Please turn the car around!"

"No sweetie! I got a surprise for you. You're gonna love this surprise." I kept looking around hoping to see the police behind us, but there was no one.

We ended up at the house he and I used to live in. He had put boards all around the windows as if a hurricane was coming. He pulled a rifle out and ordered me in the house. I panicked. I knew this was it. It was over. God! He had really lost his mind. He locked the door and pushed me into the room and showed me everything he had done to prepare for this moment. He threw down the gun and took out the rope and tied me up and ran and got his Winchester rifle that he loved so dearly.

"Sweetheart, we're gonna both die tonight. I don't wanna live without you girl. Don't you understand? I've thought about this for a while now and this is my conclusion." I begged him to reconsider and that he had so much to live for and that we always see stuff like this on the news, but never for it to actually happen to us. I didn't know what to say really. I was scared to death! "Get up goddammed! I might as well get me some of that gooooood stuff baby, before I pull the trigger."

"Please don't do this. You don't really want to do this Dylan." Chances are, if he doesn't kill me, I'll probably end up pregnant for him again and all my plans for the future, entering the armed forces would be out the door.

I'm thinking, will my family be smart enough to know that he brought me back here. Will they really call the police and get here in time. My cousin was a policeman – someone said he had made detective. If only they could've reached him. Dylan's torturing me now. He's biting my face and telling me that he loved me more than life itself. He said "Since we're gonna die, I might as well do some of the things I've always wanted to do." As the screams were shouted, they came no more. I couldn't speak anymore. I had no voice. I started talking to God. Wanted to know why he put me on this earth to go through such horror. "Why me, Lord?" I was a good person and still very young. All I wanted was someone to know that I existed. Someone to love me and really care about me. I wanted someone to care – doesn't anybody understand? Suddenly, he stopped, and got off of me.

Some hours had passed. I'm wondering, what's next? He pulled me up and pushed me into the other room where he had the Winchester laid out on the other bed.

"I'm tired baby, it's time, then he took the Winchester up with one hand and squeezed my neck with the other hand – then said, - "Open your f**king mouth - I ain't playing - open wide!" I opened my mouth and he put the rifle down my throat. He started crying saying that I screwed up everything.

"Why don't you want me? You got my folks thinking you're so innocent. They don't know you don't talk to me half the time. They don't know you won't make love to me ever, ever! Why is that? Why you always have to make me take it – huh? All I want is for you to act like you want me."

By this time we heard a loud noise at the back door. Somebody's saying –

"Open up in there! I know you're in there Dylan!" It sounded like my Brother, Dino. He had been in so much trouble with the law. I knew he would hurt Dylan and not mind going back to detention. He had never tamed his demons, and was always into trouble. Dylan took the rifle out of my mouth.

He said, "Shut up – okay?" Little did he know that I couldn't speak even if I tried, then I heard Trevor's voice; he was the policeman – my cousin. They broke the door in. My Brother ran for Dylan with a knife. My cousin broke them up and backup came. They got me to the hospital and Dylan was taken to jail.

They wanted to know the next couple of days when we were in court if I was gonna press charges. Nobody was worried – they just knew without a doubt, I would press charges. All I wanted to do was go to the Air Force. They would get me out of there really fast and I could start a new life. They even promised to put me through college and take care of my dependents.

My recruiter told me that he got approval to skip me ahead of all 400 recruits. He said, "This is the last year that females can enlist and take their dependents with them. You're in luck kiddo." I was so excited!

Thursday, was the day that I had to go for my physical.

He said - "Jade - is there a chance you might be pregnant?

I said, "No."

56

He said, "You wouldn't be able to go in if you're pregnant, you know that -- right?"

There I was, ready for my physical. Please God, don't let me be with child! My prayers were answered. I wasn't pregnant.

My bus would be leaving on Tuesday for San Antonio for Basic Training.

Saturday, I was sworn in and now belonged to the United States Air Force. My new life had finally begun!

We arrived around 7:00 at night. My heart was pounding so fast I thought the others would hear it, but it appeared they were just as nervous. I had heard so many things about the military, now was my chance to see them in action. Then came this loud voice asking everyone to get off the bus. In a way, it was kindda funny. We were not to say a word. We were told to hurriedly get in line according to height. I couldn't tell from most of the individuals the age differences because it was dark and I was tired, hungry, and, scared. Before I could say a word, in marched this very attractive person in uniform with two stripes. I thought she was somebody very important. Her name was Airman Dreynolds. She was very sweet, but pretended to be rude in order to get respect. She called out everyone's name and told us as much as possible about the future and what was expected of us.

The people in the back where I was standing kept talking while she was talking and she became very angry.

"You – in the pink – give me a 341." I was surprised! She was actually talking to me. I started digging for $3.41. Everybody was laughing.

She said -"Oh! We've got a comedian amongst us." She yelled for me to get to the front of the squadron. A 341 was a form of discipline. She then picked Squad Leaders.

"Since you like to talk so much ma'am, you'll be a Squad Leader." I was trying to say I wasn't doing the talking back there.

"Lord, what next?"

"Did you say something?"

"No ma'am."

"Well then, get back in line, Airman!"

She then marched us all to a large room so that we could all get fitted for uniforms. We were told to give up our civilian clothing, because, tonight would be the last time we would be allowed to wear them. We were told that our sleeping quarters would be called "Opened Bay" meaning, there were no doors or petitions separating us from one another. Everybody slept together, openly.

When it was time to shower, we still had no privacy. You shared the shower with hundreds of girls without doors. It was told to us that all lights would be out at 9:00 and all Airmen would be in bed. This was so different. The lights went out, but we all kept whispering, all still in a state of shock.

The next morning, we got up at 4:00 and was told to be dressed and outside in formation in 20 minutes. Man! You gotta be shitting me! I had just closed my eyes. And now this! We had to march to the mess hall or chow hall. This was the place where we all ate for free. There were so many other people already eating when we arrived. When did they get up? Jesus!

It was late 1973 and things were moving rather slowly. I wanted to call my family. I had promised to let them know we had arrived so they wouldn't worry. A phone call - well, you had to wait in line to use the telephone and were only allowed 3 minutes. It's my turn, but time's up, so we had to go back inside and shine shoes. The beds had to be made tight enough for a quarter to bounce off of it.

They made me Squad Leader all right, meaning I was basically in charge of making sure our squadron did everything correctly in hopes of getting some kind of Base Liberty. Base liberty meant the possibility of shopping at the Base Exchange. At that time, the Exchange was better than any department store in the private sector and cheaper. Liberty, also meant going to the NCO Club (Noncommissioned Officer's Club), to get our dance on, or catching a bus to go into town and act like civilians.

I believed in following instructions, not making waves. In other words, I was what they called "Gung ho."

Just as I imagined, we had a weirdo in our squadron named Teresa. She was from Pensacola, Florida. She gave me some pretty nasty looks, asking me if I swung both ways. I didn't know what that meant until one of the other girls filled me in. We all went into the Latrine. The Latrine consisted of commodes and showers in one big room. There were no dividers. Everybody had to strip out in the open and privacy was unheard of. There we all were. Stark naked! Eagerly, waiting to shower. In walks Teresa.

She said to me, "I can make you my queen. I want you so bad I can taste it." What the hell was she saying - talking bout she wanted me. Want me how? Boy! Did she ever disgust me! She looked like she belonged with the members of "Planet of the Apes."

"Get out of my face, you retard," I yelled. She came towards me as if to assault me.

"Come on mister. Let's dispense with the bullshit! You wanna be a man. Kicking your ass will be a pleasure." I had to check myself. Was I giving out the wrong signals? What on earth made her think I would ever want to be with a woman, anyway? Perish the thought!

There were six, other Black females in our Squadron of 300 - who were all single and without dependents.

I was the only Airman in the Squadron with children. The other girls felt compelled to protect me and kept me out of trouble because they wanted me to get through training without fail because of my kids. I really appreciated that. Being around people that I really didn't know that wanted to protect me. Now, that was a first and the beginning of a closeness I knew nothing about before. Brenda was the most out-spoken of the group.

She said, "We got your back – Squad Leader. Be cool. Let us handle things." Teresa came towards me for the last time. The girls ganged up on her and pushed her head in the commode and held it there for about a minute. She swore, screamed, kicked, and promised she'd do the right thing if they'd just get off her back.

"Apologize to Airman Jade."

"Ma'am! I'm sorry, dammed!"

They let her go. I had no problems from then on. We gave her the nick name, "Latrine Queen", and she lived up to her title by making sure all towels were kept clean, all commodes were scrubbed, and all showers were spotless, on a daily basis.

As leader, I had to delegate other chores. I asked the young lady from Washington to make sure all our shoes were shined and she freaked.

"Shine shoes! I've been a contestant in the Junior Miss Pageant representing the state of Washington. I don't shine shoes! Besides, my parents told me, Colored people were supposed to honor Whites. Looks like you should be shining my shoes." My girls were standing by when she made those stupid remarks, and as promised, to keep me from being discharged by retaliating, they stepped in.

"First of all, they said, we ain't Colored you witch. We're Black." Then, they grabbed her by the hair and threatened to beat the White off of her if she didn't participate. All I could do was shake my head. They were doing this to help me because of my children. I wanted to slap the shit out of her, but knew I had to remain focused because of Paige and Toury, my two babies. They didn't want me to lose my temper and jeopardize my career with all of this pettiness. They were great!

It was mail call the next day. I received a letter from my children's Father. He wanted us to reconcile. It made me sick to my stomach. I missed my babies something fierce. It was a deep emptiness inside, being without them. They were so little and extremely smart.

It's 8:00, and they've informed us that if we get no discrepancies tomorrow, we all would be able to have Base Liberty – meaning, we would be able to leave the Base and shop, go to the club, etc. Check it out! We won! But somebody had to pull Dorm Guard. I volunteered. I wasn't really into the club scene - so I wanted to pull Dorm Guard in case any of the girls in my squad came in after the curfew, I would be able to run interference. This was one of my ways of thanking them for coming to my rescue when needed.

Sure enough, they were coming in one by one, after hours. I let them in. We had to whisper in the dark. They were so – so excited and wanted to let me know what had happened to each and every one of them. Arlene had found herself a nice young gent and decided to let him hit a home run. Sharon said her guy smiled and cast a spell on her and anything after that was a blur. Brenda just wanted me to know how she was the best dancer in the club, all night. She said she really got her groove on when they played "If I were your Woman," By Gladys Knight. She ranted how her engine started running hot and some sergeant she encountered promised her a major tune up. Justine lost her underwear. We made her prove it as we shook our heads with subtle laughter.

I wanted them to be quiet, worried that we all would get caught and would give up any future Base liberties. I took the flashlight and escorted the girls on tiptoe to their bunks so that they could get some sleep. As I shined the light towards the bed where I normally sleep, (it was all open bay), I couldn't help notice the girl across from my bunk. We called her "Big Bird." She was about 6 feet tall and hailed from Minnesota. She admitted she had never met a Colored person before. She said her parents had told her that Colored folk were dirty, low-down nasty people, and to make sure to be careful of them. When I finally got into bed, the girl from Minnesota raised up on her stomach and held her breath until she turned blue. I stared at her with my eyes bucked, and said - "Boo!" She lost it! We couldn't get her contained, so we called the ambulance and then called

Airman Dreynolds. They came and took her to the hospital. A few days later, we were told she was discharged dishonorably. Some people!

There were others that wanted to get out of the military. They tried to commit any acts necessary to make it happen. Jessica was extraordinarily, beautiful. She hated the military, and decided to take four laxatives and did her business up against the wall. She was caught and also, discharged dishonorably.

This is crazy. I miss my little girls. I wondered what they were doing. I know Paige is trying to color in her coloring book and Toury is beating her in the head with anything she can find. I can see Paige trying to feed her when she's hungry. They are so close. They always sit together and rock each other to sleep. I'm so proud of my babies! I got a letter saying that Aunt Kemme and Uncle Francis picked them up and took them to the park. I know they'll be really spoiled because my aunt and uncle loves children and they've got plenty to do at their place.

Today, we have our final test. I was sick from all of the studying. I couldn't believe it. We all did so well. I guess all the coaching and drilling one another every night really paid off.

They came to tell us to line up because we were going to find out where our Technical Training Assignments were going to be. My heart was pounding so fast and loud, I was embarrassed that someone might hear it.

The screams from everybody came one after the other. California…. Hawaii…..Japan….then, somebody said, "Shephard, I'm going to Shephard Air Force Base. Big deal! What's so great about Shephard? We later found out, this was her hometown and, that's why she was so happy. I thought to myself – Jesus! That's not a bad deal. Then I wasn't afraid anymore. Since everybody else was getting good assignments, maybe, I might get one too. No such luck! I was going to Keesler Air Force Base, in Biloxi, Mississippi. Nice Base! Just too close to home and Dylan. Even though I belonged to the military, it wouldn't stop him from wanting or trying to harm me being that close to home. The man was possessed. I stayed there for ten weeks in the beautiful white sands of Biloxi to learn a trade for my job. I chose to become an Administrative Specialist, which meant I had to learn how to type and perform other clerical duties as assigned.

We went to the NCO Club (Noncommissioned Officer's Club) to celebrate our departure into the real world. Someone grabbed me from behind to dance to the tune, "If Loving You is Wrong, I Don't Want to Be Right," by Luther Ingram. It was my Block One Instructor from typing class. Not only was he a fantastic trainer, he should've been a dancing instructor, as well. His friend Ted cut in. He was very smooth. I felt free and relaxed. We had an incredible time dancing. Training was over. Lord knows we deserved this R & R.

We graduated, and assignments were given out. I was excited because mostly everybody was being stationed somewhere pretty cool. My assignment was to Holloman Air Force Base in Alamogordo, New Mexico. Imagine that!

"Jade, where's your assignment?"

"I don't wanna talk about it. Okay! It's Holloman."

"Where?"

"Alamogordo, New Mexico."

"We never heard of that. Where is it close by?"

"I don't know. Now, can we just get over it, already." I'm convinced I must've really pissed off God, somehow. I was sure this was a remote assignment. But I can handle it.

I sneaked home with the help of my family and picked up my babies. I can't tell you the joy of our reunion. We cried and hugged and laughed. I trembled uncontrollably. I had to keep touching Paige and Toury. They had gotten so big! Unbelievable! We kept hugging and hugging and wouldn't let go. I reassured them that it was okay. We were gonna be a family again, just the three of us. We're on our way.

It's Wednesday, and we finally arrived. What a hideous Base! I hardly slept. The bus ride was long and awful. This place had a Saturday afternoon kindda, deserted look about it. Tumbleweed was blowing everywhere and every thing seemed to be in slow motion. My God! What had I gotten us in to!

They came and got me and took me to my first job assignment. I couldn't help wonder what the people would be like. I walked in and everybody was enthusiastic. They appeared to be very happy to see me. They seemed like genuine - nice, people who were assigned there from all over the United States. As you walked into the office, there were about six different desks in one big room with file cabinets everywhere. Everything was the same drab color and the atmosphere seemed chaotic.

My Commanding Officer was very down to earth. He walked in and everybody jumped up. He informed them to make sure that I was taken care of and to make sure that I had adequate housing. Little did I know everybody lived off Base in a Trailer Community about 5 miles away! Boy!

Was I in trouble! I had no transportation and didn't know the first thing about driving. I mean, literally, I had never driven before.

I told my First Sergeant and he said, "No problem, kiddo. We'll get you fixed up in no time." I had no idea he was serious. He called in one of the Airmen and asked him to take me down to the DMV to get me a license. He was told to let me drive around the block a couple of times until I got the hang of it. I couldn't believe it! Sure enough, I made a 94 on my driving test. I passed! My driving instructor looked to be around 75 years of age. He could hardly hear and said this is what keeps him alive. It was all happening so fast. I got my license! I had a real driver's license. "Lord - I can't believe it!" All I did was drive around the block twice and they gave me a license. Unreal!

The Airman said to me, "The Commander wants you to buy a car – so we're going to the Credit Union to buy you a car." "Forget about it," I said. "It just ain't no way!" I just got here, and didn't have any money, especially to buy a car. We were at the Credit Union and they acted like this was no big deal. They said they do it all the time. It was 1974, and I was 24 years old. I told them to give me the cheapest car there. I got my wish. It was a 1973 Vega. What a joke! But, I was grateful. My own car! Then, I had to have insurance. It was almost 4:00. He let me drive back to the Base. My under garments were wet from the nervousness. It was happening all too fast. I knew then, for sure, I was dreaming

I picked up my girls who were extremely, surprised. They yelled, "Mommie's got a car!" They kept saying - "Go fast Mommie. Go fast!" They had no clue I had never driven before today. I was beginning to get the hang of it; I had no choice.

I drove to work. They were all very pleased that I was doing so well. They trained me on my first job. I was responsible for processing newly assigned Airmen onto the Base and into the Squadron. If they were leaving the Base for good, I had to out-process them, also.

I was glad to see that Terry was a part of our squadron. I felt as though I already knew him since he was partly responsible for me getting my driver's license. Things were going pretty good.

I went and picked up the girls and took them home from day care and was blown away as I found out my ex-husband was here from Alabama. He found out where we lived and where the baby-sitter lived. He went over to her place and told her a bunch of lies and said that the girls were supposed to go with him during the day since I had to work. She didn't know whether he was telling the truth or not – since we had just arrived on Base.

Later that night I called the Chaplain of the Base and explained to him what kind of person my ex was, and that I expected big trouble. I told him that he had come up from Alabama and I was scared. He told me not to worry. I couldn't help thinking, why on earth was he here? How dare this maniac of a person try to interfere with my life just as I'd begun to get the girls and I on the right track!

I had just finished putting the girls to bed and rolling my hair when I heard a loud knock. I went to the door and asked, "Who is it?" There was no answer.

A minute later, the door was kicked in! In rushes my ex-husband. I tried to scream but the words wouldn't come out. The first thing he said was, "You Bitch – surprised to see me, huh?" I told you I was gonna get my babies. Then he shoved me up against the table. I begged him to stop and that I didn't want any trouble. He laughed in a sick sort of way. He said, "All your little friends and all the Colonels and Majors you've been screwing are gonna see who you really belong to." He said, "I came for my kids and there's nothing you can do about it, you slut! I don't want my children around anybody as whorish as your ass."

I begged that he was hallucinating and that there was no truth to any of his accusations. He said, "Better yet, I'm gonna screw you myself. It's been a long time." I panicked, because now, I really knew he was totally out of control. I began to think that this was it. He was really going to kill me and take the kids. Very calmly, I tried to talk to him. That wasn't working. I saw out of the corner of my eye that my lamp was close by. Without thinking I grabbed the base of it and struck him in the head as hard as I could, watching as the pieces crumbled to the floor. I thought he'd fall out or something, but it didn't seem to phase him. He snapped out of it, then dragged me into the room and began to choke me. Blood was coming out of my throat and I could no longer scream. He hit me extremely hard in the chest and, I started praying. He rips my underpants off and begins molesting me. By this time, I was kicking and screaming, choking off my own blood. Then, as I kicked, I knocked over the floor lamp. The noise woke the children. They walked in and started crying. Their Dad jumped up and ran to them, – hugging them saying, "Mommie is having a seizure and that's why I'm here. Let's call the ambulance. Hurry and get dressed girls. We have to get Mommie to the hospital." I was lying there unable to move or speak. My rollers were hanging from my head into my face and blood was all over the front of my gown coming from my throat. He ran to them and said, "We can't wait for the ambulance. Hurry girls! Let's get Mommie to the doctor." I still couldn't speak.

We were in the car, going about 90 miles an hour. A policeman pulled us over and asked for his license. Dylan lied that I had – had a seizure and we were on our way to the Base Hospital. The officer said, "Follow me." He phoned the Base to expect us, and to get the emergency room ready.

When we arrived, I could hear Dylan telling lies to the nurses and the doctor. They asked him to leave. While they were cleaning me up I wrote down on a piece of paper for them to get the Chaplain. The male nurse was trying to fix my rollers and clean my face. He gave me lots of tissue to blow my nose. As he wiped my face, he asked, "Did that man abuse you?" He told me not to be afraid and that I was in good hands now. "Nod your head if I'm right." At that moment, the Chaplain walked in. He was baffled! He wanted to know what had happened. They scrubbed my mouth and gave me a throat culture. I still couldn't talk, but wrote down my responses. They were all very upset. The male nurse was really pissed. "Press charges honey. That bastard was trying to kill you." The Chaplain held my hand and agreed with the nurse. I wrote that I was concerned about my children. They told me my children would be taken care of. The nurse said, "Do the right thing and have that son-of-a-bitch locked up, girl." I did. He was ordered out of New Mexico and ordered to stay away from me and my family after his release from jail.

Two months later while at work, Dylan sent a certified letter saying that he had a right to see the girls and that the divorce decree stipulated that he be allowed to keep the girls during all holidays. His lawyer stressed Dylan really wanted full custody. He wanted to drag me through court and I didn't want the trouble nor did I have the leave time. He was not permitted in the state of New Mexico so I would have to drive the children to Alabama. My superior wouldn't hear of it, so he asked Terry to drive us there and to help look after us. Bill came over and brought me his Smith & Western and told me to use it if need be. He said, "Here's the key to unlock it." I'd been a sharp shooter in training, but this was the real deal. He taught me how to use the gun and assured me not to be afraid. "Your ex is a monster - I mean, the things he's put you through! Please, shoot that muthaf**ka, if he violates you in any way, I mean it! Better yet, First Sergeant, please, let me go with her. I'll blow that f**ker's balls off, without hesitation." "That's what we're afraid of Bill," said First Sergeant. "You stay here."

Terry did most of the driving. I had just gotten my license and just learned how to drive. There was no way I could drive the distance alone.

The girls were so excited. It was the Fourth of July and you could smell the smoked ribs as we turned the corner. Judging from the noise and the amount of cars parked in front of the house, the majority of his family was there at his Mother's house.

I didn't see my ex-Father-in law's car. Usually, if there were any kind of problems, he would nip them in the bud. We pulled up to the house and honked the horn.

Paige and Toury were jumping for joy because they recognized the area.

Ramsey, Dylan's brother, ran from behind the house to the car as we unloaded and gave me a bear hug, commenting on how the military had done me great justice. Then followed the rest of the cousins, aunts, uncles and their dear Grandmother. They grabbed the girls and picked them up and took them around the back where everyone else was. Their Grandmother was very happy to see them and mentioned how good they looked.

I introduced Terry as my co-worker who offered to help me drive.

She nodded – "Pleased to meet you." She asked us to come inside. I said no because I didn't want a confrontation with her son. Oh well, what the hell. I'm a part of the Air Force now. Dylan's crazy, but not stupid. I don't think he'll be dumb enough to cause trouble. Anyway, Terry had to use the restroom. Then, up popped the devil! He came on to the screened porch where we were and Terry excused himself. The Grandmother went to check on the children. Dylan started in right away.

"Well looka here! What's going on, my little ho? I see you're screwing little children this time" – referring to Terry. I didn't have to explain anything to him. I tried to keep silent hoping he'd go away. Then, without thinking, I told him that Terry was 19 years old, from my office, and was asked by my superior to escort us on this long journey. He kept on with the nasty remarks. I stared him down. How was I so blinded to have married someone so insane! Women didn't have the resources for abuse back then, as we do now. I had the gun in my purse. I remained calm because I felt justified that whatever happened, I would be well within my rights.

We were divorced and had been away from one another for approximately eight months since he put me in the hospital and was barred from the state of New Mexico. He jumped to his feet as he asked me over and over again -- "Are you still f**king the Colonel, and the rest of them Dick's out there, honey? Huh? Huh? Answer me!" When I ignored him, he knocked my earring off, pushed me against the screened porch, as I begged---"Let me go to the bathroom. I promise I'll be right back." He followed me to the back where it was located and his Mother observed that I was crying so she immediately started yelling to the top of her voice --- "Noooo! Dylan! Today is a holiday. Y'all need to quit! You said it wasn't gone be no trouble." I looked back at his Mother as I finally approached the restroom and said --"Whatever happens, I want you to know, it's not my fault."

I knew then, I was going to kill my ex-husband. No regrets! I had - had enough- and was more determined than ever. I'm not sure how this train got derailed. I just knew I had to end it. I went into the restroom and opened my purse. I took the gun out to make sure it was loaded like my co-workers taught me. At that moment, I was surprised - I wasn't nervous. I felt a calmness that was unfamiliar to me. It was like an inner peace, that was indescribable. I flushed the toilet as I summoned all my strength and courage. Then, as I began to say, "God, please make sure my babies forgive me for..."

I was interrupted by a loud bang on the door ---"Come on outta there!" I pushed opened the door and pointed the gun at him.

His Mother looking on - hysterically screaming --- "God! Lord, have mercy! Jade! Stop! Baby, please don't! I'm gonna call the police!"

I said calmly, "Please do."

By this time, Dylan was slowly walking backwards to the front door, his eyes glued to the gun as I followed - pointing the gun towards his head hoping it would discharge if he made a wrong move. By this time, his brother and others ran to try to help. I repeated myself.

"Call the police! Tell them to bring the ambulance so that they can take this piece of shit to the morgue." I wished his Mother would shut up. Her yelling made me nervous. Dylan was her favorite son and couldn't do no wrong, so she was flipping out. All I could think about were flashes of this maggot abusing me day after day, because he could.

We were on the outside now.

Dylan begs, "Put the gun down, girl. You betta put it down, I ain't playing with you!"

All the neighbors gathered around. I blocked everybody out. All I could think about was some of the despicable, awful things he had done to me in the past. I despised him. I was now 24 years old and didn't care at that moment if I would have to spend the rest of my life in prison. It would've been worth it. I couldn't think about Grandma and what she thought of me. I refused to think about my babies. I knew they would be taken care of somehow, and that, some day, they would forgive me for what I was about to do. It was time. In a matter of seconds, I pulled the trigger - all I could hear were screams coming from every direction. It was chaos personified. Nothing happened! The gun didn't fire. I was petrified! I forgot I was supposed to use the key to turn the safety off. "Oh hell!"

Dylan jumped in the air and kicked the gun out of my hand knocking me to the ground. He grabbed the fallen gun and pointed it at me. He said "I oughtta blow your brains all over this cement!" By this time I could hear the sirens approaching. He grabbed me up and dragged me across the street to his brother's house where he held me hostage. The policeman that finally arrived, was a friend of the family. I didn't know where Terry was. All I knew was that something really ugly was about to happen. He then said, "You are a sick woman. Don't you know you'll never be rid of me? I don't care if you turn 50, you'll still be my woman, and I'll kill anybody who tries to take you away from me." He wiped the mucous from his nose, proclaiming how much he loved me. Muttering that I had the best sex he'd ever had in his entire life. He started bragging about being one of the Captains of his school's football team in the past and having his share of women. He kept saying, none of them compared to you. I knew he was mental, at this point. I begged him to let me go because I had to be back on the Air Force Base. He said not until I have my way with you. Before he could yank my underwear off, the screams and knocks came for him to open up the door. His friend, the policeman, begged him to open the door and not to do anything stupid. Reluctantly, and unbelievably so, he opened it. I ran to the officer and Dylan began telling him how he was just trying to calm me down after I tried to shoot him. The officer kept telling him that it wasn't worth it and that this time he would have to take him in and needed him to give up the weapon. Dylan said, "I ain't got it man! I left it in my Momma's yard and somebody must've picked it up and ran off with it, I swear." Lying was second nature with Dylan. He still has that gun to this day. I was surprised. The policeman handcuffed him and took him downtown. We watched him take Dylan away. My children's Father, who pretended frequently to the public that he was this soft spoken, shy man that wanted to do anything for anybody he could to help them out. The image he portrayed even fooled his Mother. God! She worshipped him.

I heard my baby, Toury say, "I want my Mommie." I, then, ran from the apartment across the street. I didn't want to leave my babies there, but knew they would be all right. I knew that in the state of Alabama, they would try to take my children if I didn't abide by the stipulations of the divorce by letting the children stay with their Father. I was surprised his friend the policeman, arrested Dylan and he would be released in an hour. I knew this would go on and on and I would never win. I wanted to grab my babies and get the hell outta there. But I knew, also, that this is why we made the long, long journey for them to stay for the summer. I was nauseous.

"Lets go Terry...now!

"Are you okay Jade? I mean, you sure you're able to travel?"

"We're outta here y'all!" I grabbed and held the girls tightly; Paige didn't want to let go. I kissed their tears as I pretended to be brave and promised to be back before they knew it. "Take care of one another like I taught you, okay? Give me another kiss."

I tried not to look back as we drove off. Terry had to drive. He begged me to stop crying and to try and get some sleep. He then brushed my hair back and said, "I'm glad you didn't kill your children's Father, Jade. The guy is scum, don't get me wrong; but nobody deserves to die till God takes them away. Why don't you get some sleep, okay?"

When we returned, Terry became very emotional trying to describe and explain what went down.

"Man! You had to be there! I'm telling you, it was like outta some kinda movie. I'm proud of Jade. She didn't crack, man. She held her grounds. I don't think that punk'll try her again. This time, she showed him she ain't taking no wooden nickels. I'm talking kicking ass and taking more than names - Huh, Jade?" They all hugged me and said, it's a good thing the gun didn't discharge. I think he got the message.

The weeks went by and I tried hard to push myself at the job so that I wouldn't have time to think about my children. I even went to bed early.

The next morning at work, I heard a lot of commotion about the plane coming in with a bunch of new people from overseas. Some special assignment, or another.

My job was to in-process these new people into our Squadron. The next person in line was Innis. I didn't look up.

I asked - "Name?" He said – "Innis."

That voice! Jesus! I had never heard such elocution. I knew it wasn't Barry White. Instantly, without looking up, I tried to figure out where he was from. Definitely, East Coast! I was right, he was from New Haven. I looked up and saw that the voice did, indeed fit the face. Yeah! Boyfriend was plenty -- sexy! I tried not to let it show cause I was literally, out of control.

With a straight face -- I said, "First name?"

He responded -- "Johnnie."

I looked up and said, "Is it Johnnie, with a "Y" or an "I?"

He replied – "Whichever you prefer." So, I smiled.

He leaned over and asked --- "What's a fine young thing like you doing working in a place like this?"

Okay! So I blushed. And said, "Next, please" -- but he refused to leave and all the other guys kept saying, "Come on man! Give somebody else a chance." But, he wasn't having it. He turned around and said, "I'll leave if she'll go out with me." One of the other guys screamed - "I'll go out with you man." We all laughed as he walked away.

I couldn't wait to finish my work. It gave me time to reflect. I had no girl friends yet, but I liked talking to Bill. He was like a girl and very out spoken. I ran over and told him I wanted to talk to him about something. I mentioned the new guys that had processed in this morning and that one of them was quite interesting. He smiled and said – "Did he look delicious?" I laughed because this was a whole new ball game for me. I had been in prison - married to a maniac. I had never talked to anyone on the serious side before. I told him that I had never - ever -- been attracted to anyone like I was attracted to this Innis character. His voice was like magic and he had the personality and looks to match.

The next day on my way home, I was headed downhill and he was headed uphill and stopped me as we were side-by-side. It was the new guy, Johnnie. I had just processed him into the Squadron.

He said -- "My goodness -- my prayers have been answered. Hello angel!"

I told him I was in a hurry and couldn't talk.

He said "What a coincidence! Do you know somebody over here?"

I said, "I live here and so does everybody on Base."

He said - "Wow! This is gonna be a pretty cool gig." Then he asked if he could come home with me. He said, "Have you noticed, there's nothing to do around here? I'm bored out of my mind, man."

I told him I was about to take a drive to clear my head. I told him that I wasn't going to see anybody for a couple of years and that I just wanted to focus on my kids.

He said --"How many do you have?"

And I said –"Two beautiful girls." He wanted to know where they were and I explained they were on vacation and I would be picking them up soon.

After he left, I knew I probably would never see him again since he knew I had children. The next day he came to my office and brought me a rose.

He said -- "Girl, I can't stop thinking bout you." I asked him to give himself a couple of weeks and he would know everyone on the Base with that personality of his. He asked me to stop pushing him away. I told him he didn't want to get mixed up in my mess and that I would do my best to introduce him to someone really nice. He kissed me on the forehead and left. Nobody knew how I was feeling at that moment. I watched as he left, feeling intoxicated by his charm. I couldn't move. Indeed, this man did something to me whenever he came around. The feeling I had was totally unfamiliar to me. I liked it.

The next week, he came to my job and asked me to go shopping with him to help him pick something out for his Mother. He was crazy about her.

"If you won't be my lady, Jade, will you be my friend?"

"Friendship has to be earned Johnnie, and we seem to be off to a good start."

"Can I go with you to pick up the girls?"

"No. But thanks for asking."

I arrived in Mobile around 3 O'clock, p.m. Everything was quiet. Seemed almost deserted. Everybody was at work. I pulled up to the driveway and both dogs barked ferociously. The noise brought my ex-Mother-in-law to the door. I was surprised to see her smile when I jumped out of the car. She ran and hugged me and told me the girls were anxiously awaiting my arrival. She said she wanted to get the girls right away because the sooner I get them, the sooner we could be on the road and back to the Air Force Base. She let me know that her son was at work and was expecting me tomorrow. She didn't let him know I would be arriving today. This was the first time I'd ever known his Mother to side with me, and not her favorite son. She didn't want any more trouble. Their Grandmother had no idea the role she played that day giving me a peaceful departure and reuniting my beautiful babies with me without any additional drama to their young lives. With her help, maybe it's finally over. God! I'm so grateful and blessed.

I told the girls on the way home about my new friend. They were so excited and wanted to know if he was small like them so that they would have somebody to play with. I explained that he was a big person like Mommie and that he made me laugh a lot, which made me very happy. Toury yelled, "Yippee!" We laughed and they fell asleep till I pulled up to the trailer. We slept till noon the next day.

John called to make sure we had made it safely. He was so excited, and wanted to meet my girls right away. He came over and picked us up and took us to get ice cream and hamburgers and then he took us to see the mountains. I couldn't stop laughing at his jokes to the children. They all liked each other right away.

The next day he wanted to take them to see the horses. Everyday that he came was a new adventure. He was so easy to talk to. The kids started depending on his arrival, and just like clockwork, he showed up on time. This time when he came over, he came in and asked the girls to come into the living room. He told them that he was growing to love them and wanted their opinion about asking Mommie to be his special friend.

"I thought she was already your friend," Paige said.

"I want to ask your Mommie if she'll be my girlfriend. Y'all know what a girlfriend is, don't you? I know the both of you got some boyfriends –right?" Then, he started tickling the both of them and the laughter warmed my heart. He was terrific with them.

Toury looked up and out of the blue asked, as she played with his mustache, blurting out the unthinkable -- "Are you gonna be our Daddy?"

"I'm trying sweetie. I mean, I'm really trying!"

That night, I became his woman. It was an experience indelibly planted in my memory bank forever. After seven years with Dylan, I was now with a real man!

He gave up his trailer and paid all the bills at my place so that I could have more to put on the girls. He knew that I refused to take child support from my ex, because I didn't want him in our lives in any way, whatsoever. It worked out perfectly.

We became the talk of the Base and were the most popular couple there was. It was the happiest I'd ever been in my life. Every weekend, all our friends came to our house to party. We had moved out of the trailer and into our own home.

My First Sergeant wanted to see me the next morning. He said that the information that he was about to give me was Top Secret and most confidential.

My curiosity was at a new level. I said, "Go on."

"The Commanding Officer is really impressed with you." He said, "We are having some appalling problems among the female crew chiefs and their superior officers. It's been rumored that several indiscretions have taken place and a Task Force has been designed to alleviate the problem." Word came from the Pentagon to make this top priority. They wanted me to head up the Task Force at this Base and Major Badelt, from Washington, would be my contact and would visit us for findings in two weeks.

"We will give you your private office to interview and, or interrogate personnel. Discretion is crucial because of the sensitive subject nature. By all means, take heed," he said. "Yes sir."

One of the airmen I interviewed disclosed that she was very, very afraid. She said often times it was extremely hot on the flight line and it was necessary for the female airmen to remove the top part of their fatigues, leaving only a "T"- shirt on. The shirts would expose the anatomy of the female airman's breast, then unsavory remarks were constantly made.

One of the female airmen disclosed that the Officer in Charge forced her to come into his office. He required her to pick up his telephone exposing naked pictures of females spreading their legs without underpants. Some of the poses were of women on their knees performing oral sex and, he explained that in order for her to receive an outstanding performance evaluation (APR), she would have to act out what was in front of her on his telephone." She was terrified! The officer threatened that if she divulged any information about what was taking place on the flight line, he would make sure she was kicked out, dishonorably.

I interviewed two more airmen before submitting my findings and established that we were way over our heads.

One of the airmen was repeatedly, molested from the anus by two lieutenants during the same night. She tried to handle the situation alone, but couldn't. She went AWOL (absent without leave), and left a note attached to her dresser addressed, "To whom ever gives a damn." Her roommate brought the note to my office. Nobody has since heard from her.

My report was given to the Commander and we met with the overseer from Washington and they declared it a job well done.

This special project taught me a lesson. All that glitters is truly, not gold! - And, shit does float to the top. These people had a full career ahead of them, but chose to take advantage of innocent people for their own personal, sick gain. I was happy to learn that the officers involved received court-martials. There was only one enlisted person involved. He was a Master Sergeant who was discharged dishonorably.

Then came the dreadful news - the military decided they wanted to separate Johnnie and me. He got orders to England. There was complete silence. He turned to me with tears in his eyes.

"There's no way I'm gonna leave you and the girls here in the states without me." "Will you marry me, Jade?"

I vowed I would never, ever marry again, in this lifetime.

"Sweetheart this is an emergency. I want us to stay together, no matter what it takes. Besides, your first marriage wasn't a real marriage. This time it'll be the real thing."

I was still in a state of shock. I wanted things to stay as they were. Every day Johnnie would make marriage a priority in our conversation.

Fred and Barbara came over to help make the topic a reality. Fred would often grab me from behind and jokingly say - "Man - you guys are the greatest together." Then he would try to harmonize the tune - "There's No Me, Without You" - and we would crack up cause he really thought he sounded great. He was Johnnie's best friend and could roll the biggest joint I'd ever seen. The door- bell rang - it was his other best friend, Maison. We called him with the news and he came right over. Maison was ruggedly handsome and would make open passes at me, in front of John. He'd always say - "Man - you'd better never mess up, cause I'll be on her like flies to doo-doo." We laughed, but I knew he was serious. He'd always want a kiss and, I'd try to get out of it by hiding behind John, but he would say "Give him a peck, baby - he's, harmless."

The following week was most chaotic. Every body pitched in to help prepare for the wedding. It was over before we knew it. My heart was pounding. Lord, what have I done? We were leaving in a month.

I took the girls to Alabama to live with their Grandmother until I was situated then we'd all be reunited. The coast was clear. Dylan was on assignment in Florida building pre-fab houses and his Mother didn't tell him I'd remarried and the girls were on their way. What a great break for me! His Mother was finally keeping peace.

I'd heard an awful lot about England, and boy - was I excited!

We had a very long flight across the pond and I was truly tired. We were escorted to our dorms. Everything looked gloomy, maybe because of lack of sleep.

Johnnie and I were separated. He went to the male dorm and I went to my dorm. There, I met my roommate Jessica who later became my very best friend.

Being overseas was different. The idea of being so far away from home made everybody seem closer. The Blacks really stuck together. It was an unusual kind of unity.

The Base was eerie. All the buildings looked the same. Every building was painted the same color --- an ugly tan. I was assigned to Headquarters. Going to work became a routine. Afterwards was the real trip! When we flushed the toilet, we pulled the handle from above the head. The English referred to an elevator as a lift. And so many other things I found fascinating.

I missed Johnnie and wanted to see him. I had told Jessica about he and the children. Sometimes we stayed up till morning talking and laughing. The other girls were nice, too. Ernestine was hilarious.

I was on my way to the bathroom, and to my surprise, I saw a guy in the building. I had on a robe - so I gasped! I Ran back to tell Jessica and she said -"Girl - before you guys got here, they were spending the night." She said - "Wait until the weekend. As a matter of fact, let's go to the market and I'll show you around." Before I could check with Johnnie, I said, "Okay," with much excitement!

My supervisor was a cool kindda guy. The airmen I worked with were really nice. All they talked about was the Ojay's concert next Friday in London. I was definitely gonna go to that. I was finding myself not missing Johnnie. I didn't really want to be with him. My life was full. We weren't getting along, anyway. Since our arrival, he had become pugnacious.

I had promised to marry him only if he agreed for us to divorce once we arrived here in England so that we could be together. He began to change. Arguing became second nature to him. I just wanted to have fun!

Hastings mentioned going to the NCO Club Wednesday night. He said that it was off the wall and that it was like a ritual for the Bloats from England to come over on the train from the city to party on the Base.

He said - "Girl - wait until you see those Englishmen dance! They put us to shame child!" I laughed.

While at work, I couldn't help thinking about tonight. It would be my first night at the club since being on Base and being here in the Motherland. Johnnie kept trying to get my attention. He called and called. Finally, he took a brick, threw it at the window and broke it. We couldn't believe it.

He said "You'd better come out or I'm coming in!" I went outside. When I stepped outside, I was shocked beyond belief. People were making out in the grass, not giving a damn about being watched. I stepped on a condom. How disgusting! Naked butts were all over the place. They told me about this on the plane, but never in my wildest would I have believed this until I had seen it with my own eyes. I explained that I didn't want to fight and that I was going over to the NCO Club with the rest of the girls. He said he'd be there.

The phone rang down the hall. I could hear them yelling, "Jade! You got a call from the states!" I rushed to the phone hoping it wasn't bad news. I couldn't take it if it was. The voice on the other end was my dear sister, Zoe. My God! I missed them something fierce. I needed to hear her voice. She had something to tell me. She wanted to tell me that our little brother, Ian was graduating from High School, from an all White school, which had been quite an easy task for him to achieve. He was staying with her at the time. "That's not all, Jade." She said, "I called to tell you that not only is he graduating from this all White school, he's graduating as the Salutatorian." I couldn't believe it. I said, "Are you sure? Our little brother! The one that used to sit and read and read." I was too proud of him! Zoe was responsible for him being focused because she provided a stable environment for him. We were on our way! I wondered if Grandma had heard. I knew she was probably pissed. Not quite what she expected!

I was more than ready to kick up my heels. I mean, the mood was right for some real partying. I told Jessica about the news as we swore to tear the roof off the sucker.

The music reminded me of home. The crowd was hyped. It was all new faces. I looked for Johnnie, but didn't see him.

Jessica introduced me to the wildest dancer in the place, no doubt. He pulled me to the floor. I tried to be coy; didn't work. They were playing, "That's the Way I like It," by K.C. and the Sunshine Band. The mood was hyped and I was ready to strut, my stuff. "What was he doing? I mean, what kind of dance was that? I had never seen this dance before." I looked to the side, and they were doing another strange dance. I liked it. It didn't take me long to mimic what I saw combined with my personality and we had a hit. He tried to find out where I was from in the states while dancing, and I ignored him so that I could really shake my groove thing. Everybody was clapping. What a show off! I felt a tap on my shoulder - to my surprise, it was Johnnie. "Hey baby!"

I let him know how happy I was to see him with a lingering hug. He led me through the crowd whispering how he'd forgotten what a great dancer I was. He said he found me because of all the comments he overheard from the crowd about me, and my partner. I said, "Nice try; but it was the outfit; not the dance." Then, out of nowhere, they played "Memories" by the Temptations, and I, like everyone else, nearly, wet my pants. We were mesmerized with one another. He whispered how much he loved me and couldn't wait for us to get a house off Base. I didn't want to argue so I savored the moment. I was really happy with the news about my brother, Ian, and decided to reward myself.

It was time for me to buy a car. I went to the dealer and purchased an "MG" (Midget). It wasn't fancy enough, so I went with some of the guys off Base to Liverpool, England, where they put customized, removable tops on cars to match the bottom. This was in 1975. That same car would slightly resemble a 2002 convertible Mercedes. This little car was the transportation needed to go to the concert on Friday to see the O'jays.

My car only seated two people so I only had Jessica to pick up for the concert. Neither one of us knew our way around London. It was so foggy. Lord, I was driving down a one way street. I don't know who screamed the loudest. Jessica covered her face as she yelled, "You're gonna kill us both!" I pleaded -- "Hang on" as we circled the round about and somehow ended up at the concert. Go figure. The Four Tops and the O'jays were headliners. We were too late. It was already over. I was pissed. It was the first time I had been out of uniform in a long time, and my black leather jumpsuit was more than ready for this concert. I turned the car around in hopes of trailing somebody that looked military to lead us back to the Base in this thick, nasty fog. Suddenly, we smelled smoke. The car was coughing. I can't remember being this scared.

I stupidly, stripped the gears and tore up my car. I had no idea how to drive a stick. I took it back to the dealer and without question, they gave me another new car. "Hush your mouth!"

It was time to go to London for some real shopping. We saw the "Changing of the Guards" in front of Buckingham Palace. I wanted to go to the famous Piccadilly Circus I had heard so much about. It was horribly busy. People were everywhere. I wanted to go shopping. Some of the guys on Base told us if we really wanted to get our shopping on, go to Regents Street. We managed to get to Trafalgar Square. I wanted to take a picture in front of the monument. Johnnie wanted to go back and see Downing Street to check out the Prime Minister. This was like a dream. I couldn't believe it. London became my hang out for all my shopping.

My God! I miss my babies. I called the states to talk to both of them. We cried and cried. I told them it wouldn't be long. I found out from my Commanding Officer that I wouldn't be able to go back home and get them because I didn't have the time or leave. I asked for special provisions and was denied. I found myself suffering severely because I wanted to be with my children.

Johnnie found a house off Base, but didn't realize I had contacted a lawyer in New Mexico that had annulled our marriage per my persistent request. I didn't tell him until two months later.

He had purchased some hashee from some Turks off Base and said he would not try to make me smoke it. He said I never participated in any of their exploits when we were in the states and figured since we were away from anyone that knew us, I wouldn't be afraid to try it. I told him again, "I wasn't afraid; I just don't do drugs. Anyway, they slow you down." I told him he should know by now that I had a natural high. Anything else was unnecessary. He took a couple of hits and mellowed out. I felt it was a perfect time to break the news to him about the annulment. What I didn't know was that he was gonna lose his mind completely. He really injured his fist as he punched the wall.

"Why, baby? How could you do this?"

"It won't change anything," I pleaded. "As a matter of fact, I think it'll make us better."

He said "forget it. Just forget it! You've destroyed me." There was no reasoning with him and I was afraid.

The next day at work, they could tell I hadn't been to sleep and my supervisor let me off. When I came back to work, the alarms went off. We were having a Disaster Preparedness Exercise. I was in charge of teaching employees how to dawn their gas masks in case of a war or a terrorist situation. It was serious and practically all the guys on the Base attended the class. Boy, I was a nervous wreck!

The next day we watched our first football game. We were at Lakenheath Air Force Base. Next to us was Mildenhall. Other Bases, like Upper Hayford, came to watch, and, some - participated. We sat on the ground in the grass, on top of the hill. I didn't particularly like sitting in the grass and being dirty, but it turned out to be fun.

Jessica was excited about going to see Ben. He was the love of her life and I was excited for her.

Jessica was a class act. She said I was her idol. I couldn't see it, but tried to be exemplary anyway.

Being in the military was the best thing I could've done. Here I was in good ol' England. Who would've thought? If I had been still in the private sector, I'd still be dodging Dylan trying to find a job without furthering my education. The thought of that man made me ill. I looked to the right of the bulletin board and saw advertisements for martial arts. Yes. I enrolled. It was one of the hardest things I'd ever encountered, but tripled my confidence. We were taught not to use what we'd learned unless faced with the possibility of death. Of course, he was talking about Dylan, I'm sure of it. I couldn't wait to get back to the good ol' U.S. of A. I had a new walk - a new talk - and, a definite, "in your face kindda attitude, since my affiliation with TaeKwonDo."

The military afforded me the opportunity to enroll in college while in England. I started night school. Johnnie couldn't stand it. Again, we had no time for one another. He was so smart. I wanted him to go to school with me, but his job wouldn't permit it. He couldn't get off early enough. In spite of that fact, he ended up getting his Masters, and I didn't. Go figure! I was very, very proud of him. We had grown apart. It seemed all I could think of were my kids and making something of myself. He wanted our lives to include just he and I.

It was time for me to leave England. I needed to see Paige and Toury really, badly.

In another year, my oldest daughter would be starting first grade. That's all I could think about; The lives we were gonna lead with just the three of us. I hadn't told them about Johnnie and me because I didn't think they would understand. They were so crazy about him. I started having nightmares about my babies, so I went to the Chaplain to see what he could do to help me get back to them. I had everyone from home to write in my defense, including our pastor.

It took a long time, but finally, my Humanitarian Reassignment became a reality. I was going home to see my children!

My follow-on assignment was to Hurlburt Field Air Force Base, in Fort Walton Beach, Florida. It was the auxiliary to the famous Eglin Air Force Base, which was right down the street.

It was a small town and I was very pleased. All I wanted was some peace and quiet after being in the Motherland. Down the street from the Air Force Base was these nice apartments called Westwood. It was ideal for me, and my children. The apartments were a referral to me by someone that had lived there before, and, was now stationed in England.

I was told by the Commander of the Base that it would take another year or two before I would be able to acquire my own housing. The apartments I decided to live in were about two years old, and full of young adults from the military. You could hear the laughter half a mile a way from the pool. My kids loved it. I was relieved that it was so close to the Base and an ideal location until Base housing became available.

The next day I had to drive to Jacksonville to the Port to pick up my car. It finally arrived here from England. It was weird driving down the freeway after being on the left side of the road in England. But it was good to be home. I mean, really, good!

Today was my first day on the job. I was assigned to the Gunner Squadron. The squadron consisted mostly of guys flying helicopters. I missed the F'4s, and T-38's (airplanes) at my other Base. Again, the crew was wonderful. They made my job very special. I had heard so many negative things about the military that I just knew it would be oddly unsettling to be a part of this major conglomeration. Nothing could be further from the truth. I loved watching all the guys come and go with their flight suits on and dark sunglasses, making suggestive, flirtatious remarks. They would walk through the office on their way to an excursion in another city or country and we never knew from one day to the next where they would have to go. I wished many times that my sisters could be with me to experience this intriguing adventure, but knew they preferred hearing from me instead.

No one knew me here or had any incline of the horror I'd lived through in the past. I was quiet and appeared very shy. I wanted to block out the fact that I missed out on playing with other kids because I was always trying to make money so that we could have what other kids had. I missed out because I felt guilty about us running away, and, not looking back. I felt guilty that we would never find out if we could have been doctors or lawyers if we'd stayed with the troll of a Grandmother and our Father. I felt sad that I might have been responsible for my sisters becoming pregnant when they were still children themselves. If only I hadn't insisted on us staying with our Mother and never going back home. Oh God! I've never lived down the guilt. I was the one that always talked back to Grandmother when I felt she was being a true Bitch. I was always talking back when I felt Daddy was being unfair towards our Mother. I worked hard as a little girl because I felt bad that our lives had changed so drastically. We hardly had money, and sometimes not enough food, but I wanted to prove that we didn't need my Granny or Father in order to live. I promised myself that I would live down the lies and gossip that we would never amount to anything because of what we did by leaving that old lady. I promised myself that I would look after Little Zoe because she wanted to be just like me when we were 9 and 10 years old. When she got pregnant, everybody thought she had seen me in the act because she mimicked everything I did. I cried so many nights because I was still a virgin until I got married, but no one believed me. I had been quite bawdy about sex anyway. Well, I did let two boys have their way with me with our clothes still on, and quite frankly, we didn't know what the heck we were doing.

My goal was to prove them all wrong. I was on a mission. As I lay there reminiscing, my heart's broken because I had not yet accomplished my goal to really make it big so that I could reunite my sisters and brothers and all our families and just be together and love one another.

When I awakened, my pillow was soaked from the tears I shed in my sleep. I had to pull myself together and get ready for work. I was to ask for a week off to get settled. My supervisor was very understanding.

Again, I could not have pulled this off in the private sector. The girls and I went home to see my family. My sister, Zoe seemed happy. She was still married to her second husband and on her fourth child. I was surprised at the realization that I no longer fit in. I had outgrown this small city. I was afraid of myself. I had become too driven and my instinctive behavior led me away from Alabama and back to Florida on my Base at Hurlburt.

When I returned to work the next day, I discovered something drastic had taken place on the Base. We had a new Wing Commander and, surprise - surprise - surprise! He was Black. His name was Colonel Teddy Armatel, Jr.

My Commander informed me that his Protocol Officer had gone around the entire Base and gathered all Black females for an interview with the new Wing Commander. He wanted an all Black regime within his command. I understood that he was dissatisfied with everyone he had interviewed. My Commander phoned the Protocol Officer that he had forgotten me because I was on leave. He came over immediately. Once he and his crew arrived, they hovered over me like I had stolen something. The next thing I knew, he was on the telephone to the Wing Commander making arrangements for me to be interviewed. I was stunned. I said, "No!" I was satisfied with my position right where I was. I didn't want any extra attention.

My supervisor informed me that I was to report to the Wing Commander's office at 0800 hours the following morning, promptly. It gave me a headache. I didn't want this kind of change. I made up my mind that I would be a complete bitch and the Commander wouldn't like me and there wouldn't be a possibility of me changing jobs.

The next morning, there were no butterflies in my stomach. I arrived promptly and made the appropriate salutes.

Their offices were beautiful and intimidation was not a factor for me. I had no intentions of staying. I treated them like they really didn't matter. The door opened, I stood and saluted. There he was. The distinguished gentleman I'd heard so much about. Not bad! Little did I know that this person, Colonel Teddy Armatel, Jr., had probed into my life and found everything he wanted to know about me. He had found out that I was born on the first of April; he was born on the second of April. He had found out that he and I drove the same year and model car. He found out that we were both born in the state of Alabama. He bragged that he had several children and a beautiful wife that he was most proud of and knew about my eight siblings. The list goes on and on. There were so many similarities. Everything he had to say, I matched. He laughed and commented that he was impressed that I wasn't afraid of him. I asked, "Why should I be," and, he said, "You're a tough little heifer." I said, "A heifer had four feet, sir, and,

I only have two." He told me I was hired and I was to take care of him. I was to move to his office starting tomorrow. I asked if I could stay in my office another week, and he said, "Two more days; not a minute longer."

As part of his team, I was responsible for chauffeuring around all VIP's. My first driving experience was about to happen. The entire Base was buzzing. General James was expected to arrive at Colonel Armatel's office tomorrow. The excitement was overwhelming. I didn't really see what the hype was all about until I actually met him. He was one of Colonel Armatel's closest friends and colleague. His friends often called him Chappie. I got out of the car and extended my salute to this very tall General and tried to remain composed. He smiled and returned the salute.

He asked, "What is your name airman?"

I replied, "Jade, sir. How long will you be staying, sir?"

He said, "Overnight and off to Washington." He asked, "What's it like working for my good friend Colonel Armatel?"

I told him this was my first day on the job and I was sure it would be rewarding. He told me to stick by him because Armatel could help me get to Officer Training School. My heart was no longer beating fast. He was very easy to talk to and I smiled with ease as we finally arrived at the Command Post. I jumped out to open his door and he said, "I got it Airman Jade."

"Now, don't forget. If you're ever in Washington, feel free to come by the Pentagon and I'll get someone to give you the tour."

"Thank you sir." I enjoyed meeting General James. He was very down to earth, and Josie and I would jokingly comment on how Colonel Armatel had to look way up when they were high-fiving. I made sure their favorite cigars, doughnuts, and coffee were available, then I had to drive them in the Staff car, back to Billeting. He asked me what were my aspirations and I replied, "Commander, soon, sir." He laughed and said, "Very good and it shall be so if you stick with ol' Steady Teddy." He asked me if I knew this was Col Armatel's nickname and I responded that he'd mentioned it in the interview before I was hired. "Good man, good man!"

General Daniel "Chappie" James was the first Black, Four Star General of the Air Force. He was born, I believe, on February 11, 1920, in Pensacola, Florida. He retired on January 26, 1978 after 35, resplendent years of service. Gen. James was at a speaking engagement in Colorado and shocked the entire world, when he had a massive heart attack and died. He died on February 25, l978, and, is buried at Arlington National Cemetery.

Whenever I was seen on Base, people would salute me because they knew that I worked directly for the Wing Commander. They also saw me in my car and immediately assumed that my car was his car because we drove the same model and year, automobile. Rumors saturated the Base that we were somehow involved. I was livid! I was asked to prepare slides for the next big retirement party - and at that party, all the brass attended.

I was introduced to all by the Protocol Officer and the rumors that had been made about my mentor, Col Armatel and I, were topic of discussion. I let them know in no uncertain terms that there was no truth to the lies being spread. I reiterated that the Colonel was the most gifted, brilliant, true professional the military has ever known.

The Vice, Wing Commander asked me to dance, and I obliged. He and Colonel Armatel had their work cut out for them. I was Colonel Armatel's confidant. Josie was his personal secretary. She was a dynamic civilian secretary. On the military side, I was his most trusted Wing Administrative Specialist, and accompanied him on some of his TDY (Temporary Duty Assignment) assignments.

We sometimes flew to the Pentagon, in Washington. Colonel Armatel was an awesome pilot and did his own flying. Man! He was so great! We often stayed around in the command post with the other brass. Real fascination is an understatement. Colonel Armatel is now retired military.

Today, I decided to go to the chow hall for lunch. What a treat! I had no idea the fun I was missing. As I tried to cut my meat, someone bent down and whispered in my ear -- "May I join you?" I looked up curiously, hoping he wasn't a monster. Suffice to say he was a hunk. His name was Javi and everybody called him Jay. He had the cutest laugh. There was something about him that was very pleasant. He wasn't a tall person and often wore clogs with heels attached to appear taller. He said Prince was one of his favorite entertainers and was known to wear heightened shoes, also. I had a feeling he was going to be a lot of fun.

I had taken my children home for their quarterly stay with their Father. It was the first time I'd laid eyes on the children's Father since returning from England. As he walked down the steps from his home, I got a good look at this man that put me through hell. He looked retarded to me, somehow. He spoke, but I didn't say a word. I just stared with my chest stuck way out, hoping for a wrong move from him so that I could send him to meet his maker with my TaeKwonDo self defense. I kissed my sweet babies, goodbye, and smiled as I entered my car. I was no longer afraid.

There was no reason to rush home to my apartment. Nobody was there. Jay asked if he could come over and I replied, "Don't think so." Then he asked if I would consider going out with him to the Sugar Shack. I said "Yes." He picked me up and when we got there, I was tired from laughter. He was a hoot! He said, "I forgot to ask if you could dance." And I kept laughing without a response. Oh my God! What a cute little club! The place was surrounded with palm trees inside, giving it that tropical kind of atmosphere. I saw a few familiar faces from the Base and felt comfortable. They were forming a line to dance. This was like Soul Train. I loved it! He smiled really big because he could tell I approved so he forced me onto the dance floor. For a few seconds I just stood and smiled as he portrayed his version of Dance Fever. Not bad! Well I guess I had to show off. He clapped his hands with approval and said -"I knew it! I knew it! Work it girl!" We moved liked we'd been practicing for months together. Then, everybody gathered around clapping. What fun!

On the way home, he asked if I'd be his woman. His woman! I laughed at him and said, "You mean just because we're good on the floor you want me to be your lady?" He said -- "Nah -- come on - I didn't mean it like that." Then he pulled out a joint. I said, "No" and he became suspicious. He wanted to know how could I be so cool and not want to smoke. I said, "I have a natural high." He smiled and lit up.

He called four times the next day. He insisted on me meeting someone very important to him. I said, "Okay." Pick me up around 11:00 on Saturday. We went for a ride and pulled up in front of a well-manicured house with his best friend kneeling down washing his car in the driveway. I could hardly see his face. It was obvious he didn't know we were coming.

Javi yelled -- "Hey man! Come here! I want you to meet somebody." He looked up and stared really hard trying to see if he recognized anybody in the car.

Then, he yelled, "damn man! Why ya ain't warned nobody? I don't wanna meet nobody when I'm smelling stank, man!" We laughed. As he approached the car, he turned his head to the side and made a strange face - then remarked - "goddamn! Where you come from?" Javi cracked up. This is Jade, man! He said, really softly, "Hello Jade. You ain't from round here? Huh? Where's home?" I replied – "Mobile." He said -- "Git the f**k outta here!" We laughed again. He said - "Git out Mobile. - Let me take a look at cha." I was still laughing when Javi kept insisting I get out for a little while. When I got out, he went berserk -- yelling and screaming -- "Look at that ass -- Jesus -- you gone be mine girl!" Javi said -- "You too late bro." Javi informed him that I was an Airman, and he said, "Is that so?"

We went inside of his home and I was more than impressed. Immaculate would not be enough to describe how very neat and resourceful this new man was. He went and got a towel from the back to wipe his face and then pulled out this elaborate box he bought from over seas which contained hashish. He said, "I only pull out the good shit for the classy, people." Javi said -- "She don't smoke man!" He said -"No shit? Come on -- try it -- ah! -- come on!" I said, "No" -- then he said --"I gotta pee, anyway. F**k it! You sho she ain't no narc, man? Damn! In a minute, man."

We cracked up and waited for his return. He was magical. So real! So down-to-earth, and very invigorating. I couldn't stop thinking about him. Javi kept calling, but I wasn't interested in him. I was interested in his friend, Zane. Both their nicknames were "Jay". Most unusual! I didn't see him for months after that encounter.

Everybody I met after that seemed corny and turned me off. They were sort of pretentious. I didn't like that.

I decided to throw my own party and invite him over. I called him at his job and invited him and he was delighted. He responded, "I called Javi several times and asked for your number, so check this out, he refused to give it to me because he said you were his woman." "No! God no! We're just friends." "For real?" "My man, Javi was serious, so I told some of my partners, it'll be tough, but I'll back the f**k off." I thought to myself, I have to somehow make him believe it's not true. So, he said, "Tell me more about this party. When is it?" In my mind, I knew I didn't have the foggiest. I just wanted to see him. I told him I'd get back with him on the details.

I called my sister Coda and asked her to come down from Alabama, and she was delighted.

Two days later, I was coming off the Base and Zane was coming on to the Base and we passed each other and stopped. He said -- "What's going on Mobile?" He told me he admired my car and I smiled and said I had to go and I left. Actually, I was embarrassed that I didn't know what to say to him and didn't want to spend too much time with him for fear he'd see right through me.

I daydreamed about this man. He was so nonchalant, mellow, and surreal. I had a desire for him that I didn't understand. I was a little inept when it came to men and didn't want to blow it.

Zane showed up at the party with two women. Not one woman, like normal people, but two. I was not a happy camper, but didn't let it show. The girl on the left was his girlfriend. Rowdy as hell! Totally, unlike anyone I would have picked for him. He brought his own bottle and introduced us all. He wanted to dance with me and I refused, as I didn't want any problems with his insecure date. Coda told me that she thought he liked me and I said, "Don't think so girl. You saw that nut he was with."

The next week, I'd decided he was out of my league, when a knock came to the door. It was Zane. The girls ran to the door and he was shocked beyond belief. He said, "Hello Mobile. I remembered where you lived from the party the other week. Who are these little people?" I started to laugh and replied that "These were my daughters." He was still shocked as he let himself into the apartment. I looked out the door wondering if his girlfriend was on the way in, and he said that they had broken up months ago, he just needed companions for the party. He said, "I wasn't bout to come over here by myself to your little party. You blame me?" The children were hugging my legs and asking who he was. They liked him right away. The first thing they wanted to do was play in the pool. I thought he was gonna say nice meeting you little girls, now run and play, but he did quite the contrary. He went to his car and got his swimming trunks. "Come on girls, get your suits on and let's go swimming. Bring your Mama too." They said, "come on Mommie."

I watched them swim for hours and was really impressed. Paige got out of the pool and yelled for Toury to follow. They went inside and began plotting. Paige found Zane's keys and they decided to hide them so that he wouldn't leave. They were truly smart for their ages.

It was time for him to leave and we searched for an hour looking for those keys. Finally, I looked at the baby and asked her if she knew where his keys were. She looked at her big sister and I knew they had something to do with the disappearance of those keys. Toury broke down and started crying. She looked at him and asked, "Why do you have to go?" Paige joined in and told him that he didn't have to leave and that he could stay right here with us. "Right Mommie", she asked? I had to do some hard explaining and Zane interrupted and told them he would be back next weekend and we would all go to the beach.

They counted the days until his return. I must say I couldn't wait either. He was prompt; and on top of that, brought the picnic basket full of chicken and other goodies. It had been a long time since I let a man take charge of my life. I mean a long time. The weather changed abruptly and we had to leave. I couldn't help looking at him. He was not at all like the men I ended up with. He was a red bone. I'm talking - real, almost White, red bone! I remember what my Mom used to tell me many years ago. She would say - "The Blacker the berry – the sweeter the juice." I believed her but had many reservations now that I had met Zane.

We made it home and the girls were fast asleep. He came with me to tuck them in. He sensed my bashfulness and pulled me close and swore that he couldn't get me off his mind. I leaned backwards as he stroked my hair with his hand and stared into my eyes. He confessed that I made him very nervous. He made me tell him why I wouldn't kiss or become intimate with him. He promised not to push.

The next day was exciting for me because at work, we often spent time after the weekend, reminiscing about what we did. Josie said, "Tell me more about this new man."

My Wing Sergeant Major walked in on our conversation and told me to be careful because Col. Armatel would be angry with anyone I wanted to date. I disagreed and told him it was my personal life and nobody else's business. He said, "The position you're in is almost like being in the White House. The Colonel sees you like you were his own daughter." I said, "Yeah! Right!"

Sure enough, after the Commander returned from his trip, he called me in and said, "I've heard rumors that you've been taking up with some Staff Sergeant." He said, "I'm gonna introduce you to this really nice Major that I think you would like because you deserve much more than you think." I told him thanks but I was capable of taking care of my own personal affairs. He told me to remember that my life would be scrutinized, even under the most microscopic situations. Everything I did was a reflection on his office. I told him I remembered. I, also, tried to make him understand that I didn't want my friend investigated and he acted like he understood, but told me in no uncertain terms that he cared about me and wouldn't stand still for any foolishness. He said, "You've become like a daughter and I'm very proud of you and want only great things to happen for you." My head hung low, I blushed with deep gratitude.

I forgot today was the day for all, the young officer's meeting, and the Colonel had to attend, which meant I had to go, also. There were three Black Officers present and I wasn't interested in any of them. Captain Woods was the most eligible officer there. He was 6'5", dark and everyone thought he was incredibly handsome. I found him to be arrogant and self-centered. A total, turn off! The Colonel walked over and introduced us. He said, "I want the two of you to come over to have dinner with Andrea and the family." Ms. Andrea was a beautiful, determined, intelligent young lady that didn't take any stuff off anybody, whether she was the Colonel's wife, or not. I declined, and the Major asked for a rain check.

Three months later, I accompanied him to a Gala, and when we returned to his apartment he automatically assumed I would be intimate with him because he was an officer. Perish the thought! I told him he was distasteful and to call me a cab. He apologized and asked if I would not tell the Colonel. When I arrived home, the baby-sitter informed me that Zane had called three times and was very angry that I was not available.

The next day, he came over unannounced. I told him about the Gala and how uneventful the evening had been. He lifted my face with both hands staring into my eyes. Before I knew it his mouth was over mine pressing hard with his tongue following no rules. He was holding me so close I could feel his nervousness. I tried to pull back as he kissed my neck, grabbing my face with both hands, breathing very hard and shaking his head, "I love you baby, and I don't want to lose you." I begged him to stop and he kept saying, "Don't say anything – it's okay – you don't have to feel the same about me. All I know is that I need you desperately." My heart melted because he seemed so genuinely sweet. It's a night I will never forget!

The next week was a nightmare. He called and wanted to come over. He said he couldn't tell me over the phone. In his hands were orders. He was reassigned to Ankara, Turkey and leaving immediately. I ran to him and revealed how I didn't want him to go. He said, "I know baby; I don't wanna leave you and the girls, either." He said, "I feel like you and Paige and Toury are my family. Just when my life was taking a turn for the better, I get a remote assignment." He said it was for 18 months and he could get a return back to the states. I was feeling sick and wanted to be alone.

We spent every day together. Then he was finally leaving. We went to see him off and I cried all night long. I hated being by myself and so did he. I knew that 18 months would go quickly and we would be together again. He said he would call as soon as he was settled on Base. The phone rang. I looked at the clock – it was 2:20 in the morning. Who could be calling at this hour? I said, "hello" - there was silence, then, just as I was about to hang up, that voice said, "Hi baby...I really miss you." There was an echo and sounded far, far away. Before I could say anything he was steady talking, leaving no time to get a word in edge wise. Then he said, "before we get cut off - Jade! Can you hear me?" I said, "Yes." And he said, "I love that sweet voice. Send me some pictures so that I can make love to them every night." He said, "I'm so lonely for you, baby." Then, out of nowhere he said, "You know – I've had a lot of time to think while I was traveling cross the pond to get here. Jade - will you marry me?" He said, "I know you're gonna be my wife anyway, so you might as well say yes." He said, "Come on baby, we belong together, we're so good together." So I said, "Okay" and he screamed to the other guys and I started laughing and he said, "I have to go, but I wanted you to know you've made me the happiest man alive." I didn't want him to hang up - I missed him so.

I told the girls that Zane and I would get married and they yelled with excitement, "Yippee! Way to go Mom!" I knew they would be happy with him and I couldn't wait for us to become a family.

Two months have passed and I had bad news. I got orders to go to Davis-Montham Air Force Base in Tucson, Arizona. Man, was I upset! I told Col Armatel and he said he had gotten orders also to go to Luke Air Force Base in Phoenix, Arizona. I became very suspicious.

Why was he leaving when he was in charge of the entire Base? He had gotten in so much trouble and needed me to testify in court before the judge advocate that he had never flown the Air Force plane to Alabama to see his Mother when she became ill. I knew it wasn't true.

They also wanted me to testify that he had secretly been taking female civilians to the Billeting Office and having his way with them. I knew nothing of the sort. I knew the real source behind this entire incident was someone he trusted and this individual was jealous of Col Armatel's position as the Chief Commanding Officer of the Base. It was proven to be false, anyway. He was the only Black Officer to ever hold such high office at this Base. There was so much corruption going on. Everywhere you turned, somebody was lying on him or trying to demean his position as the Commander in Chief. He was such a great leader! I tried so hard to protect him because I loved him as my adopted Father. He taught me so much. I was overjoyed that he was vindicated, and at the same time, sad to be leaving the Base.

It felt weird to be traveling to another Base. We'd only been there for a year. Interstate 10 was a good route, but everything was beginning to look like the desert. We finally made it to the Base and it was nothing - I mean nothing like Hurlburt. I wasn't excited because I didn't want to go. Not after I had - had it made working for the Wing Commander. As soon as I arrived, I went straight to the Commander's office and explained my situation. I told them how I was in dire need of housing being a single parent with two children. I had heard how hard it was to get Base housing so I wrote a letter to the Commander. Guess what? He obliged.

We stayed in Billeting for a while, then we were assigned housing and I knew I was truly blessed because sometimes it took a year or two before anybody got housing.

I also found a baby-sitter for the girls and I was feeling like this might not be a bad assignment, after all.

Once I went to Base Personnel to process in - I could tell this was the bomb. I received an extremely warm welcome. Most of the guys were letting me know if I needed any assistance, they would be more than glad to help me with getting adjusted.

Word spread fast that I was a single female and I was assigned to one of the most popular Squadrons on Base. I finally went to my Squadron, and whoa! I had never seen so many men. They were coming out of the wood works. My Commander asked me to come in and he told me that word came down that my housing was available and that I could move in on august 7th.

Right away, I made lots of friends and I couldn't wait to tell Zane. He couldn't call me until we were in our new place, but we wrote to each other every day.

When we moved in, all of the neighbors came over to help. Jason's parents were most memorable. They lived right across from us, and Jason was always over to the house. He was the cutest, two- year old, I'd seen in a long time. It didn't bother me that there were no other Blacks living near me because since it was military, I felt a little safe. They had informed me that the phone would be on in two days, and it was.

I was so excited I called my family to let them know that we were okay. My sister Zoe was excited, too. She kept me informed about everything and everybody in the family.

Then, my sister Coda always came to see me when she could because she felt it was exciting being on the military Base. I called her to let her know about the Base and she wanted me to look out for the eligibles for her. We laughed and I had to remind her about Zane. She was shocked. The first thing she asked was "how tall was he?" I said, "You remember,

Coda. The party I had. The guy with the two dates." She couldn't believe when I explained, "We're getting married!" She wanted to know where he was and I explained that he was still in Turkey. She said, "Dang man! You really believed that stuff Grandma said about you betta not have sex till you're married." She said, "Seems like you should be able to relate to that movie star, you know the one - and we both laughed.

That same night Zane called. God! I missed him. He was quiet that night. The first thing he asked was how many guys tried to hit on me. I said -"Honey - you're calling long distance, we don't need to talk about other men." He agreed. I told him I had met some very interesting women. One of them was in my Squadron and, named Cheryl. She was part Filipino and Black - quite beautiful, and openly, gay.

I also met a guy that was really smooth and most influential with everybody on Base. His name was BP. This guy was really fine with one of the most beautiful wives I'd ever seen. She was part Japanese and part Black. I never saw anyone that was so married, but, yet, still very single. Quite disturbing! But, he became one of the best friends I've ever had. Nobody messed with us because they knew BP and I were tight. I often confided in him about my husband to be and he was always there - putting in a good word for Zane. He turned me on to some really nice people and parties. BP had some rather dynamite parties. The man had it going on.

The guys started coming over to the house for me to corn row their hair. Some of the other guys wanted me to cook red beans and rice with ham hocks because you couldn't get it on Base at the Chow Hall. One Brother asked if I would cook him some turkey necks with gravy and onions on top of rice to remind him of home. Then somebody else asked for ox tails. The nerve! Who did they think I was?

One sergeant offered to pay me a large sum of money to hide his marijuana so that when the dogs came through the barracks, he wouldn't get caught. I asked him if I really looked that dumb and he apologized. Everybody wanted to take the girls out for hamburgers and fries trying to get next to me.

Time was flying. Zane wanted to know what kind of wedding I wanted. I said I wanted to get married at the courthouse. It's been six months and he wanted to fly home and get married, then fly back to Turkey.

He asked me to get everything lined up because he only had two days and he wanted everything to run smoothly. I wanted to wait. But, he had this superstition that he was gonna lose me and didn't want to put it off until his tour was over. I was having so much fun. I was having second thoughts. But, he convinced me again, how great we would be together as one.

Later that night, Cheryl asked me to go out with her. The most exciting place to party - was called, "The Boat." The club was a ship and very exotic on the inside. We walked in and the poor guys were in awe. They called us Charlie's Angels. The dancing was incredible. The guys were all over us. I was kindda tired of the same old scene - Immature little boys trying to be men and promising something they could never deliver.

The next week I would be a married woman. My heart raced wildly. Should I? Oh Lord - this was forever! Married to the same man for the rest of my life! There was so much negative talk on the Base regarding marriage. I just wanted to bump into one couple that was happy together. Never happened. What was I thinking? I had so much to do, to get ready for the wedding. I called the courthouse; went and got my dress; got the cake taken care of; and made the hotel reservations. We decided against a reception - he didn't want one. I contacted all my girlfriends so that we could scream with joy, and went and bought the camera.

Cheryl was to be my witness and take care of the kids, afterwards. Zane would leave immediately afterwards and return to Turkey for twelve more long and agonizing months. How was I gonna get through this? I wanted to wait until his entire tour was over but he feared I would forget about him.

This is my first time at the airport. I'm almost late for his arrival. Butterflies can't express what I'm feeling.

I haven't seen this man for seven months. He doesn't know a single soul at this Base and I'm not the same person he left before; I've grown so much more. I kept replaying the last week we spent together - it was pure sweetness I didn't want to end. He was my very best friend. I was able to share with him - from whence I came. He knew that I had never had a real childhood. He knew that my sisters and I had to raise one another along with our other siblings without any assistance. He felt really bad for me but couldn't relate. He said I appeared to have been sheltered with all the finer things in life. He kept saying how resourceful I was. He said, "Jade - baby, your life story is so unbelievable, and by looking at you nobody would think your past was a reality." He said that all the things I went through, living in the Projects; working two jobs at the age 13, and continuing to be an honor roll student without parental guidance was far fetched, and to forgive him because he couldn't see it. He would often say that we could have easily fallen into the wrong hands and become drug addicts, prostitutes and God knows what else. He brought out that we should have had very low self-esteem, but did quite the contrary; He marveled at how calm - very calm we remained. He knew that I - especially, loved to dress nice, loved to be neat, was totally conscientious about hygiene, had complete self-worth and wanted all of us to remain discreet and appear well taken care of so that suspicion wasn't aroused and we weren't thrown into foster care. I had explained to him that my Father and Grandmother cursed us -"saying that nothing good would ever come of us - especially me." My objective was to totally prove them wrong. I wanted so badly to let them know that they didn't know whom they had produced and being second best was not an option.

Our other relatives were all whispering and gossiping about us but nobody really knew what was happening in the house. He knew that I felt horrible about my Mother and about how she never had a good life, either. I always sent money to her begging her to come and live with me wherever I was assigned in the Air Force, but she always declined. He just kept saying - "That's an amazing story sweetheart. Truly, amazing!"

Oh God! There he is! He looked thinner, but nice. "And what is that on your face? A Van Dike? I love it." He hugged me as if I was gonna run away and he was trying desperately to prevent it. There was so much to catch up on. We talked for an hour. The girls were happy. He seemed sad and distant, and I learned later that he had been in some trouble with the Turks and was frightened about the outcome. I assured him that everything would be all right. He appeared under nourished but pretended everything was fine.

I just wanted to take care of him. I had prepared a big meal that he did not eat very much of because he said he was not used to eating. He said he was too excited. Mercy! How I wanted to protect him; he seemed so vulnerable.

I wanted my friends to come over and meet him, but he wanted me all to himself. The ceremony was very brief. We didn't seem married, but we were. I couldn't believe it.

Col. Armatel called because he was now situated at Luke AFB – He called because he wanted to come down to see the girls. I broke the news to him and he congratulated us and asked to speak to Zane and made him promise to take good care of us. He promised to meet him upon his return.

Tomorrow he would be leaving to go back to his assigned Base in Turkey. As we held each other close, I could hear the loud beat of his heart as we stared in each other's eyes making plans for his final return from Turkey. He reassured me that life would be sweeter now that we had made that final step to become one. We vowed to remain focused.

As I stared at his flight climbing the clouds, my eyes tightly shut and burning from lack of sleep, I prayed for his safe journey back to Ankara. A remote assignment I wouldn't wish on anyone.

Two days later, he called. "Ahhhh - baby! It's so good to hear your voice! I hadn't slept because I needed to hear that you were okay." I reminded him that I hated to write even though the phone bill would be enormous I didn't care because I loved hearing his voice and being able to express my feelings verbally. He didn't mind. He told me the semi nude pictures he brought back of me were not like the real thing but helped somehow to calm his agonizing longing for me. I missed him so much. He said the guys stayed in his room wanting to hear every detail of the wedding since they were all so lonely and in dire need of female companionship. They threw him a small congratulatory party upon his return and he promised pictures real soon.

My friends seemed to multiply. I was more popular than ever. Jerome was a dear friend and always trying to get some play, but I'd always let him know it was much better for us to remain friends and that I cherished my vows as a married woman, so I'd often match he and other single males to eligible females. I was very good at it and word spread like wild fire. They kept saying I should charge a fee and I laughed that this was something I liked to do. Some of the acquaintances turned into real relationships and I was pleased. I had to let everybody know that I wasn't responsible for any differences being that we were all adults. Even though I initiated the introductions, I was not responsible for any conflicts that soon followed. I became a relationship counselor - giving advice to everybody. It was fun and kept me occupied so that I wouldn't mope unhappily that I couldn't be with my husband.

I enjoyed my last name. During this time, in 1977, the name "Tyson" was revered all over the world. If I went to a restaurant and the maitre de loudly announced the name - Tyson - party of three, everybody would turn around and stare. I made sure I was always stunningly attired, and they swore I was the boxer's wife, without setting the record straight, we'd eat for free. Those were the days!

I had worked really hard talking with personnel and my Commander trying to get Zane reassigned as a follow on, from Turkey. He was trying on his end, also.

Later that night, he called so that we could discuss possible joint assignments if my present Base was not a possibility. A week later, to both our surprises, he got his orders. The news he presented me with was too devastating, so I broke down crying. He kept apologizing and promised to try and get his orders changed. We were assigned to Minot, North Dakota. They changed his orders all right! He ended up being assigned to Loring Air Force Base, in Maine. I couldn't speak. The news was too upsetting. I kept saying - "there are no Black people in Maine!"

He assured me it would be okay as long as we were together. I cried all night. The next day, everybody was telling me about their experiences with Loring or what they had heard. It didn't matter what anyone said, I knew it wasn't a good assignment.

Then I received a phone call from my sister, Zoe. Our baby sister, Mace, was graduating. It was one of the happiest Moments of my life. She was the last daughter to finally graduate. Oh what a joy! She was so smart. I used to see that same determination in her eyes that I had. But, wait! As if that wasn't enough, on September 27th, that same year, she gave birth to a handsome baby boy we proudly call Arias. When I finally saw the baby, I knew he was destined for greatness.

As far as the military Base was concerned, I thought to myself, okay! I can do this and I can make this move. It's really not that bad. Being the optimist that I am, how bad could Maine be?

The movers were on time. We couldn't wait to get there because in October, everything is orange and yellow and very pretty during fall. We drove both cars and I thought we would never get there. If ever there were a wilderness, by God, we'd found it! People were waving like they were in a parade and staring as if they'd never seen Black people before. There were so many potato trucks. We laughed. What had we gotten ourselves into? We had automatic Base Housing and it was ready to be moved into.

The neighbors were quite friendly and everybody had a story to tell. They enlightened us to hurry and gather all the food we needed because starting next month everybody would experience "cabin fever." Meaning, it would snow long, and hard, half of the year and virtually impossible to do anything, lasting nearly six months. When summer rolled around, most babies are born.

My new job was working with the Wing Commander, again. It was completely different from working where I'd been. They were very biased and couldn't hold a candle to Hurlburt Air Force Base. They couldn't understand why I was so cocky. Actually, I was very confident and exuded total professionalism. My performance evaluations backed up my abilities.

Then, one night as we were trying to make it home in the snow, I caught a pain I had never experienced before and couldn't move. Zane gave me some aspirin and put me to bed hoping the pain would go away, but it got worse. We searched the house for something a little stronger. We found Excedrins, but they didn't work, either. I was getting worried. We called the Base hospital, and was asked for a description of the problem and they told us to get there right away. We had a problem. We couldn't get out of the driveway. It was snowing really badly! I could never become acclimated to this horrific weather. The girls were worried. They wanted to know what was wrong with Mommie. They wanted to call Col Armatel. I had to endure the terrible pain.

Toury asked Zane to make me stop hurting so that they could go outside to make a snowman. He said, "I wish I could sweetie, but your Mother is going to have to go to the hospital." The neighbors helped to shovel the snow out of the driveway so that we could get to the hospital.

They ended up keeping me, and emergency surgery was imminent. I had so many fibroids they had to operate immediately. They kept me longer than the norm.

Paige often called to say how much they missed me. They said, "Hurry home Mommie! Zane is so mean!" I said, "You guys are exaggerating because you're spoiled."

Doris, all the other gang, and the entire office came to see me with so many goodies I couldn't eat them all. I told them the best thing they could do for me was to get me the latest record out called - "Freak Out." I didn't care how they did it, I knew it would help make me well, just to hear it. Doris granted my wish.

Before I left the hospital, my sisters called to tell me that my baby brother Kendrick was graduating and going to the Coast Guards. Hallelujah! We were free at last! We had all graduated. This was my dream.

My Grandmother said it couldn't be done, but this was a great day! I was so happy I wanted them to release me from the hospital immediately.

When they did finally let me go home, everything seemed so different. I didn't want my husband to put his hands on me. I found myself not wanting to be in the same room with him. What was happening to me? I discovered things about him that were not to my liking. I noticed that he was not very nice to the girls. His excuse was he was just trying to be a disciplinarian so that they would grow up to become responsible adults. That, I deeply understood. The manner in which he went about it was incorrect. Constant yelling is not the way. I'd been through enough abuse to last a lifetime. This was not the way.

We argued over everything. This was the first time we were together for a lengthy period of time under the same roof, and we didn't have very much, in common. I hated being home on sick leave. I had six more weeks to go and for the life of me, didn't know how I was gonna make it.

I enjoyed having everybody over to see about me, this way I wasn't alone with him and I felt relieved. He was such a wonderful person otherwise. He didn't know how to handle my illness. I believe if he had stayed in counseling and continued to talk with the doctors, he would have understood what was happening to me as a female, and we would still be together today. He's truly an outstanding person and a dear friend.

Five and a half weeks passed. We were watching television and a sharp pain hit me again and wouldn't let up. The pain was exasperatingly excruciating, and he hurriedly called the ambulance. We arrived at the hospital approaching midnight. I became suspicious that perhaps he was poisoning me. It wasn't true. I didn't understand why I was falling apart. Then I passed out.

I was awakened with hard, slaps to my face by my doctor, begging me to snap out of it. He said I was very blessed - and that I had a close call with my appendix rupturing, causing damage to other organs in my body.

As I recuperated, I was still having pains in my stomach. This time, I asked for a second opinion and they flew me to Wright Patterson Air Force Base, in Ohio. I had to stay a week for very thorough tests. I found out that their recommendation was for me to have a hysterectomy right away. I said "No" and they ordered a Laparoscopy in which they had to go into my navel and probe around to find out what the problem was. I asked for them to quit treating me like I was some kind of guinea pig. I wanted to go back home and stop hurting. An infection set in and I was ill for a while again.

Four months had passed and I had not been back to work. I demanded to go back to work and I did. Once back, I realized I had trouble sitting up. I went back to the hospital and found out that the anesthesiologist was on temporary duty somewhere else and they wouldn't be able to operate on me again without one available.

From what I understood, a young trainee decided to take on the job without permission. He decided to cut on me without my consent. He said there was no time and when he realized he was over his head, he panicked and they transferred me from the military installation to a new hospital in Caribou, Maine, not affiliated with the military. They explained everything to the doctors there and the next thing I knew they had given me another major surgery. I was devastated. I was 28 years old and had my whole life ahead of me. I had not been prepped for this kind of surgery. Psychologically speaking, I was not prepared for what I was feeling. Again, I had to stay in the hospital for an extended period of time.

After two weeks, I was released and ordered to stay off my feet for six more weeks. I had been away from work approximately six months and felt really bad for my husband because here we were still considered newly weds after a year, and I was an invalid, and we hadn't had a life together, yet.

Zane was left to take care of my children and me. He had to deal with no sex since my first hospital visit. I knew we were growing apart. I needed my sisters. We talked and cried and talked and cried. They wanted to see me something fierce! I hated the distance between us. Somehow, I knew in my heart, I'd see them real soon.

Zane came to me with some news. He said he was due to get out of the military and wanted me to get out too. I said I had two more years to do and they wouldn't let me out. Zane had four more months to go. I wrote a letter to the Commander and whomever else I could write to, that would hear my case.

My mind was blown. The Commander approved my early out, but before he signed, he said, "Sergeant, you sure you wanna get out? You know if you stay, the military will take care of your medical bills for free, and if you get out, the military won't have any obligations. Why don't you think about it some more, I mean, you're still very young, and looking at your records here, I see a really bright future, Sergeant! I believe I saw something in your files about Officer Training School. Now, what happened to that idea? Why are you so eager to get out? Is this you talking or is someone else making up your mind for you?" "I have to obey my husband, sir. Officer

Training was a dream for me sir. Maybe, I can come back in later. I'll come back and talk to you next week, sir." As I stood up to salute the Colonel, I knew I wasn't coming back. I knew that this would be the last time I'd see or stand in this office. I looked around at all the medals of honor and all of the photographs of different events that the Colonel had accumulated over the years. This could be me, I thought, but my husband wanted me to stay home and recuperate, then do something comparable to the military and make more money in the private sector.

I felt I'd been hypnotized with all the medication I was taking after all my surgeries. I knew I wasn't thinking straight but also knew I was plain old tired and worn out from working since I was thirteen years old. I'll figure everything out later.

Zane and I decided that Florida was a place where we both wanted to settle down. He wanted to go to Gainesville where he was born, but I overruled with a suggestion to reside in Tampa where there was a veteran's hospital and a military Base where we could both get jobs really quickly as civilians. He agreed.

We arrived in Tampa and both enrolled in college using the GI Bill. I got a job right away at MacDill Air Force Base as the secretary to the Chief of Civilian Personnel. He got a job with The US Geological Survey. Whatever happened to me just resting and recuperating.

I thought we were set, but I became severely despondent. I didn't realize that there was a name for this depression. I had not been prepped for my last surgery and I was out of control. It was too soon after surgery. I didn't understand these feelings and soon realized I needed help. I couldn't stop crying. I felt like the world was caving in on me and I needed someone to tell me it was going to be okay. I wanted to be petted and pampered. I had gone through some rough ordeals with one surgery after another. A few people I had confided in kept saying you'll get over it, but it never happened. I wanted to be close to my husband, but he kept pushing me away when he found out I couldn't have his son.

We were in a new place with new people and I didn't know a single soul, except for my husband and children. I felt very alone. I needed my sisters.

He later started calling me names like "Blackie" which brought back memories when I was a very small child. I was often called Buckwheat and Stymie - because I was so ugly. Right now wasn't the time to make me feel less about myself. He didn't understand what was happening to me as a woman, so I asked him to go with me to my visits to the doctor. I really felt less than a woman, and wanted the doctors to explain to my husband why I was having so many problems. I wanted us to be the way we were when I first met him, but too many things had gone wrong.

I had heard about all the myths of not being wanted by the opposite sex after you have this type of surgery. I needed help and support from my husband. He decided I would get over it and that all we had to do was graduate from college and everything would fall into place.

I threw myself into my work. I played with the girls and often went to events after school, then went straight to class - trying to forget.

One day, in a major conference with most of the officers on the Base in my civilian capacity, I was taking minutes of the meeting and broke down crying hysterically. They adjourned the meeting and took me in the other office to try to find out what the problem was. They called my husband to hurry and come and get me because by now I was out of control. He was unsympathetic and made matters much worse.

Later on that night, I decided I wanted to end my life. I had been reminiscing all week about my life as a teenager and as a young girl. I didn't see why I needed to continue this existence if I wasn't going to function as a woman. I didn't feel like a woman. No one made me feel like a woman. I certainly couldn't have the son I sincerely wanted. There was no need to go on.

Zane had school. There was no way I was going to attend school the way I was feeling. I convinced him I would be okay and he left. When he had gone, I went to the medicine cabinet and found some valiums and sleeping pills. I took them all. After I took them, I panicked, got in the car and amazingly, drove myself to the hospital. I knew I was going to die. But in a creepy kind of way, I wanted someone to rescue me. I knew it was too late when the man asked me if he could help me and I said, "I took too many pills," and all I could remember is him asking, "What kind of pills - ma'am, ma'am? Can you tell me what kind of pills you took?" Then, faintly, I could hear all the fuss. My memory of the incident was a blur. I could hear and barely see all these people surrounding my room, then passed out.

When I woke up - all these tubes were inside of me. Zane was sitting there with his head in his hands. I didn't know if I was in heaven or hell. So I closed my eyes again. I volunteered to stay in the hospital for 30 days for observation and counseling. I didn't want to be married any more.

I didn't want my life the way it was. I just wanted to be around happy, positive people. I missed my babies. They came to the hospital everyday.

The Veterans Hospital took me in and was very thorough. Some of the people there were really freaked out. I saw how unfortunate most of the patients were and I tried to stay away from them but they would all come over to me and ask if I was some sort of movie star or another. I felt really uncomfortable, because they would stare at me and stare until I'd have to move from room to room.

We had to gather in the day room and stand up and tell everybody who we were and why we were there. After listening to some of the people, I was sick. I mean really sick.

I had been there three days, when somebody said, "I'll be glad when Seth gets back because when he sees you, he's gonna flip out." I had no idea what she was talking about until he showed up. Seth was one of the orderlies. He was on vacation. All of the nurses were trying to talk to him, but he refused to mix business with pleasure. Besides, he was very, very, religious. There were some really cool men on the ward who took care of everybody, but I wasn't interested in all the attention.

We had four doctors - two of them Black - one Italian - and the other one was Indian. They all came to my room to see who I was. It was so unbelievable to everyone that somebody like me would be in the nut ward, because this is where they put you if you try suicide. One of the doctors was very interested in me, but I wasn't interested in anybody. I just wanted to heal.

The next day, Seth returned from vacation and you could here the commotion all over the floor. Everywhere he went, they were telling him about the new patient. "Man, you need to go to room 312, I'm telling you, that's where she is, man." "That's where who is? What are y'all talking bout? Why is everybody talking bout this patient? I mean, what's so special bout this person?" God is the only one that deserves that kindda attention from me. So, anything else, I ain't interested." "Okay, man, don't say I didn't warn you." It was time for everyone to be in bed. I saw him walking my way very slowly, and sexy. Later I found out it wasn't pretentious. He was just fine as hell and a super nice human being. I had only seen bodies sculptured like his in magazines. He wore his hair long and had tiny lips and a pointed nose and piercing eyes.

We had to stand in line for our medication and I could see that he had my files in his hands. When it was my turn, he stared at me for a long time.

In the back of my mind, I wondered what his voice would be like. Then, he spoke. He said - "Hello, and how are you? My name is Seth, and what's yours, I've heard a lot about you?" I was in a daze and didn't care what anyone thought of me or perceived me to be. I answered by saying - "You already know who I am, I see my files in your hand." I'll talk to you tomorrow." He smiled and said, "Now, you sure you gone be here tomorrow?" I smiled flirtatiously and turned around to get to my room. Some of the others were teasing him that he would be smitten. I could here him laugh.

As I lay in my bed, I tried to think about my husband. We were separated and I knew I didn't want to be with him anymore. I thought about when I first met Zane. I thought about what it would have been like if I had said no to him when he asked to marry me. I was so screwed up. I remembered when my sick Grandmother would tell us when I was nine years old, over and over again, not to have sex with anyone unless you were married to him. I then asked God to forgive me because I really tried to make Zane and I work but I didn't want to be with anybody that lacked compassion and romance. To me, it wasn't hard to be nice. He had switched gears on me and was like a whole different person. Zane hadn't expected a lengthy illness from me and refused to deal with me being out of commission for sex. He said he didn't feel like it was his duty to have to pet or pamper the opposite sex in order to get along with her. I told him all I wanted him to do was to be nice, and it would surely be reciprocated. Why in God's name was it so hard for some people to be nice? I mean really nice.

Then, I thought about Seth. It wasn't a turn off that he didn't have a really nice job or that he wasn't rich. He appeared to be a genuinely kind, pleasant, and sweet person. The next day, I decided to avoid him, but he found me anyway.

They were serving lunch in the cafeteria and he came over and sat with me. As I wasted my hot chocolate, I let him know that it didn't look good for him to fraternize with a patient and he said he didn't care. He wanted to know more about me. I found myself, reluctantly, attracted to this man.

That night, I saw him staring at me again. He came by the room to ask my religious preference. He said he wanted to share something with me tomorrow. We talked every day about the Lord. It was really refreshing. Seth was very religious and loved his Mother, dearly. He couldn't wait till the morning sessions were over. He was right there waiting for me. The moment came when I knew he wanted to know what brought me to the hospital and how I got to this point. When I finished, he wanted us to read two chapters of Psalms.

Seth and I were getting closer. I tried to fight it with all my might, and, so did he. When he left at 11:00 p.m., he'd always call back and they'd put him through to me knowing it was against the rules. He was worried sick about me. We'd talk forever and just hearing his voice was medicine enough for me. He pretended to be the godfather - because he knew it made me laugh. That night, he wanted to know where I lived but I wouldn't tell him. I didn't want to go into any details because I had just legally separated from Zane and the divorce was pending.

Zane and I had purchased a very beautiful home in a brand new subdivision. The girls loved it. They were always excited over the Pomeranian I had purchased for their birthday since they both were born in the month of August. His name was Pasha - German, for general - and he looked like an orange ball. Toury was mostly fond of him and took him everywhere she went. They had promised me that they would always take good care of him, but as soon as he pooped, they went the other way. I didn't want to be bothered with the cute little puppy, but as soon as I arrived home, he'd jump all over everything, scratching the windows, and turning flips, making me crack up.

The girls had so many friends and were very popular with the teachers, and the other children. I was very proud of them, especially, Toury. She was my little track star. I knew she would be the next female to represent the United States in the Olympics. Man! That child could run! She won first place. The next week she came in second. I thought we'd have to hospitalize her to calm her down. Second place was not an option with her.

Paige was my other daughter. She liked to draw, was a natural, and smart as she could be. She was unusually quiet but came alive when reminded that she looked like my twin. They were complete opposites. I wanted to stop talking, but Seth wanted me to go on. He said my life was interesting. I told him how I hated my life. How I became bitter, lonely and frustrated and was still married. I told him how I knew that finally, I was over the edge. I had asked my husband for a divorce pointing out the reasons why we should part, when he kept screaming he would never let me go, I lost it and put a coke bottle through the wall of the new house. Everybody freaked out. I knew I needed help, but nobody was listening. I just wanted to be free of this person that reminded me of the failure I'd become. I told him I just wanted my husband to be nice to me and say nice things, even if they were not true, therapeutically, just, to help me out. I explained to him what a wonderful man my Zane was and how we needed to be with other people and not live under the same roof. I told him that since they'd taken my insides out, I saw things in a different perspective.

Seth saw that I was really reliving the situation and asked if I wanted to stop. He was so easy to talk to. I told him to be quiet and let me tell him about some of my past. He said, "I'm all ears."

I remembered that I had just started working at the Control Tower for Air Traffic Controllers at the Air Force Base. My supervisor was Capt Bowers. The brother was really smooth. He came at me also, but when he found out how professional I was, he backed off. I told him I would watch his back always, and he appreciated that.

There were many, many officers and enlisted personnel always coming to the Air Traffic Control Tower to see Capt B. Then, came Capt Rollins. Capt B. was always making fun of him because he wasn't built like the rest of the crew. He was about 6 ft 3, and 160 pounds. He kind of reminded me of Barnie, on the Andy Griffith Show, but once you got to know Rollins, he was nothing like that character. He was very cool. He walked in and saw me and put his hand over his heart. Capt Bowers told him to forget it. He said, she's my little sister, dude, and I ain't letting no stank dog like you talk to her." He laughed and said - "Shut up man!" "How you doing baby?" I smiled. He said if I became bored in any shape, form, or fashion, to please give him a call.

I didn't realize that the big thing in Tampa was happy hour. The majority of the Base went to happy hour right outside the Base. I had never experienced this kind of partying. Military personnel kept their uniform on and did their thing. The civilians and military really came together after work.

Rollins came back when he knew Capt B. was at lunch and asked me to accompany him the following evening for happy hour. I agreed. What an experience! We went to a revolving bar that was famous for their beautiful waitresses. I never laughed so hard. What excitement! Everybody came over to our table to beg me to stay away from the Captain, which made me laugh.

Rollins was all about fun; I mean big fun; and I was ready for a major change. He took me to lunch every day. He was a Squadron Commander and I began to meet a lot of people through him. He introduced me to the Base Commander, who was White, but had Black characteristics. He called the tower and asked if I wanted to attend a function at the Officer's Club and I said I would think about it.

I did accompany the Major and to my surprise, the brothers' didn't appreciate it. They were like - "Damn - where did she come from?" The attention was more than I could handle. Rollins and the Major became rivals. They both competed for my attention. I was having the time of my life.

Zane was trying to get up with me, but I wasn't having it. I noticed that I began to tense up again. He was a really nice guy (my ex), but we just didn't mix under the same roof. I wanted him to be a part of my life as my dear friend because he was still very special to me.

Seth said - "Girl! I knew you were attached. You're just too beautiful not to be surrounded by people who can appreciate you." He said it sounds like you've brought us up to date or, "Is there more?" He said, "I wanna know if there's somebody that's got your heart." He said, "I can deal with, the wanna be's; I just want you to tell me whether or not you're in love with any of these cats." I said, "No, they're just close - close, friends."

I told him how surprised I was at the amount of people that smoked marijuana. I asked him if he was a part of that number and he responded - "That was my past." He asked - "What about you" - and I said - "I had a natural high." His reply was -"Praise the Lord!" And we laughed.

The conversation with Seth filled a void that I so desperately, longed for. I love to talk - and, when reciprocated, it's refreshing. He asked, "Do you want to hang up Jade?" "I'd better, before you get fired," I said.

The next day, I couldn't wait to see him. I felt closer to him after divulging all that information regarding some of my past. He came to my table during lunch and stared at me a long time and said to me, "Jade, I feel as though my God has or never will fail me. I prayed and prayed and asked him to guide and always direct my path." Wow, where was he going with this? It was hard for me to finish my food. He said, "Sweetheart, you were included in my prayer when we finished talking. I expressed to my God what he already knows about you. I told him I wanted to talk to him about one of his angels. He let me know that you were gonna be all right, Jade." He kissed my hand as one of the nurses passed by and as she spoke, her smile, and wink to Seth, made his day.

I had stopped taking any of my medication because it made me drowsy and I didn't want to fall to sleep when he and I talked late at night. I suddenly realized that I had one more week to go.

They came around and asked if I wanted to stay in the hospital another month and I declined. I felt I was ready to get back to my life and was truly unrepentant about the events that led me to this place – because had I not gone through the fire, I never would have met Seth. I felt there was a special reason why our paths had crossed. It was almost time for him to get off from work and I became sad because I wanted to be around him continuously. He was such good therapy. He said he had a revelation and that it may cost him his job, but he was willing to risk it. He had aroused my curiosity. As he spoke I, was all, ears. He said, "How would you feel if I came back after hours instead of talking on the phone. Would it be all right if we talked in person?" He said he was not trying to take advantage of me; just couldn't help himself. I accepted the offer. The nurse came down on my end to give me a rose that was left by someone. She wouldn't tell me who it was. She smiled big and said – "Trust me sweetheart, you'd be well pleased to know who it was."

That night, he came back on the Ward. I was afraid he'd hear my heart beating loudly. He took my hand gently and said, -"Jade - I know I'm out of line but I think I'm falling in love with you. I've only known you a short while, but I feel I've known you all my life. He said, "I love the way you keep me looking forward to the next day. What a beautiful spirit you have; One of God's finest creations."

There was nothing I could say or do except blush as I tried to calm my nervousness. I was filled with euphoria and couldn't help but ask if he had left me the rose with the nurse, and he asked if I liked it. He said he was leaving, but wanted to look into my eyes when he divulged - without me - life would be imperfect for him. He asked if he could hold me for a minute and I froze. He slowly walked towards me, pressing his well-built body against mine. His large hands left my waist and slowly found the arch in my back. Just like an artist knows his subject, he circled my round bottom then explored the curve of my hips as he tried to contain his breathing. In an instant, his tongue searched mine sending moans and whimpers of ecstasy as I disappeared into seventh heaven. He whispered as he brushed my lips with his mouth – "There's nothing in this world that feels as good as your touch." He confessed that he was quite overcome. We knew danger was near, so I asked him to leave and he stood in front of me without a word - shaking his head and kissing the palms of my hand. He revealed that because of his work for the Lord - he'd stayed focused and had been celibate for two years and eleven months. He said the flesh was weak sometimes, but he always maintained, because through prayer, all things are possible.

I couldn't sleep; the evening had been most memorable and very intense. As I closed my eyes, I replayed how my body cried out for his, wondering what it would be like to go beyond his powerful kisses.

Today is the day for my departure from the hospital. I went around to all the patients individually giving them a bowl of confidence. It was kind of sad to be leaving but I knew I had to get back to the real world and put all this behind me. I had laughed a lot since my arrival and decided that laughter from the comedy had healed my soul.

Seth arrived to take me home, but I wanted to go to his place first. His apartment was cute and masculine, almost as I'd imagined. I didn't want him to see my home, but he insisted. When we drove up, he said - "I knew it! I knew it! This place is unreal!" He asked if I stayed here, all alone. I told him my daughter Paige and my sister Mace would be coming back tonight. Toury, my youngest daughter had gone to live with their Father in Atlanta. There were so many messages on the door and on my answering machine. He was, without a doubt, very impressed, and wanted to come back that night, but I needed to rest.

My daughter and sister nearly fainted when the knock came and they opened the door. It was Seth. He said, "You must be Paige - and she blushed.

"How did you know my name?" My sister, Mace was oohing and panting hilariously, as I hit her on the head. She asked boldly if he had any male friends or relatives that looked like him and we laughed violently. Mace was really humorous. She was my baby sister who seemed older because of her wit and intelligence. I often times reminded her of her excellence as a child and knew she'd go far with her amazing intellect.

There was another knock at the door, and this time, it was Capt Rollins. He wanted to know where I'd been and why I didn't tell anyone I'd be gone for awhile. I introduced him to Seth and he gave him an unappreciated stare.

Seth volunteered to leave and I was not a happy camper. Later that evening Zane came by and a few of the guys from the Tower. My neighbors were having a field's day trying to figure out why all the visitors. I waved and watched them turn their heads as if I wasn't there. Nosy bastards!

I didn't care about all the visitors; I just wanted to be with Seth. I couldn't shake that burning desire I had for him. I didn't know what to do about the other men in my life. They were all very nice, but didn't affect me the way Seth did. But, I'd never interfere with his walk with the Lord. When he got home, he phoned me to see how I was and, wanted to see if I was exhausted from all of the other company. I told him I was okay, just really missing him. It was 8:30 and the wind was blowing something fierce. Without warning, a blazing thunderstorm arose. It was lightening and thundering so I jumped and he wanted to know what was wrong.

"I wish you were here to protect me baby."

"You want me to come back, he asked?"

"It's too far and I know you're tired Seth. You want to wait till the weekend?"

"I can't wait that long, baby, he said. I'm hanging up. I need to see you now. I promise I won't stay long. I just wanna hold you. Please. Please Jade."

I whispered, "Okay. Be careful my love. See you in a few. Bye."

Seth lived an hour away. That gave me time to call my sisters Bria and Zoe. We were on three-way trying to catch up on all the juicy gossip. I told them that Mace and Paige were doing well. I had to tell them finally about Seth. Zoe asked if he had any uncles or brothers and we laughed. I looked at the clock and didn't realize we had been talking for 30 minutes. I suddenly explained I had to go because it was almost time for Seth to arrive, and Bria said, "Jade, it's been a long time for you, so use your better judgment and decide what to do."

Zoe said, "The heck with that. Throw your legs around that hunk of a man and give it all you got." We couldn't help but crack up at Zoe. She was hilarious. The doorbell rang.

"Oh my God! You guys I have to go!"

"All right Jade, we love you. Let us know how things go."

"I will. Hang up you guys, I'll call tomorrow! Bye, Bye."

I looked through the peephole. Sure enough, it was Seth.

"You made it here so quickly, I said. Can I get you something?"

"Yes. I want a hug. Ahhh baby! You feel soooo good!" I felt dizzy as he whispered, "Let me make love to you Jade." "No! Absolutely not! I believe in you Seth and your walk with the Lord."

I tried to convince him that it wasn't a good idea because he had been abstinent for quite some time.

"I'll risk it. This is the first time I really feel like it's right and I'll take my chances. You're not responsible for me baby, so please, don't feel guilty. This is between me and my God." I led him to my room and took off his shirt. He slowly removed my robe. Seth scared me as he stepped back to check out my body. "Ah man! You are so fine, baby. I mean - seriously! You are really built baby!"

"So are you Seth." I gave him a delicious smile, and as I parted my lips, he thrust his tongue deep into my throat sending a definite message of burning desire. He then took my hand in his and asked me to kneel down and pray with him. After prayer, he whispered, "Trust me Jade...I need you so very badly. Please don't make me go away." I was speechless as he lifted me and gently laid me on my carefully, made bed. As he undressed me, my breathing was out of control. He then kissed my entire body, sucking my fingers slowly, one by one...watching as I squirmed with passion. He gently caressed my breasts, then moaned that the firmness gave me away. He confessed, you've got to be at least twenty, baby. He whispered, I don't want to hurt you Jade, just let me know and I'll take it slow." He then used the strength of his legs to open my thighs, then thrust hard against my love walls, igniting passion beyond surreal! "Dear God...he's all I wanted and much more." He took my head with both hands and stared into my eyes as he shouted out to me..."I love you Jade! Please don't ever leave me baby!" I then flipped him over and straddled him as if riding my favorite horse bare back. I continued to flex the muscles of my love canal as he gasped for breath. As we detonated together, I knew this was what I wanted for the rest of my life. We were incredible as one.

I was crazy about his spirit, his personality, his kindness, his heart, his humbleness, his arms - his hands - his neck - his shoulders - his chest - his legs - his thighs - his butt - his eyes - his lips - as he touched mine - were - magical! I didn't want him to leave, but begged him to go before day broke. Reluctantly, he left, and I re-ran every moment in my mind - over and over and over again. I could still smell him - I could still taste him. He was in my blood.

Thirty-five minutes passed. The phone rang. He said he had arrived in an excited and ebullient mood. He went on to tell me that he'd fallen in love with my every being. He wanted to know where I had learned to move like that. He confessed his deepest fear of when and how he would be punished by the Lord for disobeying him. I didn't want to think about it. How could God be against something so beautiful? Seth had been celibate for quite some time wrestling with the flesh, but acknowledged that he had to have me or else die on the inside.

He wanted me to meet his family. His Mother - now that was a real lady! He was crazy about his Mom. That made me care about him even more. I was so nervous. He thought my shivering was from the cold. His Mom was everything he said about her - a devoted worker, and member of the church, a fantastic cook, and a real sweetie. We liked each other right away. She shared with me some of the works she had accomplished in her bible-study class. I was amazed! Her enthusiasm was infectious because she was on fire for the Lord.

He told her, "Mom, this is the one."

She laughed and said, "You all have my blessings." I couldn't help but hug her. What a doll!

Seth had two brothers. They were very close. One of them had been in the psychiatric hospital for eight years and was to be released in a week. He would be staying with their Mom until she determined whether he was stable enough to be on his own. He was released to their Mother on Friday. Seth said he looked good. His Mother didn't allow any loud music, smoking or drinking in her house, and she reminded the brother constantly about her house rules.

The sixth night home, his brother went out on the town with some old acquaintances. He returned home approximately two o'clock that morning. Seth's Mother got up to open the door and complained to her son that she didn't appreciate the loud music and him coming in stinking drunk. She reminded him of her works for the Lord. He ordered her to leave him alone and she wouldn't stop. Seth jumped out of bed to rescue his Mother from the brother's loud and drunken behavior. He was a loose cannon! Seth asked him to go to bed and told him that he'll talk to him in the morning about disrespecting their Mom.

"Come on man, sleep it off. We'll talk about it tomorrow. It's gonna be all right. I love you. See ya in the morning, man. Be strong!" Seth went back to bed and shut the door because he thought he'd heard the last of it, and fell back asleep.

An hour passed. His brother became deranged, somehow. His brother got up from his bed in a trance, went into the kitchen, got a knife, turned the music up loudly, and butchered their Mother to death. He stabbed her so many times no one got an accurate count.

When I received the phone call, I knew something had happened. I thought, perhaps it would be my family calling to report bad news. There was silence for a second. I almost hung up. The somber, weary voice on the other end sounded familiar. Was it Seth, I couldn't be sure? "Yes. It was Seth sobbing hysterically." I was bewildered, and mystified. "What on earth is wrong sweetheart? Talk to me! Seth, what is wrong? I'm on my way over." I hung up the phone in a frantic state and couldn't imagine what this was all about. I didn't dress; Just jumped in the car. On the way over, I tried to visualize all sorts of reasons that Seth would sob uncontrollably. Never, in all my days was I prepared for what I was soon to envision. I could hear his loud screams from my car. It sent chills through my body. When I arrived I could see all the police standing around, lights flashing from every direction. It was 2:45 a.m. My God! What could be wrong? Before I went in, I thought to myself, maybe his Mom had a heart attack or maybe his brother had become really ill. I inhaled and blew it out really hard. I said to the policeman, "I need to see Seth." The door was open, so I walked in. I disregarded the other police as I saw Seth sitting in a corner on the floor. I ran to him and held his head against my chest.

"What happened? Somebody tell me what happened." The police asked who I was and said only family, were allowed.

Seth said, "This is my fiancée and I want her to stay." Then he divulged the horror to me and I couldn't stop the gag as I listened in disbelief.

Needless to say, just like that, the man I was recently with, was indeed a changed man, and understandably so. This, he said, was his punishment for having intimacy before marriage. The tears wouldn't stop flooding my face, for I knew, instinctively, we would never be the same with one another again.

He stayed in counseling for several months. I tried to stay in contact, but he wasn't the same. I wanted to be near him, for I felt his pain, but he hated himself, and the world. He wouldn't see me. He wouldn't see anybody else, either. Life was not worth living without his Mother. I wanted to be there for him just like he was there for me when I met him at the hospital after trying to end my life. This is my twentieth time at his house. He's still not there. The phone's been disconnected. I went to his job to locate him there. He never returned after his Mom's death. No one knew his whereabouts. I continued to pray. "God! Please let him be all right! I miss him so!"

It's 9:12 p.m. I craved for some jazz to soothe my soul. Billie Holiday was in arm's reach. I think I played "Good Morning Heartache" eleven times, as she so beautifully expressed - "Stop haunting me now, can't shake you no how. Got those Monday blues, straight from Sunday blues," - Suddenly, I realized I needed Seth just as I needed air to breathe. I couldn't change what had happened, but wanted to be a vital part of his life.

Three months later, an acquaintance of mine and Seth's, informed me that he had seen him at an ungodly place with acquaintances that were users. He told of how disheveled he seemed, not at all, the same man I knew before. Indeed, I had to see for myself.

The next day, I went to his apartment - low and behold, he came to the door completely out of it. I couldn't get past the smell in the place, so I sprayed it down, opened the drapes, put him into the shower, cooked a meal, fed him and talked and talked until he promised me he would get help again. He looked at me for a long time - then, admitted how much he still loved me and wanted us to start anew. I knew that I still loved him too. I explained that I would always be there for him, no matter what.

I cried all the way home thinking of what could have been and how very cruel life had been for him. I knew he missed his Mother, because she was his world. He often told me how he loved her more than life itself. I tried numerous of times that year to contact him again, but to no avail. I'm telling you, I just became uninterested in the opposite sex. I mean...really.

The following Saturday night, I saw headlights from my window, but couldn't imagine who it could be. It was good old Capt Rollins. He knocked, and knocked. I yelled through the door that I was ill and not up for company. He kicked the door in and I called the cops. My God! He was inebriated. He said he couldn't stop thinking about me and that I kicked him to the curb without warning. I assured him that it was his imagination. We didn't have a relationship. We were just friends.

I didn't press charges against him because I knew he wasn't in his right mind. We were friends and I didn't want his reputation ruined. I was still distraught over Seth, and didn't want anymore drama. I just wanted to be alone. He came by again with fifteen apologies and the money to repair my door. I felt lost. I hadn't felt this way for a very long time. I wanted to be loved - just anybody to care about me - not in a physical way. Just care about me. I missed Seth. He was someone that God was going to really use to get his word out.

Today, I can't stop reflecting about my past. It is unbelievable - I tell you. Why can't I forget about this? Why can't I get over it? I'm feeling bitter. I used to dream about a normal childhood. Sometimes when I was 12 years old, I used to go to the library and read up on growing up and becoming a woman. I still wasn't sure why I was having a period at such an early age back then. I really don't understand why nothing happened to me as I hitchhiked across the Bay every night (30 miles away) trying to make it to my job so that we could eat. I really don't know why I didn't get raped as I traveled alone every night on my ventures. I really don't know why the eight of us children didn't get stabbed as they continuously broke into our home and stole our small check. I realize, truly, that it was the works of the Lord. He had something better in store for us all. We just had to find out individually, what that something would be. I decided I wasn't gonna feel sorry for myself anymore that night. I concluded that it would be better if I relocated away from it all. I thought if I was far away from Seth, I wouldn't think of him so often.

The next day, my daughters wanted to play with me to cheer me up. My youngest daughter, Toury, had joined us from Georgia and wanted to race with me on the bicycle. I hadn't been on a bike since I was ten years old and had a terrible accident of splitting my vagina open and almost bleeding to death. I climbed on - a little wobbly at first - and wow! It came back to me. I was riding again - it felt good. Then I got cocky. My daughter said, "Let's race Momma." I raced ahead and was winning. As I looked back - I didn't realize that a truck was on coming, so I swerved to avoid collision and ran into a parked vehicle. I was thrown onto the cement. My face burst wide open as I came down really hard. I couldn't move. All I could do was lie there. I heard all these screams. I just couldn't move. I wasn't sure if I was alive or dead. It happened so fast. My daughters were panic-stricken. They yelled -"What are we gonna do?" The man jumped from his truck. They called an ambulance. I was unaware that my girls had called my recently divorced husband, Zane.

I was unaware that he rushed me to the hospital. They called in a plastic surgeon. The doctor explained to me that because of the severity of the injury, I wouldn't be able to talk for a couple of months. Communication was to be done in the form of sign language and writing. No laughter! He told me that unfortunately, I would have a huge - long - protruding scar on my left jaw extending to my nose - and that people of color usually scarred in this fashion. I didn't care anymore. I knew I would be deformed. It didn't matter. I was just glad to be alive.

As I recuperated, ten to fifteen people a day would come by to visit. I was exhausted because I wasn't allowed to laugh. It was so painful. Two days after surgery, I decided to disobey the doctor. I laughed until the tears nearly drowned me. The next day, I did the same thing. I disobeyed the doctor. My ex continued to come over and tried to help nurse me and made sure I was obedient. My sister, Mace assured him that she would keep me in line.

Two months passed, and I was sure I would relocate to California. I told Mace and Paige I no longer wanted to live in Florida. I had to get out of there. I had healed enough to travel, and my ex-husband, Zane, decided he'd spend as much time as possible with us before we would relocate. His first suggestion was for all of us to go to Disneyland and have some big fun. I kept rubbing the scar on my face. I wasn't afraid of it. I just wanted to see it grow like the doctor said. But it didn't happen. I never got the large, protruding scar that was promised. It was a miracle!! I was eternally grateful to the Lord for blessing me that way.

Disneyland was a blast. We had a fabulous time. Zane and I promised to be friends for life. We hugged and road some of the rides together and decided we had made the right decision to just remain great friends. We said that we would always love one another and he made me promise to contact him if we ever needed him and he would come running.

I made one last attempt to see Seth. I found him. He looked good. He couldn't believe that I was taking off to another city clear across country. He revealed that we needed to try again. I couldn't make any promises. I told him that he and I would talk when I got settled and we would figure out if we had that date with destiny.

We packed and packed and headed for California.

My baby sister, Mace promised to help drive. We hadn't slept in two days. We knew the journey would be a long one, but had no incline as to what it really entailed. A small U-haul was attached to the new Volvo.

I was 32 years old with two children, divorced and didn't know what my destiny was.

When we arrived in the city of Houston, I knew we couldn't go any further. I was too tired. I started seeing double. Mace decided she'd rather be a passenger instead of a driver. I could've choked her, but I understood.

We decided to pull over to the first hotel we thought reasonable. I got up the next morning refreshed, ready to take on the world. I went down to the lobby to find out when was checkout time and saw a newspaper. The paper was so thick it shocked me.

I asked the concierge why was traffic so bad in this city and he wanted to know where were we coming from. I said, "Florida", and immediately, he knew this was a rude awakening for us. He asked where we were headed and I replied - California. He said, "That's all well and good little lady, but you ought to give our town a chance and I guaran –damn- tee - you won't wanna go way out yonder." I laughed and purchased a Sunday paper. He said - "Word of advice - go to one of them temporary places and they'd put cha to work right away." I said, "Thanks, and would give it some thought." I was excited. I had never seen so many people. Traffic was horrific!

We looked through the classifieds and went crazy. There were so many jobs. I convinced my sister that we should stay, if only, for a little while.

The next morning, I went to one of the top temporary agencies in the city. They tested me all day and called me back that afternoon to see if I would be interested in a fund-raiser for a hospital that would be willing to pay a large amount of money hourly for word processing. I was excited for sure, then asked what I needed to do.

I was to report to the Stehlin Foundation for Cancer Research at 8 0'clock. The people were nice. The job was simple. I had to type one letter and let the word processor spit out copies as if it had been typed individually to look like originals for each letter.

This hospital was preparing for a Gala at Jones Hall with famous singers and actors donating their time and talent for free in order to raise a million dollars for cancer research, followed by dinner for the stars at the Four Season's Hotel. Tickets were from $50.00 to $1250.00. My ticket cost $500.00, but I didn't have to pay for it because I was an employee.

The stars ranged from Crystal Gayle, Ann Margaret, Liza Minnelli, Marvin Hamlisch and Alan King. My job was to mail out letters individually, to fortune 500 companies and movie stars. Dr. Stehlin was asking for donations ranging from $50 to $10,000.

Dr. Stehlin is well known for his emphasis on treating people rather than the disease. He is a phenomenon.

It was Monday, and everybody went to lunch. The phones were ringing off the hook. I decided to answer one of the lines and didn't want to get into any trouble, so I disguised my voice. Suddenly, I was British. I convinced this star's agent to pledge $5,000. I knew the information to divulge because of the letter I was typing and what I had over heard. He complimented me on my made-up accent and said he would be more than happy to donate for his client. I was ecstatic! When the staff returned from lunch, the man called back and explained that he had just pledged $5,000 and wanted to speak back with the British female. The administrator explained that he must be mistaken - that no such person existed in this fund-raiser. The guy was insistent and called my name. The administrator immediately looked me up, saw that I was Black and demanded to know what was going on. I broke down and told him the phones were going crazy and I tried to help by answering them. I explained that I was from the temporary agency. He said - "I don't know what you did, but if you can do it again, you're hired permanently as assistant to the Director of Administration."

Carolyn Farb was chairperson for the fund-raiser to raise a million dollars for cancer research. She was one of the city's most prominent charity fund-raisers. She was responsible for taking care of all the little extras that escape obvious attention. She made the corporate presentations, and sold the expensive seats and helped to plan the "Supper Dance" at the Four Seasons for big-ticket buyers. This was the first time that a million dollars had been raised in Houston. Ms. Farb wasn't trying to set any records, even though she exceeded her goal, she was only trying to raise what Dr. Stehlin asked for, a million dollars because she appeared to be a very caring and compassionate person. She wanted to make everyone aware of Dr. Stehlin's Clinical Cancer Unit and Research Laboratory at St. Joseph's Hospital in Houston, Texas. Dr. Stehlin explained his philosophy: "A tri partnership exists between the patient, doctor and the researcher in which the patient is supreme. The patient is not a case, not a number, and not a statistic. That's critical because their biggest single complaint is that they're treated as just another statistic and patients are tired of it."

One of the stars that donated their time for free in order to raise a million dollars was Marvin Hamlisch. He is the one that got the ball to rolling. He met Dr. Stehlin at a party given by Carolyn Farb. He was so captivated by him, as a person, he described Dr. Stehlin as a very loving and a very caring person. Mr. Hamlisch is one of the most gifted composers of all times. He decided then, that after meeting Dr. Stehlin, he wanted to participate in the Gala. He is noted for winning 3 Academy Awards, a Pulitzer Prize and international fame by the young age of 31. He's most remembered for composing the Score of the beautiful song, the Way We Were, song by Barbara Streisand.

The night of the Gala, Marvin Hamlisch brought the house down as he performed his award winning score for A Chorus Line.

Liza Minnelli was the next star to donate her talent for free. Liza is the daughter of movie director, Vincente Minnelli and the fabulous, Judy Garland. She was the winner of three Tony Awards and two Golden Globes. She is a good friend of Mr. Hamlisch and proved this night why she is a very loved, and larger than life, entertainer.

The next performer was Ann Margret and her dancers. Ann is also a friend of Marvin Hamlish, too. What can you say about Ann Margret? She was married to her long time romantic husband and lover, Roger Smith. I remember Mr. Smith as known for his movies with James Cagney in Man of a Thousand Faces and his character as Jeff Spencer, a detective in 77 Sunset Strip. He was Ann Margret's manager, and a darn good one at that. In 1975, she won the Foreign Press Association's Golden Globe award, for Tommy. I remember her mostly, in Viva Las Vegas with long time, good friend, Elvis Presley. Ms. Ann was very blessed with a remarkable talent. Her performance, the night of the Gala could only be described as, truly incredible!

The next performer that donated her talent for free was Crystal Gale. I don't think I've ever seen anyone more beautiful. Crystal is the sister of Loretta Lynn. She used to travel with her famous sister many years ago then married Bill Gotzima who was known for his long hair too. She not only mesmerized the audience with her wonderful singing, we were fascinated with her long, beautiful hair.

Last, but not least, the Gala could not have been a success without the great Alan King as Master of Ceremony, and man! Was he funny! Alan King was cast opposite great actors like James Garner, Jane Wyman, and Tab Hunter. He was often found in the companies of legendary comedians like: Dean Martin, Jerry Lewis, Danny Thomas, George Burns, Jack Benny, Gary Moore, Billy Crystal, Bob Hope, Milton Berle, Carol Channing and Whoopi Goldberg. I heard the people behind us say that they were about to wet their pants with laughter. He was that funny!

After the Gala was over, everybody went to the Four Seasons Hotel for dinner. We were told to be hostess to the stars and to dress like a star, too. I was so excited! Dr. Stehlin was the guest. Stars had flown in from all over.

I was escorted by Sean who was my companion at the time, and, drop-dead gorgeous. He looked like a much younger Billy Dee Williams with really long, shaggy, hair. When we walked in, they thought I was a celebrity. Ann Margret gave me a hug. I tried not to speak because of the British accent, but had to because different people kept asking me questions. Someone in the crowd thought Sean was one of Ann Margret's dancers and gave him a big hug for a job well done. I told Ms. Minnelli she was, without a doubt, an amazing entertainer. She thanked me and remarked, "How sweet." Crystal Gayle announced her pregnancy and introduced her husband as her Manager to us. As I made my way through the crowd, I bumped into Ms. Margret again, and gave her another hug. I told her I'd never seen anyone so fabulous. Susan Stafford was there also looking incredibly stunning. She informed me that she was with the 700 club now and very happy. She invited me to come to California and visit. I did visit Susan at her Gallery. She was magnificent. While I was there, I visited my Father's daughter, whom we had not yet met. She was wonderful. I enjoyed she and her daughter thoroughly. Man! There were so many people there. Along with the stars were Presidents and CEO's of Fortune 500 companies. I rubbed noses with the majority. The event was a smashing success! We all applauded Ms. Farb, for an incredibly, successful evening. (We went over the quota of a million dollars). I was impressed with Carolyn. She had done the unthinkable of exceeding her goal. The lady was amazing. I often assured her that she was one of the most beautiful women I'd ever seen. She graciously thanked me and said I was much too kind.

The next day, the media was all over us, and the administrator called me into his office. He gave me a breakdown of the job offer, what it entailed, my benefits and salary. Wow! It was a handsome salary, but I declined. I was just passing through. I had to gather my thoughts. My career had only been with the military and I wasn't really ready for anything else permanent. I wanted variety, then off to California.

My next assignment was with Citadel Properties - a commercial real estate company. As I printed out mailing addresses, day after day - I realized I could do this on my own and do word-processing and create resumes, etc. I learned so much about the business.

Then I got a call to go Downtown to LDX Net, a Fiber Optic Company. It was ground floor all the way. The Branch Manager was the only official person in place. He gave me total power to organize and restructure the office. I hired the rest of the employees and he made me the Branch Administrator. I had developed a wide range of contacts and wanted to branch out on my own. So I opened my own secretarial service.

My office was inside of the Brown and Root Building, in the Westchase area, which created a lot of traffic. I worked day and night but became very bored with typing. I enjoyed music. I wanted to be involved with the entertainment industry.

After days of brainstorming, I decided to include a Talent Agency. Word spread like wild fire. There were other production agencies in the area that were run by men, but when they found out I was a female owner, they all came running to find out what I was about. I had entertainers that had played with Duke Ellington, toured in Europe and wanted a change. One of my accounts had jammed with James Brown before.

Today was really wild. I had to turn down four people who walked in my office with a snake act. Scared me to death and the other tenants, too. But to make up for it, in walked a classical pianist. His repertoire was phenomenal! I had contacted several people to make them aware of what was available with my company. The Great Caruso was in dire need of an opera singer. His singer was unavailable, so I sent my people over; A car was sent for me to observe my singer at the Great Caruso, and his performance rocked the house.

The next day, I made some contacts. I remembered Ms. Farb from the Gala. I let her know what kind of business I was running and she said she'd keep me in mind.

The next week, I received a call from Ms. Farb saying she needed some singers to perform the song - "Oh Carolina". She was having a party for the Maestro and his wife. She suggested no money. Just exposure for the first performance and she would circulate my name. It was a good move. I convinced the group and they went for it. The performance was excellent. My company was now becoming popular.

My kind of business was a difficult one for females, back then. I started receiving unpleasant phone calls, according to my receptionist... from unsavory characters that made inquiries through other channels about the company. My receptionist was afraid. Then, I found out that the Mafia paid me a visit and wanted to take my office. I became afraid. This was getting out of hand. I needed more money to stay afloat.

I decided to get a full time job, let the receptionist stay full time and have my Marketing Director run the place. I raked the want ads and found this big ad from Keith, Katonn, and Payne, looking for a receptionist. I was not beyond working for somebody else so that I could realize my dreams. So I convinced myself to get that job. It was downtown, and far away from my office...no one would ever put two and two together, and suspect that I owned my own company.

I went for an interview. The storm was horrific. When I stepped foot into the law firm, I knew I was way - way - out of my league. The office was plush- beyond belief. I started to walk out, but wanted to use the restroom before getting back on the road. I approached the receptionist and asked if I could use the ladies room. She looked up in disbelief because of the British accent and also that I was a Black female and asked where I was from. These people didn't know anything about me so I decided to continue the charade of being an English woman. It was only temporary.

Then Shelby came out in the receptionist area, then asked the receptionist, "Are there any more applicants?" The receptionist looked up at me and asked if I was here for the position, then remembered that I had to use the powder room, as they called it. Then she said to Shelby, "You should hear her speak. She's from England, right?" Shelby was the Administrator, and a vision of class, impeccably attired and, obviously, astute. When I returned from handling my business, the receptionist told me to go to the left door and don't be nervous and good luck. When I walked into Shelby's office, which looked like an elegant living room in New England, decorated by Better Homes and Garden, I couldn't control the rapid beat of my heart. I asked her to give me a minute and she gasped, complimenting the accent. She wanted to know what brought me here to America and I continued to fabricate. I didn't let on that I drove a Merccdes and owned my own firm. I thought it'd be best to divulge that information later. I asked about the job and she said, "You have it, my dear, providing you're still interested." She made a handsome offer with all benefits, including parking, an expense allowance, and after 90 days, there would be a review and the Partners would decide if I would get a substantial raise. She almost forgot bonuses were given during Christmas. I tried to remain calm and stood and shook her hand. I wanted to make sure, so I repeated the offer. She asked if I had time to stay and meet everyone and I said I felt uncomfortable since I was still wet from the rainstorm and it had obviously ruined my "Fabulous do."

"When can you start?"

"Next week will be better for me."

"They'd be most grateful if you could start before the week is out."

"Granted, Ms. Shelby. It will be my pleasure," I replied.

When the elevators landed on the ground level, I blurted out a much suppressed, scream! "Am I dreaming, or what?"

The Partners were awesome. Mr. Payne, the Senior Partner became my good friend. He would often stop by my desk on the way in...just to tell me how I looked. He wanted to know what brought me here to the states. I wanted to confide in him so badly that I really wasn't from England, I only pretended to be so that I could get this job, and decided to give it another month. I felt I could trust him and wanted him to know the truth about me. It was so hard to continue this travesty. He would tell me war stories and tell me how he got started in this business. Mr. Payne was a combination of Henry Fonda and Jimmie Stewart (both wonderful, warm actors), just better looking. He was gentle, kind, witty, happy -go -lucky, and a part of the singles club. I found him to be most inspirational. Even though he was a millionaire, you'd never believe it by his mannerisms. He was very smooth. He said I impressed him because I wasn't easily intimidated. He told me "Charming" should've been my middle name.

It was amazing watching the Firm take on very difficult tasks, and always, but always, winning!

I was centered in the middle of the entire office and could see and hear everything that was going on. I watched as Yasmina, the Paralegal, was verbally attacked by two of the secretaries. I intervened, explaining that ladies really don't act like that and that it was totally unfair for the both of them to attack her without warrant. They went to lunch graciously and Yasmina leaned down to the desk in laughter and thanked me from the bottom of her heart for the rescue. We became inseparable friends. She was Puerto Rican, and flawlessly, beautiful.

Shelby, the Administrator kept the place immaculate. She maintained organization and total control of the office and expressed that dignity, was a must! She overheard what had happened and promised to speak to the girls, but Yasmina declined her aid, explaining that I had gallantly taken care of the problem.

She and Mr. Payne made life in the office, bearable. Yasmina showed me around the building and took me underground to the tunnel. Unbelievable! I had been in the military and traveled all over, but none like this. We shopped in the tunnel, had margaritas for lunch and took on happy hour every evening.

It was hard for my Marketing Director, at my own office, to find me most evenings. I was so happy. I had the best of both worlds.

Then the unimaginable happened.

The next day, approximately 8:30, Mr. Payne hadn't shown up for work. He was never late. His 9:00 appointment was already there. Yasmina asked me to continue to try and get a hold of him. Still, to no avail. It was now 10:15, and Shelby and the rest of the Partners became suspicious. They asked one of the mail clerks to go over to Mr. Payne's apartment and see if everything was all right. We patiently waited then the call came in that he wasn't there.

The next couple of hours were pure hell. Shelby decided to call the police and have them search the area. Mr. Payne liked to keep in shape and would jog every morning before work.

The Partners asked the police to search the area in the park just, to be on the safe side. The call came in from the police. I knew something was wrong because he asked me to put Shelby on urgently. Then I heard this scream. My flesh started to crawl. I closed my eyes tightly and gripped the cord on the phone. They were ringing off the hook. I couldn't answer because I wanted to know what was wrong with Shelby. The others were running out of the room and crying. Everybody was sobbing and hugging. "What?" I wanted to know what happened. I knew the inevitable from their reactions. Mr. Payne had a heart attack. He was found dead on the jogging trail at the park.

"No! God, No!" This wasn't happening to me. Shelby came out to console me. She knew how much I cared about him. I ran to the powder room. I was vomiting uncontrollably.

They closed the Firm the remainder of the day. I was speechless. Suddenly, I was lost. What were we to do?

This great man I revered, had been taken from my life without warning. What about his sons! I had just met them. He had told the others that if something ever happened to him, he wanted us to celebrate his life. He said he wanted the ladies to wear red to his funeral and wanted nobody to be sad.

His wish was granted. We all wore red. They all pretended to be upbeat. But, when Shelby broke down, we all did.

It wasn't the same anymore...at the Firm. I missed him more that I can reveal. Yasmina and I stuck by each other for months to come.

I received a call from my receptionist, at my own office, who was frantic. She had received a call from a new client that wanted to talk to me desperately.

I took his number and on my lunch break at the Firm, gave him a call. His name was Mr. Hemingway. Mr. Hemingway was a famous landscaper in the River Oaks section of Houston, Texas. He had charged customers $100 an hour for his services. His divorced wife was a millionairess, and upon settlement, he became one too.

He said, "You were referred to me by a very good friend that worked in the Citadel Properties building. If you are to take me on as a client, I want complete confidentiality.

Wednesday, was my day off at the Firm, so I told him I was free that day.

I finally found his condo. The security guard let me through and I rang the doorbell. The frail man that came to the door extended his hand and introduced himself as Mr. Hemingway. Some of the stories he told me about his life were unparalleled. He told me that he needed someone to come in once a week and do his books. He went on to say that he used to have a live in secretary that wasn't very kind to him. He said he wanted me to keep things neat for him and organized. He told me that his son was an attorney and that he and his daughter wanted to declare him incompetent. The man sitting in front of me was more than sane and my heart went out to him.

He asked me how much something like this would cost him and I told him I didn't have the foggiest. He said he had discussed it with his good friend and CPA and they both agreed the amount of money we discussed should suffice.

I told him I couldn't, and he said, "Hog wash young lady! I can't come to your office and I don't wanna. Now, I expect you to come to me." He said, "Your tea will be ready when you ring the doorbell. Just help me stay organized." Unbelievable! I couldn't wait to tell Sean, my Marketing Manager at my own firm.

Months passed. The security guard knew and trusted me. Mr. Hemingway seemed to be in softer spirits. He introduced me to another friend of his. I started typing some of his friend's work on the word processor and made my office very busy. Something was going to have to give. I was going to have to let the law Firm, go. What was I thinking? This was a fabulous deal. There was no way I was leaving the Firm.

Then, I got a call from Sherry from my previous office telling me that she had landed a $3,000,000 account and wanted to celebrate. She begged me to celebrate with her the following evening. She informed me that a friend of hers wanted me to meet a good friend of his and we were all to meet at the club at 6:00 on Westheimer. We arrived a few minutes late. We fought through the crowds, and she finally located them. Her friend was with this really tall, I mean really...tall young man. He picked me up with one hand, without introductions and said, "Lets dance." Sherry was beyond ebullience. The next thing I remember, she and her friend had disappeared. I became uncomfortable and the famous athlete told me to relax, because he would take me home if she didn't reappear. He assured me that I had nothing to worry about. He told me that he loved my accent and that we should get out of there. He took my hand and led me out of the noisy club.

We got into this car that didn't have a top to it and I was livid! I told him I wasn't getting in that thing and he said, "Come on. Where do you live? I'll take you home, I promise. Hop in!"

As we drove down the street, I didn't understand why everyone was pointing and waving.

He said, "You really don't know - do you?"

I said, "Know what?"

He replied, "I play for the "Roamans.""

Then, I said, that explains everything. All the secrecy! I knew I wasn't impressed. Then I noticed this wasn't the way to my house. He said, "Relax sweetheart! Why are you so uptight?" He said, "Sherry told me you would rebel." I responded that I needed to get home. He said, "I have to pick something up and it'll only take a minute, okay?" He pulled up in the parking lot of the Galleria.

There was a really happening club at the top of the Galleria Mall and it seemed everybody was headed in that direction. He knew that I was annoyed, but asked me to come inside for a second.

"I won't be but a minute," he said.

We got off the elevator and I was sure I was in the wrong place. He asked me to sit at the bar and he would return soon. He ordered me a drink before he left not giving me the chance to share with him that I didn't drink alcohol. I wished I were home in my bed. Everybody was having such good time. I was totally out of place. I'm sure to others that weren't on the dance floor I appeared snobbish.

I kept looking around wondering whether he would return, when another gigantic man approached me.

He said, "Dance with me sweetheart." I declined and he said, "Are you waiting for somebody?"

I told him I was brought here against my will and before I could finish explaining, he pulled me off the stool and onto the dance floor. I told him I wasn't going to move and he laughed and said, "Come on baby, what's wrong?" I told him I wanted to go home. He saw how serious I was and took my hand and said come on let's find your friend. I noticed he was well known, too.

I asked him why everybody was hugging and shaking his hand and he said, "Do you watch basketball?"

I replied that I don't have time and he smiled and said, "Well, just exactly, what could keep you so busy?" He said, "I know. You grade school papers at night, huh? Come on. Tell the truth."

I told him that I was much too preoccupied with my business to indulge in sitting in front of a television watching basketball.

He said, "I love your accent. "Sho would be nice if you could talk to me all night, bet! Sorry. Just joking, all right? Looka here, on second thought, you ain't one of them nun's, are you? Okay - Okay - come on, let's find your friend."

We approached the elevator and it opened. On the elevator, with one hand against the wall and the other on the woman's head on her knees, was another very tall person whom I assumed was a famous athlete too! There he was. Pants dropped to the floor, and this woman giving oral gratification to him in a public place. I was outraged!

He was laughing hysterically, and said "Way to go man!" Then threw him the keys to his room and said, "Hurry back, man."

He said, "Come on. It's all right."

I told him it really wasn't. "How was I going to get home?" He said, "You really are upset, huh?" I looked at him and he could tell that tears were surfacing. He said, "Wait a minute. Stay here." He told me that he would take me home, and that he would be right back. He went over and talked to another team member and asked him for the keys to his car. I could hear him say - "Be right back man."

We were on the elevator and I finally looked at him in the light. He seemed to be a genuinely nice guy. I told him that I didn't approve of such behavior from the others and he said to me, "You ain't had no business up here no way. "Tell me again how you said you got railroaded up here in the first place." What kindda maniac would bring a sweet, innocent, little thing like you up here anyway?" He said, "You kindda fine though. Hope you don't mind me saying so."

We got off the elevator and he took my hand and asked me to help find the car that belonged to his friend. He pushed the alarm and there it was.

"What kind of car is that?"

He replied, "This here is what you call a Lamborghini. He confided that he wasn't sure how to drive it and that we would give it the old college try. While he was practicing, he asked if I was married and I told him "No." He asked me again, "How did you hook up with my man?" I explained, and all he could say was, "For real?" I told him that he and I had been together for well over an hour and I didn't know who he was. I told him it's obvious you must be one of those Roamans and he said "No." He said "Jade, right?" He said, "My name is Maison Elliott and I play for Detroit." He said, "You heard of us, right?" And we started laughing. He commented that I was very pretty when I was smiling and that I shouldn't try to be so serious. He said, "Life is too short, man."

We finally got the car started and I tried to remember how to get to my house. He said, "You know what? I ain't really ready to go in, just yet. You know where some other spots around here?" I told him the only other place that might be open this time of night would be the Caribbean Club. He looked surprised and said "Raggae?" I smiled and asked if he really liked Raggae and he said, "It's on now, baby!" We stayed there for a little while and were again on the road to home. He said, "You know what, I like you, Jade. You're a real nice lady." He said, "That's kindda hard to find." I told him he was really sweet also and that I was eternally grateful for his gallant behavior in trying to get me home. Maison said, "I want you to know that this was a real change for me tonight." He said he had never met anybody so straight laced before." We finally pulled up to my place and I thanked him again. He asked if he could call me the next day and I asked when was he leaving and he said he'd be here a couple more days. He gave me the number to his room and asked me to call if I hadn't heard from him by noon.

Maison and I managed not to keep in contact for a year. As I reminisced, the events that led to me knowing him, I was overcome with laughter. I watched him play several games on the tube and secretly smiled, he was my hero. Whenever he came to town, he'd call, but somehow we'd always end up missing one another.

Then, I found out that my Grandmother was deathly ill. I cannot explain why, but I packed up shop and unbelievably so, moved to take care of her, after twenty-seven years. I hadn't lived in the city since my horrible life as a child. "I know. I needed my head examined."

I thought I could handle being in the old neighborhood, but I started having flashbacks. Months passed and my Grandmother became much stronger. She opened her eyes and asked if I had - had plastic surgery since I looked so different. She said she couldn't believe how pretty I was - and that it was amazing considering how ugly I was as a child. She said I had always been the darkest and worst looking out of all nine children. She reminded me of how I chose to live in filth with our Mother, rather than being with her causing us not to become doctors and lawyers. I started crying because I knew how much she hated my Mother. It all came back. How could I have felt sorry for her and come back to help her. I must have been out of my mind! Actually, I wanted some sort of closure to my past life as a child, only to have it backfire.

Four months have passed. It was particularly hot this after noon. The window air conditioner was humming loudly and I had to yell in order for the old lady to hear me clearly. I had just brought in some pink roses and presented them to her and she replied "Put them on the table, they're nice just like all the others you've bought. Gone in there and get me a glass of water, child."

"Let me comb your hair Mom-me. I'll grease your scalp too." "Suit yourself. Don't matter to me none," she said. "Well, if ya gone do it, ya might as well get the big comb. Go in there and look in my top drawer and get me my comb. What's taking ya so long gul? Don't be in there looking through my stuff. Now, come on outta there."

"Your hair sure is pretty Grandma...just like Big Mama's."

"Sho is, ain't it?" We started to laugh. I figured she was in a good mood since I got her to laugh, so I asked her something I had wanted to know for many, many years. "Mom-me do you love me?"

"No, I can't say that I do. You remind me of your Mother gul. She wasn't bout nothing, and you just like her."

"I'm gonna ask you one more time Mom-me. Do you love me?" "What made ya think I changed my mind gul? I'm gone make ya suffer just like you made y'alls Daddy suffer when you left here long time ago.

I ran out of the house. It all came back. I was driving, but didn't know where I was going. My car was on empty, so I pulled into the next station. As I sat at the pump, I replayed, and repeated the episode that had just happened between my Grandmother and I. That woman was beyond evil and a very bitter bitch, at that. She really was wicked!

While sitting there drowning in my tears, I looked up and saw this tall drink of water. He was a well - dressed young man staring at me. It appeared he must have just left church. I knew it must've looked like I was mourning somebody's death, or in deep pain. I didn't care if mucous was plastered all over my face. I didn't care if my eyes were bloodshot and swollen from crying. I didn't care if I no longer had on makeup. I now knew that I had to get away from this person that I thought would forgive me for the past so that I could move on.

This tall man began to look familiar to me. He looked like my teacher from high school, Mr. Elliott. Couldn't be! He looked too young. I remembered instantly how all the girls used to have a crush on him. He was quite charming - with looks to match. Thinking of him gave me chills. I got out of the car and started towards the cashier and looked straight into his eyes. He tried to get my attention by beckoning to me with his index finger. I looked behind me to make sure he was talking to me, and then he smiled really big. Then said, "Am I gonna have to come over there and make a fool of myself?"

"You talking to me? What's your name?"

"Tifton," he said.

I told him he reminded me of my past teacher, Mr. Elliott, and he laughed and said, "He wished." He disclosed that he was his younger brother. Immediately, I felt as though I'd known him all my life.

He asked if I was sick and wondered why I had been crying so hard and I told him about my Grandma.

He said, "Forget about her, let's go to the movies." He said, "I wanna see that movie called, "Sea of Love." "I'm looking for an apartment and I would be honored if you would accompany me."

I said, "I just met you."

"Ah - come on, it'll help get your mind off that old lady." "Now, take my handkerchief and wipe that snot off your face. I want my handkerchief back. Them things ain't cheap no more, you know." Suddenly, I was laughing. He said, "See there! I promise I ain't no murderer. You okay? Feeling better? Let's go. You need to have some fun child."

We looked at apartments and he made me laugh for two hours. How refreshing! He begged again…"let's go to the movies woman!" "I hadn't been to a movie in years," I said. He was so afraid I wouldn't go.

I said, "Okay, pick me up at 4:00."

He said, "You must live in some big elaborate house over there off Airport Boulevard, huh?"

I told him that was the farthest thing from the truth. I explained that I had dropped my life in Texas and came back here after twenty- seven years to take care of my Grandmother. He said, "Twenty-seven years! Your folks must've taken you outta here when you were three. He said, right? Am I right?" He then asked, "How old are you anyway?"

I told him but he wasn't hearing it. I also told him about my two beauties. I explained that my oldest, Paige…is now in the Air Force and my baby girl just got married and is now in Germany…in the Army. He said, "Get the f**k outta here?" He said, "You look like you're twenty-one." He stared at my chest, and said, "Maybe seventeen," and we laughed some more. He said, "I'm good for you girl, you just don't know it. You drove all the way over here with snot hanging all off of you so that we could meet." He said, "Now, tell me where you live and give me the right address, okay?"

When I told him the street, he looked at me and said, "People still live over there? Don't nobody live over there no more." I laughed again. I told him my Grandma refused to sell to the city and she was practically the only one left there. He frowned and said, "Okay, I'll be over in Dodge City, soon."

He came long before time, very nervous that I would change my mind. I couldn't look my Grandma in the face and decided to ignore her and start living my own life till I leave.

The movie was exciting. I managed to sneak a peak at him in the dark while the movie was still going on. He looked strong and appeared confident. We talked about the movie all the way home and he asked if he could see me again tomorrow.

He walked me back to the house and he said he couldn't believe how much he enjoyed my company. He kept commenting on how beautiful I was and wanted to know my real age. He said he was a policeman and didn't want to be disrespectful by dating someone under age. I assured him I was well past underage and he argued that point the remainder of the night.

He came toward me to kiss me goodnight and I refused. He asked for a hug instead. It was warm, long, sweet, and, very sincere.

It took him twenty minutes to get home and then the phone rang. My Grandma picked up the phone and I could hear her tell someone -"It's 8:30, and we don't receive calls this late, and how did you get this number?"

I picked up the phone and said, "Hang up Grandmother."

He asked - "What's her problem? She living in the dark ages or what?" I reminded him of the reason why we met. She had hurt me tremendously. We talked for hours about everything imaginable. He was there every night for the next two months.

I decided to move out of my Grandma's. She had worked my last nerves! It was obvious to everybody that I was doing everything I could to treat her like a queen. I knew that I hadn't been back to Mobile for many, many years and wanted to come and be with her since she was seriously ill. Even though she caused much misery and hate during my early years, I decided not to be horrible to her anymore for the way she treated my Mother and our family. I had prayed and prayed and I felt in my heart that I wanted to let it go. I just wanted her last days to be like heaven on earth, even though we all knew she definitely didn't deserve it. I bought her fresh roses every day. I cooked for her daily. I combed her thick, white, hair every day. I cleaned the house from top to bottom every day like she liked it. I read to her every day. I washed her clothes and ironed them. I went and bought pastries for her everyday.

My Father said, "I just don't understand it. Nobody sent you here, but God, Jade!" It made me feel good to hear him say that. He said, "It would be hard to get somebody to come over here and be with her because she is so unpleasant." Then, he said, "Ain't nobody got time for that." He said, "You understand don't you, baby?" "She irritates me and I didn't know what was going to happen because I wasn't able to pay for a nurse for her care and was unable to come over here everyday." He said, "Bria, Zoe, and, Coda were coming over doing the best they could, but they have their own lives, so I just believe the Lord brought you here, considering you guy's past."

Next week was Father's Day. I spent the weekend looking for silk underwear for my Father since he considered himself to be a player at his age. He said that's what he wanted, and I obliged. I was very happy with my selection. I got him ten pair of silk shorts, every design imaginable, and felt pretty good about them. I had already moved out into my own place.

It wasn't Father's Day yet, but I called my Father and asked him to meet me over to my Grandmother's. He wanted to know why, and, I said, "I need to talk to you about something." Finally, he said, "Okay." He walked over and came in and I said to him, "Will you come here, please?" He said, "What do you have up your sleeve, Jade?" I said, "I want you to sit in front of your Mother and tell her that you love her." He looked at me with the worst frown I've ever seen on his face. "Come on now Jade…ain't got time for this." I said, "I'm not playing. I want you to say it." Grandma looked at me, and said, "You show is foolish gul." "I don't wanna talk to him." I told her to be quiet because she'll have her chance. So he finally mumbled a few words real fast and we started laughing and I said, "Nice try." "Go on and say it." "Look at her and say it." So Daddy looked at his Mother, and said, "I love you", and I said, "Give her a hug and say it again." Then, while he had her in a headlock, "I told her to say it back. She said, "I luv you too. Now, git outta here and leave me alone!" Daddy said -"That's what you had me come over here for talking bout it's an emergency?" I said, "Yes." Then, I told them both I had a date and would be back later. My Grandma said, "That child's crazy as a road lizard. Always have been."

I was excited because I had accomplished one small goal of getting them to admit their love for one another. Secondly, I was thrilled that I was finished with his Father's Day present.

It's Sunday and it is really Father's Day. I got up with a smile on my face and prepared to go over to our Dad's. I called first, making sure he wasn't gone to Sunday school yet. I wanted to see the look on his face when he opened his box with all his sexy underwear inside. I got no answer when I called. I called Zoe. She said she and Tinsel had been calling also. I told her the car was in the yard because I drove over there and knocked and knocked, but got no answer. We called Bria and Coda and no one had been able to contact him. We all concluded that he must've gone out with one of his girlfriends and they picked him up since his car was still in the yard. It was past 10:00. We really started to worry since Daddy doesn't miss church and it was near time for the 11:00 service. He had already missed Sunday school and hadn't called to check in with anyone.

My Grandma called Zoe and told her to ask her husband Tinsel to go over to my Dad's and knock the window out, if he had to. Tinsel went over and got into the house. He found our Dad and immediately called the ambulance and they contacted all of us to get over to the hospital right away. I was going out of my mind with worry. Nobody knew anything.

They just kept saying get over to the hospital as fast as you can. Tifton called as I hurried. I told him what happened and he said I want to go with you. He picked me up and we rushed to the hospital. Everybody was there, and I wondered why they were crying? I said, "Just tell me what's wrong? What happened?" Tinsel calmed me down and told me the entire story. He said they found our Father on the bed. He was bleeding really badly. It appeared he had been shot in the head, but they didn't really know. He said they had found a gun under the pillow he was lying on.

The doctor finally came out and spoke with us. They said that it looked pretty bad. He told us that they had to fly a neurosurgeon in to operate the next day and once he operated, our Father would probably be a vegetable, the rest of his life. They had him hooked up to life support. I was flabbergasted. This is unreal! None of this was registering. This can›t be happening!

The doctor told us to go and get our Dad's house in order. "It didn't look good."

I said, "Nah! Daddy is a fighter. He'll make it."

We all went back over to the house and started packing his belongings and getting together his important papers. It was so strange being in this house after all this time.

We all went back to our homes and Zoe would contact all of us whenever the hospital called to keep us posted. Tifton offered to come home with me for support. I was so grateful as I didn't want to be alone. All I could think about was the Lord surely works in mysterious ways. It's too much for us to handle, really. We were home for about 45 minutes and the phone rang. I didn't want to pick it up, but I did. It was Zoe. They called from the hospital and said to get down there as fast as we can.

I tried to think positive and thought maybe the surgeon had arrived. We ran down the hall. The others were already there sobbing away.

They said, "He's gone Jade. He's gone."

I said, "What do you mean, he's gone? Just like that? You trying to tell me our Dad is dead? But, it's Father's Day!" Sure, we comforted one another, but wanted to find out the extent of his injury. The doctor said that it was not a gunshot wound. He said that our Dad was on blood thinner medication for a blood clot in his leg, I'm not really sure. He missed a dose of his medicine and doubled up on it, then took an aspirin for his throbbing headache, and bled to death.

"What do you mean, missed a dose?"

He said "Ma'am, your Father was told that this is the type of medication that if you forget to take your pill, you don't double, and on top of that he took aspirin with it." He said it was written in his directions.

"I'm just not believing this! The man lying there terminated, is our Father. Three days ago, I had him over to his Mother's house telling her he loved her, and vice-versa. And just like that, he's gone? Do you know how energetic this man was? He had a twenty-one year old, for a girl friend! He wasn't sick, and now he's gone?"

We agreed to all wear white to his funeral. People normally wear black, but we decided to wear white. It was beautiful. Our Mother was present and looked really tired. She looked pretty and I was really proud of her, being she never went anywhere. You could see it in her face that her fight was almost over, too. This was the love of her life and suddenly he was gone because of an accidental overdose. He had not been ill. This was extremely hard on everybody regardless of our past. My Father's daughter, Leyla, our half sister, who is a year older than our sister, Bria, and her daughter, Josie, came too. It was amazing seeing her again. She looked a lot like our Father. Leyla and Josie have always lived in California.

The days that followed were dismal, but we got through it with each other's love. My Grandmother tried to be a pillar of strength, but I could see through it. I tried to spend some time with her, but she soon squashed that. She called all my family and told them that I had stolen her pillowcases, collard greens, and a few other things that were unimportant. Sounds funny, huh? It wasn't funny to me. You would have thought, as old as she was that she had that old timer's disease (Alzheimer's disease), but she was well within her faculties. I simply had enough of her evilness.

A month and a half had passed, and I received a call from my daughter, Paige. She was in the United States Air Force, stationed at Travis Air Force Base, where she was a Cardiopulmonary Technician. She was in labor with her very first baby. My heart was pumping overtime - my first Grand was about to be born! You can't imagine the intensity and excitement of my Grand- baby coming into this world. I decided to drive to California instead of flying. Tifton wanted to come with me. We packed hurriedly.

We had no idea the distance from Alabama to California. Two and a half days passed with me pushing the pedal to the metal, and we made it.

We went straight to the hospital. I asked for the baby and they brought him out. He was too cute! What a big boy! Nine pounds three ounces.

My first, Grandson! I was really proud! Paige was so tired. And likely so. She'd done great!

Corbis took us to the apartment so that we could unpack. He was Paige's fiancée and the baby's Father. When we opened the door to the apartment, I was in a state of shock. There was no furniture, nor food. I wondered where was Paige and the baby gonna sleep? Why didn't she contact me before now to let me know what was going on? Corbis left and said he'd be back after a while. He never came back. Paige said not to worry; he does this all the time. I became very suspicious.

Anger overcame me. I knew something was wrong. The next day, I went to the grocery store and stocked up. I also went and purchased my daughter some furniture.

Corbis didn't come home that night. I was more than apprehensive. Paige decided to clue me in. Corbis was hooked on crack. He had been on this terrible drug since he moved out there with Paige a year ago...after walking away from a football scholarship in Albuquerque, New Mexico. I couldn't believe it. What a waste! He wanted for nothing because his parents gave him the best of everything. He drove a brand spanking new Maxima, when he was a junior in high school. What a dynamic young man he was and a real leader! All of his friends looked up to him; Wanted to be like him.

Whenever he came to my house when they were in high school to see my daughter, all of his boys rolled with him. When Corbis stepped; They did too. He was Captain of the Football Team and a real go-getter.

I'm holding this cute little bundle of magic in my hands only a day old, knowing he'll be smart as a whip just like his Mom and Dad. He also had lungs like you wouldn't believe. They named him Vonn. He was a joy and the love of my life.

When Corbis finally showed up, he was out of his mind. He tried to get into the apartment, but Paige wouldn't let him. He finally smashed the large patio glass with his fist. Blood was everywhere! I called the police. He screamed that all he wanted was his son. The baby wouldn't stop screaming. The police finally arrived. I took the baby hurriedly to the back room as they arrested his Father. I can't explain the feeling of sorrow I had for my daughter and the baby. I had no idea what she had been going through. They put him in jail.

I've been here six weeks, now. There's no way I'm going back to Alabama. They need me here really badly.

Corbis calls Paige from jail. She gets him out and later that night he steals her car and goes back over to the crack house. It's 6:30 a.m., and he's still nowhere to be found.

This is Paige's first day back on the job. She asked me to take the baby so she could try and find him. I was furious. Why did she let him come back to this apartment so that he could have access to her car? Come on now? Wake up Paige and smell the tea! Is anybody home? The man needs help! It's 7:20. She finds him. He finally comes home and they're arguing.

He decides he doesn't want to live anymore so he takes a bottle of codeine. The bottle is still in his hand. She asked, "Corbis what did you just do?" He started to cry and said he had taken all the pills. The police and ambulance arrived simultaneously. They rushed into the apartment and he was unconscious. They slapped his face and kept calling his name, but no response. Finally, they got a pulse. He was coming around. They pumped his stomach and rushed him to the hospital.

I still don't understand what happened. How did things get this way? He had the best parents in the world. His Mom was really sweet and had given him the best of everything. We called her, and she rushed to get here on the next flight out from Connecticut.

Corbis was such a dynamic young, man. He was the kind of person you found in "Who's Who, of Young American Achievers." He's the individual others tried to emulate wherever he went. The boy was just naturally talented.

I contacted the Post Office back in Alabama. I had only worked there, six months. My Postmaster empathized with me and said that if there was anything that she could do for me, please don't hesitate to let her know. She granted me a leave of absence and we received prayers from the entire gang.

I had almost exhausted my savings from my business and would soon have to try to find work in California.

The next day, I went to a couple of the local Post Offices and found out they weren't hiring. The last one I visited told me I would probably have to go out of town in order to get hired. He said the larger offices usually have openings towards the holidays. I didn't know which way to go so I chose the direction away from the city, which was an hour from Paige.

I came to a small town called Roseville, California. It was quaint, and surprisingly, well manicured. I decided this would be a nice little area to live. It was three miles from Granite Bay, where President Reagan's daughter, Maureen Reagan, lived. President Reagan was our 40th president of the United States. A lot of the football players lived in this area, also.

I came home and called and asked to speak to the Postmaster of the Roseville Office. He was out of town so they put me through to the secretary. She was extremely friendly and left me with a pleasant impression. I asked if there were any openings and she surprised me by saying two openings would be available in December. She told me a little about the area and their Post Office and asked if I wanted to come in and take a look.

Two days later, I was being introduced to the staff. It was a large office that was expanding rapidly.

The interview went well and Vikki offered me the job. I can't tell you how energized I was.

I had to come up with a plan. This was too far for me to drive every day from Paige's place. I decided to relocate to Roseville so that I wouldn't have to make that long commute. I had a couple of months before I had to report to duty so I found myself a job in the private sector as a sales associate with a company that made soft drink dispensers.

While there, I received a horrible phone call. My oldest brother had choked to death from an epileptic seizure. He was two years older than me, fanatically attached to his music and stubborn, as well. We hardly saw one another since I was always traveling with the military. We didn't really know him. Griffin had been raised by our Grandmother every since he was a baby, and had stayed in the Navy and produced a beautiful family. I was speechless, and couldn't conceive he was actually gone.

It was good to see the family. I wanted a reunion with everyone really badly, but never under these circumstances. We all reminisced, cried, laughed and cried some more. I didn't want to leave my family. I tried to get my Mom to come back with me, but she said her place would always be where she was, and she wasn't about to leave it.

I found out she had a phobia of not wanting to leave the house. She was still under the doctor's care and had to report to the hospital twice a week. I secretly dropped her 3 crisp one hundred-dollar bills and found out that my brother, Dino often found whatever I sent or gave her and spent it on alcohol, marijuana and women. She was afraid of him, yet she'd never admit it. I could never catch up with his behind. Then, out of the blue, as I was leaving, Dino shows up totally incoherent, and babbling to the shady characters on both arms that I was a movie star and that I was really his sister. I gave him a lingering hug, as my heart went out to his frail, and scrawny frame. Suddenly, my scolding and disciplinarian concerns became inconsequential. We both started to cry and I gave in to his pathetic plea for money.

I then sat him down and asked the other characters to leave. I knew he was beyond reason, but decided to try anyway. I concluded my conversation by telling him that "When life gives you lemon, you make lemonade." He said, "I'll take a glass of it right now." We laughed. I shook my head, held my Mom, then left.

On the plane ride home back to California, this great determination came over me that I would always be there for my children and their children. Before we landed, I convinced myself that I would win the lottery soon and everything would be okay. Fat chance!

When I returned, I was irritated. The air conditioner was taking too long to cool and it was hot and a sticky kindda of humidity in the air.

I needed solitude, so I drove up to the mountains to think and, I saw the sign that said, "Welcome to Nevada." It was an hour and a half from Roseville. I had no idea where I was. I kept driving then saw how the city lit up. Heavens! I was in Reno! I found a parking lot that seemed reliable and walked till I ended up at Harrah's. It was electrifying. Inside, I stood in awe as I watched a very young man sitting at a $5.00 machine almost jump out of his skin. He had won $30,000.00...just like that. The lights were sounding and flashing on the other side and somebody screamed - "Yes!" She had won $5,000.00 on the quarter machine. My adrenalin was pumping overtime. I decided to give it a shot. "Why not?" I sat at a $1.00 machine, then searched my pockets for cash. I was unprepared, but still had a few bucks from my flight home. I dropped 3...one dollar coins in; Nothing happened. Someone came and sat next to me. The smoke was killing me, literally. The barmaid walked towards me and asked if I wanted a drink and I declined because I had to drive home alone once I was over my little escapade. The smoker said, put more money in and pull the lever. Don't let it stop. Just keep it coming. I was annoyed, but decided, "What the hell! You can't take it with you, so you might as well spend it." I told him to catch the barmaid and get me a drink.

"What are you having."

"I don't know."

"Just pick something for me." He asked her to bring me a girlie drink. I was then introduced to a Mai Tai. Since it tasted like Kool Aid, there was no harm in getting a 3rd or a 4th.

Moments later, I felt on top of the world. Nothing mattered. I wanted a good time and it had better not end. Clearly I forgot about gas money to get me home. Wow!" I loved the way that Kool Aid stuff made me float considering I was not a drinker, it felt good to be a lush for a change. I found $40.00 in my wallet.

"Change please!"

"Thank you." Here goes nothing. The machine ate up one of my twenties. I still didn't care. Here comes that hateful little barmaid. She looked like her shoes were too tight. Judging from her figure, she shouldda had on trousers instead of that short skirt constantly rising up her butt.

"One more Kool Aid ma'am." Her laughter was surprising.

"You sure you're okay?"

"Uh huh." I was down to the last 3...one dollar coins. I looked around, awaiting her return with my delectable Mai Tai. Before I deposited my last 3 coins, I gulped down all of my drink. God! I never felt so good!

"All right!" "Work your magic for me; You know this is all I've got." Till this day, I've every incline to believe those guys were behind the mirrors upstairs saying, "Let's make her a winner." I closed my eyes as I put my money into the slot machine. The room was spinning and I could smell the freckled smoker nearby. Ghastly! Bells went off. I was feeling sooo good! I opened my eyes to see everybody surrounding me. Puzzled, I asked, "What's the matter with y'all?" They were all happy. They kept saying, "Wow! You won! You won!" I hit 3...triple diamonds. Everybody was patting me on the shoulders, hugging, and being congratulatory. It couldn't get any better than this. I was on top of the world! Suddenly the recent burial of my brother...may he rest in peace...was on the back burner. It was gonna be okay.

I didn't leave the casino. I cashed in and had security escort me to my hotel. The hotel had a safe that secured my winnings and I was eternally grateful. They were afraid for me to leave alone the next day. Instead of the cash, I had the money wired to my account in California.

Upon my return to California I quit my job with the Drink Dispenser Company. I had enough to tide me over till I started work for the United States Postal Service.

Not working gave me a chance to spend quality time with my little Grandson. I was excited to be near my daughter again. She was so independent. Made me feel proud.

I started my new job. I had heard many things about the Postal Service. I knew just like anything else in life, you would actually have to be there to know what really went on.

The office I transferred from in Alabama, had only five people in it. I was only employed there for six months. This office had about 150 people under one roof and they were different nationalities and personalities. I was first introduced to Terri. She was a kind soul. If only everyone else could have followed suit. Aaron came to me to let me know that everything was going to be all right and if I needed help with anything, to please let him know. How nice!

The commute back and forth to my daughter's house was too much.

I got a call from home and they told me that our cousin Diedra lived in Sacramento, which is about twenty-five miles in the opposite direction. I gave her a call and she asked me to come over. It was so good seeing her after nearly twenty-eight years. I would have recognized her anywhere. She brought back so many memories about the rest of the family.

I remember when I was eleven years old, we visited Diedra and my other cousins when we lived in Alabama. We wanted to get into their pool. Bria and I had stepped in an ant bed. Uncle Sedwin sprayed us down, and we were thrown in the pool right away screaming our heads off. We laughed, then she went on to tell me that Uncle Sedwin resided in Sacramento, also. She welcomed me to stay a couple of months till I knew my way around and swore we'd have loads of fun. So I stayed a month. God! I was so grateful!

I finally moved to my condo in Roseville, California. I had to make a stop at the local market for my new place. I pulled up to park and noticed the car pulling up next to me. I sat there for a minute and waited for the person to emerge. When she got out of the small car, I had trouble trying to figure out where her legs fitted inside the small sports car. She was so tall and strikingly beautiful. My bet would be she stood 6 feet tall. I immediately said, "Hello." She hesitated for a second and said, "Hi! Do I know you?" We stood and chatted for about 10 minutes and exchanged phone numbers. I didn't know anyone in the new town and was excited that Talia was my first acquaintance.

She called, and commented on how wonderful it was meeting me at the market the other night. She said she wanted me to know that there was a really big party she wanted to attend on New Year's Eve and wanted me to accompany her.

She asked if she could come over because she needed to talk to someone and I said, "I'd rather come to your place." She told me how to get to her house and I nearly freaked when I pulled up in the driveway. What an unusually, breathtakingly, beautiful house! Talia lived about six miles from Roseville in a small town called Rocklin, California. She lived on an acre that was carefully landscaped and I couldn't imagine what kind of work she did. If you thought the outside was unusual, inside was equally charming. We talked for hours when I realized she could easily become a close friend. She lived alone in the house and even though it was incredible, it was apparent she had to be lonely out there all by herself.

It was New Year's Eve. She asked me to be the designated driver. It was okay with me since I hadn't planned on drinking. The party was amazing! My intrigue led me to believe there must be some guy she wanted to see. He finally surfaced and discretion was essential.

Guys kept trying for my number, but I couldn't remember my new listing, so I took number after number, thinking how desperate they all must be. Calling the numbers wasn't an option. I needed to get myself together first.

This was my second week at my new office. Tuesday was really horrible at work. Usually, after a holiday, the work is doubled and everybody is tense.

My supervisor wanted me to work the window. Working the window entailed selling money orders, stamps, packages and anything else pertaining to customer service.

Another supervisor came and got me off the window and wanted me to throw mail in the distribution area, which meant placing correctly addressed letters and flats in the appropriate slot so that the carriers could come and retrieve them and deliver them to the assigned homes.

My other supervisor wanted me to work in the box section putting mail in individual rental boxes before 11:00 a.m. Then, some of the carriers got slightly irritated because they wanted their mail put around to their cases a little faster than the norm and, understandably so, since there wasn't enough help available, then, chaos was sincerely, inevitable. The faster they got their mail, the sooner they could get onto the road and make accurate and safe deliveries.

The supervisor came and got me from the box section and asked me to place the thick trays of letters, and buckets of flats, which contained magazines and newspapers, and hurriedly, place them at the carrier's cases.

It was an enormous amount of mail! And absolutely no organization. Roseville was a good office with potential, but lacked good supervision. The Postmaster had it going on, but his supervisors weren't equaled.

I wanted to go home but decided to try and stick it out. Then, I heard this wisecrack from Marcus. I looked up at him as he uttered, "What's up?" He asked if I was single and I confessed that I wasn't in the market. He said that I was the new kid on the block and everybody was going to come at me. I told him I could take care of myself. His best friend was Paulo, and they stuck together like glue. I told them that I had to go to Alabama and pick up my furniture and wanted to know if they would lend a hand upon my return. They assured me they would be happy to help. Marcus said they would get some of the other guys to help and it wouldn't take any time to complete the task.

I flew to Mobile and picked up my furniture. I drove the largest U-haul imaginable. It took me three days. I didn't realize it was a big deal until after I was back in California. Some of the guys gasped in disbelief that I handled all that furniture up and down the interstate, almost 3,000 miles all by my lonesome, driving a big truck.

I was exhausted, so the guys took over and told me they would handle the rest by unpacking and unloading the U-haul so that I could return it that evening. Paulo took over. I was impressed. He helped me hang all the abstracts and pictures on the wall so that it would look more like a home. When it was time to go, I thanked him from the bottom of my heart and he told me he just wanted me to feel welcome and that it must really be hard relocating to a strange place not knowing anyone and trying to make it on your own. I appreciated perception and knew that we would become very good friends.

The next day at work, he found me and asked if he could come over to see what I had done with the place. I said wait till the weekend and bring Marcus. He smiled and said okay.

I got a call from my daughter wanting to bring the baby over because she wanted to have some R & R. I said, "Sure - bring him over." It was so good to see my daughter. She looked beautiful. Unlike someone who had just given birth three months prior to such a large baby. She was amazing!

I kept little Vonn close to me that entire weekend wanting to protect and love him. He was such a handsome baby. The guys called and wanted to come over, but I had my baby and couldn't entertain, and asked to do so another time.

Four months passed. While at work, I received a startling phone call from home. My brother, Dino had died. He was only 31 years old, and had a massive heart attack. We had just buried my oldest brother. I was in a state of shock. My Mother took it really hard; So hard we were afraid it would send her over again. He had an unusual affect on my Mother. We never knew why the strange attachment. He treated her very badly and was never around when I flew home to give him a piece of my mind. Dino was the odd ball of the family. He continuously broke the law and broke my Mother's heart whenever he could. We all rejoiced when he joined the Army because his world had been narrow. The only way for him to see the rest of it was to enlist. I remember a sigh of relief thinking things would be very different now that there was a purpose. He was such a bright, good looking young man. Dance! I think he created the Soul Train line. Just kidding. Whenever the phone rang late at night, I'd close my eyes tightly, holding my breath, knowing it was a call to report he had been killed. Dino lived a tremendously reckless, fast life that ended up being too much for him.

I can't help remembering how he stole the watch my friend let me wear as a symbol of our friendship when I was in the 11th grade. He swore on twelve Bibles that he hadn't seen it. It was crucial that we find that watch being it was an early graduation present from Jeff's Father. I can't tell you how embarrassing that was!

I went next door to Ms. Sarah's and asked for Johnnie, his best friend, and interrogated him until he finally confessed that he and my 7 year old brother had gone over to the store behind us and pawned the watch for a bottle of Boone's Farm wine. I told my sisters and we all went to the pawnbroker. I can recall, as I did like Granddaddy Alex told us to do. He said to pray to the Lord as often as you can. I told God that I would serve him till I died if he would just give me back that watch. God answered my prayer. I mean, he really answered my prayer. The broker remembered the little boys coming in to pawn the watch. We threatened to sue him penniless if I didn't get that watch back. He apologized as he gave me the watch back. I kept my promise too, as I praise and thank the Lord, every day, because he truly is the Head of my life.

Jeff got his watch back. He was a very sweet, classy, and thoughtful, young man. I liked him very much. He was also a football jock and I didn't want word to get around that something this horrid was coming from my family. Nevertheless, everything turned out all right.

Here we all were again. We had just buried our brother, Griffin, Jr. Now, Dino! It crossed my mind that maybe there might be some kind of curse on the family. The old lady, our Grandma, had already threatened she would out live us all. The funeral was short. We all vowed to stick together more than ever now that three of our family members were gone.

I was a zombie when I returned. I was glad to see the people I worked with.

I went and got the baby and didn't want to take him back home. I cried into his hair thinking how precious life is and how he had his entire life ahead of him and I wanted to make sure that I played a major role in his young life. My Grandson was the only something in my life that when my pilot light went out, it would instantly light up when he was around. He reminds me so much of my daughter, Paige.

My baby girl, Toury called. She wanted to let me know that she was going to - be - all that she could be - by joining the Army. I was happier than I had been when I heard about my baby sister, Mace and my baby brother Kendrick, graduating.

Toury was headed for Germany and would give me a call when she got there. Of course, life across the pond was nothing like being in the states. Knowing Toury, she soon had tons of friends. One of them was Mikal. They hung out famously, and fell in love. I wondered when she was going to make me a Grandma for the 2nd time around.

When they got married, the baby was on the way. She had a gorgeous little boy named Mikal Terrell. I'm jumping out of my skin, now. As if that wasn't enough, she had another handsome little boy, named Mikal Donte. Then, the ultimate happened. Yes! She had another beautiful little boy, named Mikal Darrel. Bizarre! It's okay. They're my babies (grand) and I had no idea why they were all named Mikal. Nevertheless, as happy as I was about my children, and my Grand's, something always happened to question my faith.

I knew it wouldn't be long before they would be calling to give me the unbearable news about our astonishing Mother. Zoe said, "Jade, it's over. She's gone." I dropped the phone. My life flashed before me. I couldn't move. Our dear, sweet Mother was departed from this earth.

I flew home mentally, spiritually and physically, drained. Too much had happened to our family. We had buried our brother Griffin, Jr., our Father, our brother Dino, and now, my beautiful Mother.

I couldn't sit still as the minister did the eulogy. My mind was like a computer at that moment as I rewound and replayed each chapter in my Mother's young life. She was fifty-nine years old as she lay still among us. *Here before us was the greatest female that ever lived. Here was the reason why life was bearable. Here was the reason why I fought so many years to protect our honor. Here was the reason why I have compassion in my heart for my fellow man. Here is the reason why I love the Lord.* She will no longer suffer at the hands of evil. She can rest now because as the world looks at us now, they can see that it was a wise decision for us to have followed her when we were children. A child belongs with its Mother.

I had just spoken with her two nights ago and stressed my everlasting love for her. My Mother told me that she was very proud of me, and, that she wanted me to remember that she wasn't in her right mind when she was doing unkind things to me many years ago. I whispered really low for her to rest now and told her that I always knew it wasn't her back then. I continued to whisper as I told her, "You are my angel because there has never been a day in my life that I didn't think of how much I love you." She laughed that little grin all of the family is so familiar with and told me that she was going home soon. She said, "This way I can really look out for all of you, Jade."

That night, I wanted to fly home and put my arms around her and tell her that everything was going to be all right.

I called Zoe and she said, "Coda, she, and Bria, had gone to see our Mother and she wasn't doing well at all."

She said, "I think she's given up, Jade." "You know Dino is gone and Daddy too. Those were her greatest loves."

She said, "You remember, Grandma swore she'd outlive'em all, and she did."

I'm numb now as my plane landed on California soil. "God please give me the strength to move on! I miss my Mom so much." If only she'd come with me and let me show her a better life. I still didn't understand why she constantly demanded to stay where she was. But, it's too late now.

I stayed off work for two weeks. I had made myself sick and knew I needed strategy.

The first thing on the agenda that dropped me from the stress list was the song I wrote called, "Over Forty."

Still the song wasn't enough. It was time for a change. I had won "Employee of the Month" three times in a row and was quite thrilled. Our

Postmaster had appointed me the Philatelic Manager of our front counter. That wasn't enough.

I wanted to be closer to home. It was too far from family. Nobody believed I would leave California for Texas. They were not bashful to reveal ---- "You must be out of your ever loving mind Jade!"

I was writing more songs now and desperately trying to get out of the Postal Service. Great industry ----- just not for me!

I wrote a song I really liked that I thought best described the Postal Service. The industry needed a lot of restructuring and I wanted someone to rap about it. I'm proud of that song called, "A Permanent Break." A permanent break means just that. Ten minutes or fifteen minute breaks, won't do; A permanent break entails stepping up to the plate, being creative and coming with your own business.

I requested a transfer to a Texas Post Office, excited about the possibility of being back in the place that was promising to young entrepreneurs. I was on a mission. I envisioned doing more in Texas being closer to home considering the cost of living was more appealing and practical.

My transfer was approved and I was to report to the Sugarland, Texas Post Office on July, the first. I brought my Grandson with me who was four years old at the time and a hand full! He was great company.

Somebody should have told me not to drive across that desert in the month of July. It was debilitating. We were blistering and drained from the horrible heat.

We made it three days before I had to report for duty. Vonn's Father was to meet us in Texas, then pick him up and take him back to Atlanta. We called to let them know that we had made it to Houston. Corbis said there was a change in plan. Vonn's Grandfather would be there to get him instead. I was sad to have to see my little Grandbaby leave.

I had caught the most ungodly cough and my baby did his best to take care of me. He was such a little man. I knew I needed a doctor, but couldn't move. I had a high fever and couldn't breathe. My Grandson got water from the faucet and one of the towels and rubbed my forehead with it. He jumped into the elevator of the hotel that we were in...by himself against my will and headed downstairs to get ice for the bucket. I was too sick to rebuttal his comings and goings. Once he returned, he unbelievably, on his own, called room service and told them to bring up soup for me. It's amazingly incredible, but this four-year old took care of me for two days until I was better. I wasn't cognizant most of the time and even delirious since my fever got worse. I could hear him cry, "Grandma please get better, I'm hungry." I couldn't move. My coughing was intensified. All I could do was reminisce the times in my life when I was just a kid myself left alone to shit or get off the pot. I was so proud of him, but couldn't express it because of the severity of my illness. He grabbed and hugged me then kissed my forehead and wiped the tears from my eyes. "I love you Grandma." All I could do was close my eyes and smile. I always knew he would be beyond incredible.

The next day, amazingly out of nowhere, I felt better. His Grandfather arrived and as he prepared to leave me, little Vonn stared and brushed my hair back and made me promise to go to the doctor and get better. It felt like part of me had just walked out that door. I was so attached to Vonn. He's a dynamic version of my daughter Paige. They're so much alike. I went and got some antibiotics and was ready to tackle whatever presented itself to me the next day.

The Sugarland Office was large. It was a tad bit smaller than where I had been in California, but growing rapidly. The people were really something. I don't think I'd encountered anything quite like the people in this office.

I finally met Paris and Danielle. Then, I knew I could bear it all. They became my dearest friends. We celebrated Paris' birthday. She was half a century! Go girl! She looked so young and beautiful. Danielle was the party animal and knew everybody. She introduced me around and showed me parts of Houston I was totally unfamiliar with. I was fortunate running into the two of them to keep me sane...being that I was really restless.

It's 9:30 a.m., and everybody's in the break room. I'd just lost my last 50 cents in the vending machine wanting desperately to crunch on some fried pork skins, when I was paged to come to the supervisor's office. "Ooooh girl! "Jade's gotta go to the front office. What cha done --- done now? Hurry back, and let us know what's going on up there. "Tell'em they need to call a meeting so we can let'em know what they need to do for us, okay Jade? I know ya ain't gone do it...Want me to save your seat?"

"No! I'll talk to you guys later."

I had heard about Bulk Mail within the Postal Service and wanted to know more about it. I spoke with the Postmaster and requested to learn something other than what I already knew. He explained that there were no openings in our office because it entailed extensive training and they couldn't afford to let me go. I could have stayed in the break room. The atmosphere in that office was like the North Pole.

Aida had just transferred to the Missouri City Post Office from the Sugarland Office and knew that I had just come on board from California and wanted training on Bulk Mail. Bulk Mail seemed to be a sure thing with the Postal Service and tapping into the market was uppermost on my mind. She found out that her new office had an opening so I pleaded with the Postmaster to let me transfer to the other office to expand my knowledge of discount mailings and explore upward mobility since I had only been there for a few months. To my amazement, he agreed. He said, "Go get'em tiger! Make me proud cause I know you'll do great things one day."

I went on leave for a week and went to training for Bulk Mail for three weeks at the Houston Main Post Office. Now, this was a real culture shock. I had never seen so many people. I'm talking a couple of thousand under one roof. This was the big time. Then, I heard throughout the office that only a hand full of people had passed this course. Intimidated. Yes, I was. I was horrified of testing on paper, or anybody's computer for that matter. If you asked me verbally, I had no problem. I just couldn't shake the testing phobia.

The last week of training was hands on. We had to go downstairs and actually interact with real customers. It was interesting though. One of the ladies in my class often went to lunch with me. We passed by a few guys and it was fun watching them appear interested. I heard someone say, Somner! Telephone! He was immaculately attired. I saw him from the rear and asked the student if he was a supervisor or a manager, and the student replied, "No - he's just a clerk." She said, "He might be one of the ones to try and talk to you." I said to her, "Not to worry. He's not my type." She went on to tell me that he used to be married to one of her friends and had heard he had not been very nice to her. She then introduced me to her friend and she asked, "Girl, you mean he hasn't seen her yet?" "I replied quickly, "He's definitely not my type so it doesn't matter." I never got to see his face, though. We all laughed.

We took the test, and I just knew there was no way I had passed since there was lots of information on the test that wasn't covered. I gave up. Back then, you didn't get the results until approximately six weeks later. I was literally going out of my mind. Everybody kept saying, "Don't worry, you did okay, I'm sure of it. Chin up."

Class is complete. Missouri City, here I come! My palms were sweaty from the nervousness as I walked into that office. I couldn't believe the diversity. I was so happy. I had never worked around this many facets of ethnicity before. Everybody seemed so down to earth.

My supervisor informed me that I would have to start on- the- job-training right away in Bulk Mail since I would be the relief person for our Mailing House in Stafford, Texas.

I blocked everything and everybody out of my thoughts. I wanted to do well because I was grateful to be there with the possibility of enhancing my knowledge with the Postal Service.

I still felt wishy-washy wondering if I had passed the course or not. We still had no word of the results.

One day, while at the Mailing House, there was so much mail I literally freaked. The other clerk took sick. I was on my own and had to either sink or swim. I wanted them to be proud of me so I kept my mouth shut and did the best I could. Guess what? The machine broke down! Nobody knew what to do. They had huge mail trucks waiting to transport mail to the North Houston Facility. Everybody depended on me. What was I going to do? I couldn't go any further and had to think quickly. The supervisor was calling to make sure I was okay --- The verifier of the Mailing House was impatient because I couldn't go any further since the machine was down. The truck driver was upset because he had to be off the clock. So, I thought, "Hey! I'm just one person. What would be the rational thing to do?"

I called to the Downtown Post Office. They said, "The only person that would know what to do would be Mr. Somner. He'll be back in about ten minutes. You wanna leave a message?"

"Have him call me please. It's an emergency!"

"And your name ma'am?"

"Jade." The name is Ms. Jade. Ask him to call right away. Thank you."

When Mr. Somner called back, I was terribly frustrated. I felt sorry for him as he tried to calm my nerves. He offered to give me tips over the phone, and I couldn't comprehend. I told him that I had just started working there, didn't know if I passed the test and unsure what the hell I was doing. He replied, "Yes ma'am. I'm calling to try to help you ma'am." Then we got cut off. I was petrified!

He finally got a line to call again and after everything started to work, he said, "I can give you some guidelines ma'am if you would call me back when you can talk, or I can call you, whichever you prefer."

I said, "Thank you so much and I'll be sure to call."

Two days passed. I never called Mr. Somner back.

Later that day, he called back to the Mailing House to check on me and to find out if the problem had resurfaced. He said, "Ms. Jade, you never called back. Is everything going okay? I'm concerned ma'am."

"I know and I appreciate it, I said." I told him how very sorry I was that I didn't call him back. I felt terrible about not keeping my word to call, but I was so consumed with trying to understand what I was doing, it just slipped my mind.

Guilt overcame me, so I asked Mr. Somner, "If I gave you my phone number at home, will you call me? You seem like the only person that really knows what's going on about this Bulk Mail thing."

He said, "Sure. Just remain calm and everything's gonna be fine, I promise."

Later that night, Mr. Somner called. He said, "First of all, let me say I give all praises to my Lord, and Savior, Jesus Christ." He went on to say, "Let's pray."

"I hope I'm not frightening you, but I stay prayed up young lady." He prayed a beautiful prayer for the both of us.

I asked if he was a minister and he said, "Yes ma'am, I am."

I asked him how long he'd been with the Postal Service and couldn't believe my ears. I told him it should be gravy from here on in, for him. He laughed and said "It's been a long haul, but by the grace of God, he kept me here."

I liked him. We talked every day. He called during the morning and then during the night to check up on me. We stayed spiritual.

Mr. Somner would read the word, then interpret it to me. How refreshing!

Four months passed as we talked on the phone and praised the Lord. I found myself needing to talk to this man of God. He seemed so honorable. We had not been personable and I found that to be truly extraordinary.

I only knew his last name and wanted to hear him speak of his many blessings and wanted him to know how he touched my spirit every time we talked.

I found it to be really amazing that Mr. Somner hadn't heard me say those cuss words I had learned to say on those 3x5 cards when I was ten years old. I told him that it was second nature with me and that when I was in the military, it was part of our every day language. He laughed and told me that we would stay prayerful about it. I told him I'd try to be respectful but wanted him to know it was a part of my vocabulary, and I was working on it.

He said, "I understand, ma'am."

While I was confessing, I also told him that I'd been smoking since I was thirteen years old. He said, "We'll pray about that too."

Then, something miraculous happened. The Lord came to me in a very colorful vision about Mr. Somner. He told me that this man - this man - Mr. Somner was to become my husband - and that we would know when the time was right. My heart skipped a beat. I thought of nothing else. I didn't know whether to disclose this to him now, or wait until later.

He called after work. Mr. Somner told me he had something to tell me. He said, "Why don't you go first." I told him I was very nervous and not sure about what was really going on here."

He said, "Just say it. Don't hold back. Because what I have to say Ms. Jade, it's gonna blow your mind!"

I told him I had a vision and in that vision the Lord told me that he would be my husband. I said, "It might be tomorrow, it might be next month, it might be next year. I don't know." The Lord said, "You'll know when the time is right." I told him, "It's up to you because I'm ready."

What really did blow both our minds was that Mr. Somner had the same vision. Wow! I'm telling you, it literally blew us away! I didn't know what to say. Here we were. We both had been told that we were to marry and I didn't know who this man was. He didn't know who I was either.

I asked him if I had ever seen him and where exactly he worked in the building. He asked me when did I come down town to train, and who did I train with? He told me to describe myself and I asked him to describe himself. I asked what his first name was and he said, "Mikal," and I lost it again. I told him that my daughter's husband is named Mikal. I told him that her three boys are all named Mikal, and he said, "My son's name is Mikal and my best friend's name is Mikal, also." We were blown away! This was too weird. He said "Did I hear you right? You said your daughter has three boys, so you're a Grandmother?" There was silence. He said, "Are you an old Grandmother, or a young Grandmother?"

I said, "I'm a good Grandmother." We laughed.

I couldn't wait to go to work the next day to find out if anyone knew who he was. I asked some of the employees at my office and they spoke very highly of him.

I called and asked my instructor from Bulk Mail and she said, "That's my little brother and he teaches Bulk Mail, too." I asked her to please make me know who this man was!"

She laughed and said, "I knew you guys were gonna get together. I just knew it!" I was going crazy because this was just too much for me. Then, everybody wanted to know why I was inquiring about him and found out that he was doing the same thing at his office.

He and I knew that we were going to be obedient to the Lord and marry, but we were totally in the dark because he didn't know who I was, and I didn't know who he was.

Then, I got a call from someone in the Downtown Office. She was the only one to disclose to me that he was the guy that always dressed really nice. "I don't know if you saw him or not," she said. I said, "I saw him from the back, but wouldn't know who he was." She said she overheard everyone talking about me, telling him, "Man! You remember that really cute trainee - real outgoing!"

He said, "You sure?" I believe she's a Grandmother."

They said, "I don't care what she is. She don't look like it."

He said, "I can't say that I remember anybody of that description."

They asked him, "Man, you mean you gone marry somebody and you don't know what she looks like?"

At my office, they were all buzzing, saying we must be crazy and I told everyone, "We're being obedient to the Lord."

They said, "How you gone buy a pair of shoes without trying them on?"

I responded, "we're going on faith."

We talked on the phone for a year. There was no physical contact.

Oh God! Today is the day for us to finally meet. I had promised to marry this man that I had grown to love and respect both spiritually and emotionally by telephone.

I knew to the rest of the world, we seemed unhinged, but some of their insipid remarks were no match for the enormous affection we had developed for one another. I dared not question the true works of the Lord.

Many nights passed without sleep. I was too excited about this man that our God had given to me. I had prayed and prayed and divulged to the Lord that I couldn't do it anymore by myself and left it in his hands. I asked him to provide me with the husband he wanted me to have.

I'm besides, myself! I told my daughters, Paige and Toury that I was overwhelmed with the anticipation of something so surreal.

My friends, Paris, Danielle, Kenya and Talia were still in a state of shock. They all knew my lifestyle and said there was just no way this was gonna happen. They felt any minute now, I would come to my senses and call the whole thing off. Not a chance!

I really missed my nephew, Arias. He was now in the Navy. He was living with me during the time Mikal and I had our vision. Arias witnessed the ultimate excitement of it all. I wish he were still here. His effervescence added tremendous fervor for our celibate status.

I was elated that I had waited for this man.

Today is the day! I couldn't sleep. I'm so nervous. It's impossible for me to look my best and not have slept. The phone rang. It was Mikal calling to say that he had to hear my voice so that he could go on.

He asked, "Am I really going to finally see you and hold you today?"

"Yes, I replied. I can't believe it! Today, really, is the day!" I wanted to hang up because I could no longer hold the receiver in my hand; I was too anxious and my hand wouldn't stop shaking.

As soon as I hung up the phone, it rang nonstop. Everybody equally thrilled for this unbelievable romance. I have a moment to think. The first thing I thought about was after we knew we were to be married, Mikal vowed to cook everyday for us so that I wouldn't have to. He said he wanted me to rest and always feel like royalty because he felt like, indeed, he had been given a princess. We didn't want anyone to come with us because we wanted this time all to ourselves. We were to celebrate with both families and friends later.

The doorbell rang. "Oh my God! Okay - I'm calm." Right then and there, it dawned on me that in a few seconds, it would be the last time I would ever be alone on this earth. I was about to meet my mate for life! The man I would spend the rest of my entire life with.

I opened the door. There was a calmness that took over my every being. My tranquil state allowed me the opportunity to stand and focus on my man as he walked inside my house and stood in silence. This was my girlie moment. A time I will never forget. I walked towards him eager to have his strong arms around me. I whispered how happy I was as I wiped the tears from his face.

He said as he trembled, "You are so beautiful" and I said, "So are you sweetie."

We had to hurry because we had to get to the airport in an hour.

We were flying to the Grand Cayman Islands to be married. On our way, the stewardess found out that we were to get married in three days and they supplied us with a large bottle of champagne and everyone on the plane wished us well.

Before they could marry us, we had to become residents of the Cayman Islands, first. The requirement was to live there on the island more than three days.

We finally arrived. Mikal took my hand as if I might break to make sure I wouldn't fall as we left the plane. We hugged once again as we walked on British soil. I was tired, and even so, we had to go through a great deal of red tape getting through customs.

We stayed at the Grand Cayman Hyatt Regency. It was beautiful. I was so excited and wanted to see the sites and wanted to be with Mikal alone, even more so.

I was shocked to see so many dark-skinned people. I don't really know what I expected, but the Caymanians are a mixture of African and European descent. We found out that many are seamen employed by overseas shipping companies. We were also told that the Cayman Islands were a British colony in the Caribbean Sea, which consists of three small islands – The Grand Cayman, Little Cayman and Cayman Brac. Georgetown is their capital and is located on Grand Cayman.

I was shocked to find out that Grand Cayman lies about 180 miles northwest of Jamaica. I couldn't wait to explore the entire six miles of beaches. There were wonderful restaurants inside of the hotel, but we wanted to spend as much time as we possibly could - alone.

We decided to try room service and spend time looking into each other's eyes. He wouldn't stop staring at me.

The knock came at the door for room service. Mikal took the menu and gave me one. The young man stayed until we finished laughing about our soup and sandwiches we had chosen to order. When the young man left, we gasped in disbelief over the prices we had just seen.

He came over to me and said, "I think something might be a little wrong with my eyes." I told him nothing was wrong with his eyesight because we both saw the same thing. I believe the bill for two small soups and two sandwiches were approximately $55.00. We looked at one another and laughed hysterically.

After we finished eating, we talked for hours about everything. Perhaps, we didn't know the extent of our exhaustion, because we fell asleep in each other's arms. We concluded, it must've been the champagne on the plane.

We were surprised with a phone call from the states the next morning. My daughters wanted to know if we'd made it safely. Twenty minutes later, my sisters were all on three way screaming and laughing. Then, there was a knock at the door. The front desk needed to see me. I didn't have time to wash my face. I went down to the front desk and there was this gigantic bouquet of tropical flowers and roses from my husband- to- be. They wanted to know what the occasion was and I asked why they weren't delivered to the room and she said, "Mr. Somners specifically wanted you to come to the desk."

I heard this voice say, "Good morning, baby." I turned around and it was Mikal. He had arranged for the pianist to play for us as we savored the moment. How very sweet this was! I mean - really! I was literally, being swept off my feet. I forgot all about not washing my face.

The concierge, receptionist and the others were impressed that we were getting married. When we got back to the room, they had supplied us with more champagne and goodies. He poured us champagne, and we toasted to being on British soil. He then asked if he could kiss me. I told him not until our wedding day and we laughed that we probably won't make it.

We decided no more room service. Most places were in walking distance, anyway. A taxi was always available if we decided against walking. Everybody waved and smiled as we passed by. It was plain as the noses on our faces that clearly, we were tourists and happily in love.

We overheard others coming into the restaurant predicting a possible storm headed our way. They said, "Maybe, maybe not." I was frantic.

My wedding dress had been designed to wear on the beach. It looked like a wedding gown, but opened in front to reveal a chiffon- like bikini very cleverly designed by me. All I had to do was tell my seamstress what I wanted and she sewed it. Fabulous!

Our wedding was to take place on the beach. Everything was already arranged.

As we walked out, the wind started to blow really hard and the rain was pouring rapidly. How discouraging! We couldn't go anywhere. We finally caught a cab back to the hotel. We found out that a hurricane was expected any minute, was near Cuba, and we were told it would be wise to stay in. We could not believe it! My God! It was supposed to be our wedding in another day and a half.

We contacted the office in charge of wedding ceremonies and wanted to know what we needed to do in these extenuating circumstances. They reassured us that the ceremony would be just as nice and that it was really no one's fault that the storm was headed our way from Cuba. They reiterated that perhaps we could come back again for a second honeymoon, and have a celebration on the beach. I really didn't get upset that the original plans were squashed. I was too excited to be face- to- face with my soon to be husband.

The night before the wedding was scary. It really stormed. We were up early morning. I was afraid and Mikal was really nervous. We kept laughing to try to settle our stomachs. We watched two very good movies that managed to calm our nerves.

They came over with my flowers for the wedding. The minister called and said he wanted us to dress casually, because of the weather. He said, "Regardless of how bad it is outside, we will still go according to schedule." He was on time. The storm was alarming, as the wind blew out of control.

We made it to the chapel and the others were waiting for us. We filled out all the necessary documentation for The Governor Special License. They told us when we arrived that there weren't any lights on anywhere else on the island. I looked at Mikal and he looked at me. They said, "We can do this if you two still want to go through with it. Mikal said, "Please, let's go on!"

As the trees knocked up against the windowpanes and lightning flashed angrily at the small beach community, Mikal and I pledged our love for one another, and vowed to stay as one, forever.

He asked us to place the rings on each of our fingers. He said, "The circle is the emblem of eternity; And the gold is least tarnished and most enduring. It is to show how lasting and imperishable the faith now mutually pledged." He further went on to say, "As the union now formed is to be sundered only by death, it becomes you to consider the duties you solemnly assume." He said, if these be remembered and faithfully discharged, they will to the happiness of this life, lightening by dividing its inevitable sorrows, and heightening by doubling all its blessedness. But if these obligations be neglected and violated, you cannot escape the keenest misery, as well as, the darkest guilt.

It suddenly stopped thundering and the lightening seemed to go away. Everything became calm and very still.

He went on to say, "It is the duty of the Husband to provide for the support of his Wife. "To shelter her from danger, and to cherish for her a manly and unalterable affection, it being the command of God's word, that

Husbands love their Wives, even as Christ loved the Church, and gave his own life for her." Mikal squeezed my hand tightly as an acknowledgment that he completely agreed.

The minister went on to say, "It is the duty of the Wife to reverence and obey her Husband. "To put on the ornament of a meek and quiet spirit, which is, in God's sight, an ornament of great price, his word commanding that Wives be subject unto their Husbands, even as the Church is subject unto Christ."

He looked at the both of us and said, "It is the duty of both to delight each in the society of the other." "To remember that, in interest and in reputation as in affection they are to be henceforth one and undivided; To preserve an inviolable fidelity, and to see to it, that what God has joined thus together, man never puts asunder."

We then kissed as if we were the only two people present. They clapped and broke the trance.

The Marriage Officer then certified a true copy of the solemnization. We shook hands and hugged everybody as the storm suddenly reappeared. I didn't care about the storm any longer. We kept saying - Mr. and Mrs.

My new husband said, "I love the way that sounds."

When we arrived back at the hotel, the staff all came to congratulate us. They gave us envelopes filled with money from hotel guests that had found out about our marriage. I was very pleased.

We opened the door to our room and Mikal lifted me in his arms, then put me down and asked, "Is this for real? Did we really get married? Is this legal baby?" I was glad I had remembered to put our favorite songs into the tape player before we left. I hit "Play" on the tape player, and as soon as the song said, "At Last," I turned and smiled enticingly as he began slowly undressing me. My body was begging to be touched. Mikal stood back in disbelief as he remarked with his mouth opened wide and eyes bucked, "Baby, you've been blessed!" He almost fell to the floor as he tried to hurriedly pull his feet from his pant leg. He said, I'm looking at you now Jade, and I can't believe the Lord rewarded me this majestically. He said, "I'm no saint, but, I've been trying to figure out what I did so pleasing to our God that he would bless me like this." Mikal admitted that we shouldn't question God's work and that we are constantly reminded of how he works in mysterious ways.

That night, as he slowly and sensually made love to me, I willed my soul to my new husband as he called me his gentle flower. The song "Hypnotized," by Linda Jones, recorded in 1967, was playing. We united as one - in powerful passion - that was so truly deserved from sustained celibacy. He screamed that the pleasure was immeasurable...and I surrendered willingly as he begged for mercy, speaking a languange I was totally unfamiliar with. We stared at each other for hours as we thanked the Lord for his many, many blessings. He then grabbed me as the Stylistics began singing two of our favorite tunes, "You are Everything" - and, "You Make Me Feel Brand New." He then exclaimed, "Jade, I will do everything within my power to treasure you as my one and only love without end." He then took my breath away as he kissed away my tears. I vowed, "Everything that is best in me belongs to you, Mikal."

We didn't want to let go, but soon realized we had the rest of our lives to be with and explore one another.

Reluctantly, we had to prepare for our flight home.

The trip back was frightening. We stayed in the air two hours longer because of the storm. Thunder roared and the lightning flashed into the plane, creating the ultimate scare as we continued to circle unable to arrive at our destination. "Where is that flight attendant?" I really needed a drink, and preferably something stronger than the champagne we'd been gulping the entire trip.

We finally made it to Miami, thank God! It was a miracle to be on the ground. I swore I'd never get on another plane ever again. They put us up in a hotel and we were to be notified when it was safe to board again.

Two days later, we made it home to Texas. What turmoil! I was really relieved to be home so that we could start our new life together. It was more than a treat to watch Mikal's excitement as we moved him into our beautiful new house.

It took a day to go through all the accumulated mail. There were so many cards from friends and family! One of the letters was from the Postal Service. A month before we departed for the British Isles, I had applied for a new position, and people were telling me, don't get your hopes up cause it takes forever to get anywhere in this industry because the field is so competitive. I tried to be positive, thinking - "If it's his will, then it shall be done." My new husband grabbed me from behind and held me as he said, "Trust him baby, open it. Don't be afraid. It's all right, whatever it is, it's okay." I tore the letter open. I stood there shaking with one tear falling from my eye as I recalled that morning in the first grade when I decided I didn't want to be an animal doctor (Vet); I wanted to be a Postmaster.

My dream came true. My new husband smiled really big as he exclaimed, "God is so good, ain't he baby?"

My First Grade teacher would've been really proud of me if she was still with us. I worried her sick about being the Postmaster.

Every magical day that my husband and I have been together, he has cooked our meals and brought it to me on a tray. "Unbelievable!" I thought it was an exaggeration at first when he told me that cooking was his passion and a great hobby, but soon realized, he was more than genuine.

We didn't unpack right away. He just kept staring and saying, "You are truly not of this world, and when I see you, I see Jesus!" Now that's a compliment!

Respect and admiration are foremost in our lives.

We've been married since 1996, and matrimonial bliss continues to exist in our present lives.

I finally found peace. All the pain endured in my past led to this conclusive happy ending.

God, truly, knew best!

Our Grandmother lived long enough to see that her prediction that we'd all fail in life, was not a reality.

She nodded with admiration as Bria held her hand and rubbed it gently, stroking her white hair with the other hand enlightening her about the remaining children in our family.

Grandma said, "Go on, I'm listening."

Bria said, "Mom-me - you know I'm retired, don't you?"

"Retired?"

"Yes ma'am."

"You talking bout not having to work no more?"

"That's right - Boy, you still got it Grandma - sharp as ever." Grandma laughed as she pulled the colorful quilt up to her neck.

"Are you cold Grandma?"

"It's kindda chilly in here. – Speck I'm coming down with something."

"You want me to get your doctor?"

"Nah, I'll be all right, just feeling kindda tired. Where's the rest of your sisters and your brothers? Where's that Jade at?"

"Well, let me go down the list Mom-me." "Let's see. Okay. Let's start with Jade."

"Jade is Postmaster for the Postal Service."
"Zoe owns two Health Care Facilities."
"Coda is a Telecommunications Manager."
"Ian is Director of Operations."
"Mace completed her masters as a Christian Counselor."
"Kendrick is a Chemical Engineer.

"Well, that's real good," Grandma said.
"Good thing y'all had my blood in ya!"

*   *   *   *

Grandmother died the next day. She was 91
years old.

For my incredible siblings:

Even though times were tough
We had each other's love
And that was enough
To move on to bigger and better things
You are the Queens and true Kings
Who rose above much shame -
Persecution, and great pain.
Against all odds...
Our heads are high
As we journey beyond...
Lord, you brought us through, I can't deny!